my worst
best friend

my worst
best friend

DYAN SHELDON

CANDLEWICK PRESS

Copyright © 2010 by Dyan Sheldon

First U.S. edition 2010

Library of Congress Cataloging-in-Publication Data

Sheldon, Dyan.
My worst best friend / Dyan Sheldon. — 1st U.S. ed.
p. cm.
Summary: High school classmates Gracie and Savanna are total opposites and best friends, until Savanna's lying and manipulative behavior begin to bother Gracie, who wonders if it is time she started thinking for herself.
ISBN 978-0-7636-4555-7
[1. Best friends—Fiction. 2. Friendship—Fiction. 3. Individuality—Fiction. 4. Interpersonal relations—Fiction. 5. Dating (Social customs)—Fiction.]
I. Title.
PZ7.S54144My 2010
[Fic]—dc22   2009051505

10 11 12 13 14 15 16 BVG 10 9 8 7 6 5 4 3 2 1

Printed in Berryville, VA, U.S.A.

This book was typeset in Berkeley.

Candlewick Press
99 Dover Street
Somerville, Massachusetts 02144

visit us at www.candlewick.com

For Chiqui and Judy

Before

The way I saw it when I was in high school, even though there were still millions of different life-forms left on the planet, there were basically only two kinds of girls: Those Girls and everyone else. Those Girls had hair and teeth and breasts like the rest of us, but on them they weren't just body parts that you need to keep your head warm and chew your food and feed babies. On Those Girls, hair, teeth, and breasts were these incredible, super-luxurious accessories that were designed to make men fall in love with their owners at first sight and run after them with bunches of flowers.

Savanna Zindle was one of Those Girls. When she walked down the street, heads spun and horns beeped. When Savanna smiled, hearts melted like the polar ice caps. If hanging from a roof wearing flippers and a neon-pink wig would have guaranteed a date with Savanna Zindle, Crow's Point would have been the Boys-in-Flippers-

and-Pink-Wigs-Dangling-from-Rooftops Capital of the World. I'd never had a friend like Savanna before. My friends were always girls like me. Foot soldiers in the army of The Rest of Us. Regular. Ordinary. Plain. Quiet bordering on dull. Invisible to guys unless they wanted to copy your homework or you'd just knocked them into a river. There was nothing ordinary or plain about Savanna. She was practically a natural phenomenon. You know, like sunrise over the Rockies or the aurora borealis. If I was a natural phenomenon, it was drizzle. I was the dullest thing about her. Being friends with Savanna made me seem a lot more interesting than I was.

Savanna Zindle was the best friend I'd ever had. Which made her my best best friend. Which made her way more than just a friend. She was the sister I'd always wanted; born on the same team, sharer of secrets and dreams. We were virtually inseparable. Even though Savanna had a flat-screen TV with cable and HBO in her room and a queen-size bed, she usually spent most of her weekends at my house. It was way more peaceful than the Zindles'. My dad might have what Savanna called a "tetanus" grasp on modern life (meaning *tenuous*—as in: except for the electricity, heat, washing machine, and computer, he might as well live in a cave), but he was pretty low maintenance as parents went. Especially if you were comparing him to Savanna's. Savanna's parents were both pretty insane. And when we weren't together we talked on the phone for hours. She was the one I discussed sex and boys and periods and stuff like that with. She was the only person I trusted to cut my hair, and I was the only person she trusted to tell her how she looked in something new. If anything happened to either of us—even if it was just her having another fight with her mother or me finding out that another species was on the brink of extinction—the other would be the first to know. We finished each other's sentences and got all of each other's jokes. We were so close, we walked around in our underwear together and ate off the same fork and drank from the same glass and sat in the same chair and fell asleep on the couch watching a movie, draped over each other like iguanas.

Sometimes, now, when I tell people about Savanna and what happened and everything, they want to know how we ever got to be friends. "She doesn't sound anything like you," they say. "What could you possibly have had in common?"

And the simple truth is that we were nothing alike and the only things we had in common (besides belonging to the same species) were that we were the same age, same gender, came from the same town, and went to the same school. My dad said we were a Class-A example of opposites attracting (short, quiet vegetarian who liked old movies and lizards and worried about the environment versus tall, loud omnivore who liked Hollywood

3

blockbusters and shopping and worried about her nails). But friendship isn't based on reason—like buying a car because it's gas efficient or deciding not to wear the white dress because it'll be covered in stains in about two-and-a-half seconds. Despite all our differences, we were soul sisters and cosmic twins.

"Promise me you'll always be my best friend, Gracie. No matter what happens," Savanna would say at least once a week.

And I'd laugh. "Of course I will," I'd promise. "Unless you become a baby-seal killer or run a lumber company."

Both those career choices were completely out of the question for Savanna, of course. Which meant that there was nothing that could ever happen that would end our friendship.

At least that's what I thought then.

CHAPTER ONE

Waiting for Savanna — Part One

I was waiting for Savanna by the bike shed like I did every day after last period. We lived on opposite sides of Crow's Point, but in the morning we always met at the Old Road and walked the rest of the way to school together, and in the afternoon we reversed the routine. On this afternoon Marilouise Lapinskye was waiting with me. Marilouise Lapinskye was Savanna's other best friend — the one she'd had before she met me. (Marilouise wasn't one of Those Girls, either.) She and I liked each other and everything — I'd made friends with her before I even met Savanna — but I never saw her outside school unless she was doing something with me and Savanna, which wasn't that often anymore.

We'd been standing there for a while. Long enough for us to have exhausted the topics of the gruesomeness of our gym class, how her dog ate all the candy her mom bought for Halloween, how we wished we were still young enough to go trick-or-treating, and how glad we were that we didn't wear makeup because of all the poisons and chemicals in them, and had lapsed into one of those uncompanionable silences that might possibly go on forever—or until she started talking about what her mom thought about wedges or I started talking about chameleons. I couldn't figure out why she was hanging around.

Marilouise fiddled with the strap on her bag. "You know, I just wanted to say that I'm really glad you can come out for my birthday, Gracie," she said. "It really means a lot to me."

"Me, too." I felt kind of uncomfortable. Other people might say something like it really meaning a lot to them out of politeness, but with Marilouise you knew she was sincere. "You know"—I gave her a smile—"I'm really glad you invited me. It sounds like it's going to be fun."

"I hope so." Marilouise had a nervous shrug. "I mean, I'm sorry it's not a real party or anything like that. . . . Mommy thought we could go to Anzalone's." If she fiddled any more with that strap she was going to break it. "I know it's not exactly fancy or anything, but the food's really good." Her voice brightened. "I really love their eggplant parmigiana."

"It sounds great." The only times I'd ever been to Anzalone's was to pick up a pizza with Savanna. Part of my dad's "tetanus" grasp on modern life was a dislike of eating out. "It's fancy enough for me."

"Yeah, but, you know, it's only a little celebration—

6

just you and me and Savanna. I hope that's OK." Marilouise had a nervous laugh, too.

"Of course it's OK." I hated parties. I was more a wading-through-the-river, tramping-through-the-woods kind of girl.

"Really?" Marilouise scrunched her lips together as if she was thinking of smiling. She thought better of it. "I was going to ask Jem, too, but . . . you know . . ." She kind of rocked back and forth. "Savanna and Jem don't really get along."

Jemima Satz was Marilouise's other friend—besides Savanna and me. It wasn't so much that Jem and Savanna didn't really get along; it was more like they totally loathed each other. Savanna said that Jemima was a fat, manipulative, jealous backstabber. Jemima said that Savanna was a big-nosed, judgmental, self-centered witch. (Those weren't the only things they said about each other, but it gives you the general idea.) Besides being terminally shy and perpetually apologetic, Marilouise had a real gift for understatement.

"The smaller the better, as far as I'm concerned," I assured her. "I'm not big on major social gatherings." I jingled the keys in my pocket. I was starting to feel a little nervous myself. If there were any other students left on campus, they were either in detention or in a club. "I never really know what to say."

"Me, neither." Marilouise was shyer than a monk seal.

The year before, she'd fainted when she'd had to read a paper in front of our history class. "But, you know, Savanna does. She *loves* parties and stuff like that." This time she did smile, but not much. "I'm kind of worried that . . . you know . . . that she's not going to have a very good time."

I raised my eyebrows. "I thought you weren't inviting Jemima."

Marilouise giggled. "Well, yeah, right . . . That would've been a total disaster." Her smile lost some of its pain. "But at least Savanna wouldn't've been bored."

"Trust me. Savanna's not going to be bored." I wasn't really giving Marilouise my full attention right then. I was thinking more about where Savanna was than how much fun she would have had fighting with Jemima over the eggplant parmigiana. Maybe I'd somehow annoyed her at lunch and she'd left without me. I pulled out my phone and checked the time. "I wonder what's happened to her?" I mumbled. "She should be here by now."

Marilouise shrugged. Philosophically. "Oh, you know Savanna. . . . She's probably fixing her hair or her make-up." She gave me the look one asthma sufferer might give another as she reached for her inhaler. "Or something."

"Or what?"

This shrug was more nervous than philosophical. "Well, you know, Savanna's pretty easily distracted, isn't she?"

"I don't think there's that much to distract her

between the math wing and here," I reasoned. Just empty classrooms and corridors.

"Yeah . . . but sometimes . . . you know . . . she kind of forgets what she's supposed to be doing, doesn't she?" Marilouise's bag swung slowly back and forth. "One time we went to the mall together and I waited by the fountain for over an hour before I realized she'd taken the bus home without me."

I laughed. The way Savanna told that story, it was Marilouise who'd wandered off for something and never came back. "That sounds more like a major breakdown in communication." There was no way Savanna would ever *forget* that I was waiting for her.

Marilouise glanced at her watch. "Gosh. Is that the time? I have to get going, Gracie. I have a ton of homework." She hefted her backpack over her shoulder. "I'll see you tomorrow."

I watched her shamble down the driveway the way you watch the traffic when you're waiting for a bus. Since Savanna didn't think rules necessarily applied to her, I started wondering if she was being kept after school for texting during class or something like that (Savanna belonged to a couple of clubs, but she never actually went to any meetings). I was about to leave my post to go check out the detention hall when someone rushed up behind me like a sudden wind.

"Omigod, Gracie . . . I am, like, so sorry I'm late."

9

Savanna gave me a hug, banging her bag against my hip. "Kisskiss. Please say you forgive me."

"Where were you?" I disentangled a button on my jacket from Savanna's necklaces. "I was just going to see if you'd gotten another detention."

"Nah." When I shook my head, that was the only thing that moved. With Savanna, you got a big wave of curly, shining hair and dangling, shining earrings. "I was saying good-bye to Archie." Savanna had been going out with Archie Snell since the summer. "You know what it's like. . . ."

I had no idea. I'd never even been on a date.

"For forty minutes?"

"Oh, that . . ." There was nothing nervous about Savanna's shrug. "I was behind the bike shed — waiting for Marilouise to go." And nothing apologetic about her, either.

"You *what*?" She never ceased to amaze me. Which would be one of the things I loved about her. "You mean you were there all the time?" At least she hadn't forgotten me.

"And every second was like an hour hanging by my thumbs. . . ." Savanna rolled her eyes. "I mean, like, really, Gracie, I know you have a kind heart and everything, but how could you let her drone on and on like that?"

"She wasn't droning." I unlocked my bike and wheeled it out of the rack. "We were having a conversation."

"About *eggplant parmigiana*?" sputtered Savanna. "Oh, give me a break. I mean, yeah, eggplant parmigiana is marginally more exciting than hearing about Marilouise giving her dog a bath or what *Mommy* thinks about skinny jeans, but it's still way less exciting than listening to paint dry." She sighed. "Really, Gracie — I was starting to think she'd never leave."

I laughed. "You're too much, Savanna. You knew I was hanging around waiting for you, and you hid behind the bike shed?"

Unlike those of us who were sixteen but looked twelve, Savanna was sixteen and could pass for twenty. Except when she pouted, which made her look like she was three and had lost Mr. Bunny. "Oh, don't make me feel bad, Gray. It wasn't like I was hiding from *you*. And you know that if it started getting dark or there was a tornado or something I would've come out." Savanna tossed her bag into the basket on my bike. "But I had this, like, reallyreally stressful day. And I mean *reallyreally* filled with stress. The stress was packed in there like salmons in a can."

"*Sardines.*"

"Gracie, please . . . Have a little pity." She slid her arm through mine. "I know I asked you to tell me when I get my words confused, but after a day like today linguistic perfection isn't really a major priority." We started walking down the drive. "I mean, you wouldn't believe so much crap could happen to one person who wasn't a bib-lical character. It's like everybody and his extended family woke up this morning with only one thought in their tiny minds: Let's give Savanna Zindle a really awesomely hard time today. Let's see that she truly suffers."

I poked her with my elbow. "It couldn't be everybody, Savanna. At least one person must've woken up thinking about breakfast."

Savanna grinned. "OK, maybe one person woke up wondering whether she was going to have granola or cornflakes — but everybody else was thinking about how to ruin my day." She poked me back. "And I'm not even counting the super-catalog of disasters that happened *before* lunch, Gray." Which would be the fight with her sister . . . the fight with her mother . . . harsh words from her father . . . getting her bagel stuck in the toaster . . . forgetting her English homework . . . breaking her lon-gest nail because Mrs. Pontiac wouldn't excuse her from gym . . . a surprise quiz in math . . . "I'm talking about just *since* lunch. I mean, what is that, like a couple of hours? That's not long enough for a manicure and a leg wax, for God's sake. And you know what? I even had to sit next to the window in French because Kira what's-her-face — you know, the one who looks like a cocker spaniel? — she took my seat because I was, like, half a second late, and you know I can't stand to be in the sun like that. I mean it, Gracie, if I get skin cancer I'm suing the school district. It really is sooo unfair."

I wasn't too worried about the skin cancer. Savanna was pretty much protected by makeup.

"But I still don't get it. Marilouise is your oldest friend. Why would you —"

Savanna held up her free hand. It was hard to tell if she was surrendering or shielding herself. "I know . . . I know . . . I'm, like, a terrible person—I admit it. But I just couldn't face her right now. I really couldn't." She shook her head. "I mean, I am truly fond of Marilouise, you know I am." She frowned. "And that's even though she hasn't always been the most totally understanding and supportive friend you could hope for." Curls swirled and earrings flashed. "Remember the time that psycho at Scissor Sisters cut my hair and Marilouise said I looked like a squirrel?"

"Savanna, she *was* joking."

"But it wasn't funny, Gracie. You know how sensitive I am." More swirling curls and flashing gold. "And what about how she's always defending Zelda and telling me I should be nicer to her?"

Zelda was Savanna's mother. They had a troubled relationship. (Savanna had a troubled relationship with her dad and her sister, too, but the one with Zelda was more troubled.)

"That's just because Marilouise's father abandoned them. You know, she's very mother-sensitive."

"Maybe." Savanna's shoulders heaved as though she was trying to shake something off them. "But she still makes me feel really bad when she goes into her Miss-Sweetness-and-Light-and-Two-Good-Shoes routine."

"Goody Two-shoes."

"Whatever. The point is that Marilouise doesn't live with the horror that is Zelda Zindle. I bet if she did, she'd talk to her exactly the way I do."

I wasn't so sure about that. Besides the fact that Marilouise was more the salt-of-the-earth than the salt-in-the-wound type, odds were that if Marilouise had been made of jute she'd have been a doormat. She wasn't really known for being harsh.

"You may be right," Savanna conceded. "I mean, she is like the human equivalent of boiled potatoes, isn't she?" Savanna smirked. "No butter, no salt, and *definitely* no pepper."

"There *are* worse things." I really liked plain boiled potatoes.

"I didn't say she's like this major booga-booga friend from hell, Gray. I mean, she's absolutely not the worst best friend I ever had."

That would be Lena Skopec. Lena Skopec and Savanna had been best friends when they were nine. Lena talked Savanna into giving her the pink leather boots she got for

Christmas as a friendship present, and then, when Zelda made Savanna ask for them back, Lena told everyone that Savanna had lice. My worst best friend was Candy Russo.

"But Marilouise is your oldest friend." I guess I felt about Marilouise the way I felt about the planet—you know, that I had to defend her because she couldn't really defend herself.

"Exactly!" Savanna snapped her fingers. "The important word here being *old*. I mean, let's face the very loud music, Gracie. Marilouise and I have been drifting apart since we started high school. You can't deny it. I grew up practically overnight, but Marilouise is still like a little kid. Everything's *Mommy this* and *Mommy that* . . . I mean, she still has *dolls* on her bed, for God's sake! You've seen her room. It's like Time dropped dead in there or something. Dolls on the bed . . . ruffles on the spread . . . pictures of her dogs all over the dresser . . . It's like a mega-miracle she finally got rid of her *Little Mermaid* curtains." She sighed. "We just don't have that much in common anymore."

"Yeah, but—"

But Savanna was on a roll.

"And what was the *'It's not like a real party or anything'* routine? I mean, give me a break, huh? Like there was ever a chance she'd have a real party! Marilouise doesn't know enough people to fill an SUV, yet alone enough to make a party."

"*Let alone.*"

"Don't try to distract me, Gracie. The point is that she's lucky she knows *us,* or she'd be eating her stupid eggplant with only that witch Jemima for company. I mean, omigod . . . How depressing would that be? I'd rather be put on a chain gang."

"You wouldn't say that if you'd ever seen *Cool Hand Luke.*" Savanna had a thing about old movies: she wouldn't watch them.

Savanna didn't let that stop her flow. "And, anyway, I don't know why she's obsessing about it now," she went on. "I mean, her birthday's not for, like, *ages.*"

"Two weeks."

"Exactly. I mean, like, really, Gracie, who decides what they're going to eat two weeks ahead?"

In my relationship with Savanna, she was the one who was passionate, spontaneous, unpredictable, and as emotional as a character in a disaster movie. Four more of the things I loved about her. I was the thoughtful, plodding, reliable one. I was the voice of reason.

"For Pete's sake, Savanna, she's nervous about going out for her birthday, that's all. I don't really think that's a crime. And, anyway, she was just keeping me company." I poked her with my elbow. "You know, while I was waiting for *you.*"

"Oh, that's right!" wailed Savanna. "Blame me! Everybody else does. But you'll have to get to the back of the line, Gracie. There are at least three million people ahead of you."

"Stop exaggerating," I ordered. "It can't be more than two and a half million."

By the time we stopped laughing, we were at the Old Road. I disengaged my arm so I could get on my bike.

Savanna looked at me. Askance. "Where are you going, Gracie?"

I said that I was going home. "You know, that place where I live? Where I keep my clothes and stuff?"

Savanna said she thought I was going with her. "Didn't I tell you at lunch that the mother dragonned me into doing the shopping this afternoon?"

"Dragooned."

She flicked a hand. "Whatever. The point is that you said you'd come with me."

I didn't remember saying that. All I remembered was Savanna grousing about the Zindle elders, their other daughter, and their toaster, and me agreeing it was a miracle she didn't have chronic indigestion since she never had a meal without a fight.

"Well, I can't go alone," said Savanna. With conviction.

"Why not? It's not as if you have to strap on your snowshoes and go shoot a moose, Savanna. You're just going to Food First to get some groceries."

Savanna shook her head. "Not by myself, Gracie. You

know how much I hate shopping for food. I mean, how mind-drainingly boring can you get? I'd rather be trapped in a coal mine with Marilouise. I need moral support. You have to come with me."

"But I can't. I have a translation to do for Spanish. That alone'll take me hours."

Savanna wanted to know why I always had to make things so hard. In case I hadn't noticed, this was the twenty-first century.

"It won't take twenty minutes to do it. You can have it translated online."

No, I couldn't.

"But that's—"

"No, it isn't," argued Savanna. "Cheating's when you copy off someone else. This is using the resources available. Which everyone says is, like, a major sign of intelligence and ability." Her smile was like a cloudless sky. "Anyway, it's no worse than using a calculator. It's what you're supposed to do."

I figured my Spanish teacher, Señor Pérez, would disagree with that. Señor Pérez was pretty much firmly embedded in the twentieth century.

"I wasn't going to say that it's cheating, Savanna. I was going to say those sites are—" I was going to say those sites were for morons, but I stomped on the brakes just in time. I was pretty sure she used them herself. "Those sites really don't work. Not for something like this. They're mega-literal and they get stuff really wrong." I was in the Advanced Placement class. Literal didn't cut much ice with Señor Pérez. "Besides, the whole idea is to learn the language, not learn how to find a site that'll do your homework for you."

Savanna made a face she usually reserved for a lecture from her mother. "Oh, pardon me, Pope Gracie. I wasn't trying to get you to betray your holy vows here. I just think you should give yourself a break. It's not, like, going to kill you to ease up on the drudge-till-you-drop routine just this once."

"But not today." I gripped the handlebars. Determinedly. "Anyway, it's my night to cook." My dad and I took turns.

Savanna's face darkened with disappointment. "Oh, Gracie, please . . ." She clutched my arm. At least I was wearing a jacket so she couldn't draw blood with her stiletto nails. "You and your psychotic work ethic. I mean, I, like, hardly saw you all summer because you were planting butterflies all the time."

She really did crack me up. "I wasn't *planting* butterflies, Sav." I worked on a project with the National Park over the summer doing stuff like teaching little kids about the environment and reinstating wildlife habitats. But not all of us thought that was better than sitting on the beach, self-basting. "I was planting a butterfly garden."

She rolled her eyes. "Whatever." Savanna didn't share

my worries about the environment—you know, that pretty soon we won't have one that actually supports life. Savanna had an optimistic nature. Savanna said that things couldn't be as bad as I thought, because if they *were,* someone would do something about it. She figured that if things did get really bad, then science would come up with a solution. Since this *is* the twenty-first century. Whereas I figured that was like expecting a murderer to bring his victim back to life. "The point is that I didn't get to talk to you *at all* last night."

I pretended to choke. "Because *you* were busy."

"And I haven't had more than, like, half a second alone with you today. . . ."

As if it was *my* friends who always ate lunch with us.

She gave me the Mr.-Bunny's-gone-for-good look again. "Please, I'm begging. I really need some quality Gracie time. Reallyreallyreally. Just a few measly minutes. You can't let me down."

"I want to come. . . ." I was torn. My psychotic work ethic was pulling one way, and not wanting to let Savanna down was pulling the other. "But I really should—"

"Pleasepleaseplease . . ." Savanna clasped her hands. If you'd thrown a shawl over her head she would've looked as if she was praying. "You can't abandon me now, Gracie. You can't let me go by myself. I have a very sensitive nature. You know how the supermarket stresses me out."

And I had a very pliable nature. "I don't know. . . ."

"Don't be unreasonable, Gracie. This is not like a really big deal. It's like a drop of ant pee in the ocean. I mean, the shopping's not going to take any time at all with the two of us doing it, is it?"

In my heart, I knew this wasn't true. Experience suggested that anything one of us could do by herself in an hour—like baking cookies or mowing the lawn—would take the two of us together at least half a day. Probably much longer. But all I said was, "Um . . ."

"Oh, come on." She squeezed my arm. Affectionately. "I'll be, like, a gazillion times happier, and you'll be maybe ten minutes later getting home than you would've been."

This last part wasn't true either. I rolled my eyes. "Ten minutes?"

"OK, twenty. Thirty tops." If I'd been taller, she would have leaned her head on my shoulder. She leaned her head on my head. "Pleasepleasepleaseplease, Gracie. Who can I count on in this cold, cruel world if I can't count on you?"

"All right, but we're not stopping for a drink or anything—"

"Of course not." Savanna threw her arms around me. "Only first we have to drop by the drugstore. It won't take long."

CHAPTER TWO

One of Those Girls

Omigod, will you look at this?" Savanna flapped Zelda's shopping list over the fruit section. "All it says on this is *oranges. Oranges!* What's that supposed to mean? There are, like, dozens of kinds of oranges."

Choice does have its downside. You could see why it took Savanna hours to get dressed every morning.

"Temple . . . navel . . . blood . . ." recited Savanna. "Valencia . . . satsuma . . . mandarin." The shopping list fluttered in the air. "It's like the UN of citrus fruit. And they all have the same last name, Gray. They're all called oranges. Exactly what kind am I supposed to get?"

I leaned against the cart. After several delays, we'd finally made it into Food First, but it didn't look as if we were going to get any farther than Fruits and Vegetables for a while. I didn't bother checking the time. "Well, what kind do you usually get?"

"Oh, I don't know, Gracie." Savanna tossed her hair and sighed. "Nobody, like, told me they have names."

"Well, is the kind you usually have big? Small? Dark? Light? Does it have seeds? Does it —"

"They're *orange,* Gray. That's, like, the big clue." She turned to look at me. "I don't kn —" Her eyes locked somewhere behind my right ear.

"What's the matter?"

Savanna gazed into the cart. "Don't turn around," she ordered. "But there's a guy over by the salad stuff who's, like, staring at us."

I didn't turn around. I knew he wasn't staring at me. Not unless I'd started growing antlers.

"He is, like, seriously cute," Savanna reported. "Tall and lean, but really well-built. Dark." She reached down and moved the bag of potatoes from one side of the cart to the other. "I mean, like, really seriously cute."

"Is he from our school?"

"No way." Savanna shook her head. Slowly. "You know what? Why don't you pick out the oranges, Gracie? I'm just going to get some tomatoes."

Sure she was. And right after that she was going to save the world.

I sighed. "You mean you're going to go over and flirt with that guy."

"No, I'm going to get some tomatoes." Savanna smiled. "But I can't help it if *he* flirts with me."

Needless to say, nobody ever flirted with *me.* Savanna said it was because I dressed like a boy. I said it was more like a natural law: Whatever goes up has to come down; two objects can't occupy the same space at the same time; and no one flirts with Gracie Mooney. But everybody flirted with Savanna. And Savanna flirted right back. She was a natural.

"Oh, come on, Savanna. Tomatoes aren't even on the list." We'd already spent half an hour more in the drugstore than we had to while she tested lipsticks on the back of her hand. Experience suggested that flirting could take even longer. "I have to get home *today,* remember?"

She made a face. It was long-suffering. "As if I could forget. You've been reminding me, like, every five minutes."

I pushed the cart forward a couple of inches to encourage her to move. "Savanna —"

She patted my arm. "Relax, Gracie. I'll be right back."

So if you weren't completely clear about what it means to be one of Those Girls, here's an example. A classic. In a situation where someone like me would turn red, knock thirty or forty oranges to the ground, and roll the shopping cart over her toes, Savanna merely raised her head and smiled — and sailed toward the tomatoes like a man-of-war overtaking a dinghy. She was already flirting before she'd passed the root vegetables. There was a part of me that couldn't have been more in awe of her if she could bend steel with her bare hands.

Mr. Seriously Cute was studying the tomatoes as if he

was searching for fingerprints. But only with one eye. He looked up when Savanna docked beside him. She hugged herself and swayed. He smiled. Savanna smiled back. She had a smile that could sell ice to an Inuit. And then she turned to pull a plastic bag from the roll. Her hair moved like a curtain blown by a soft sea breeze. Mr. Seriously Cute said something. Savanna gazed back at him. She said something. He said something else. He was bobbing his head and grinning like one of those dogs people put in the back windows of their cars. I'd never actually seen a guy blush before. Savanna picked up a tomato and held it out to him. He gave it a squeeze. She said something. He said something. She hit him playfully on the arm. Besides the what-you-need-in-that-igloo-is-a-big-chunk-of-ice smile, Savanna had a laugh that made people look around to see what was happening—in case she was being attacked or someone was strangling a goose. Mr. Seriously Cute joined in. Everybody else looked at them.

It was obvious that Savanna was having fun—which made one of us. Watching someone flirt is even less interesting than watching someone test lipstick on her hand. I turned my attention back to the oranges. I picked out some navel oranges, and then I took one of the free recipe cards from the dispenser. I was reading how to make lemon sauce (recommended for chicken, fish, and green vegetables) when Savanna got back with the tomatoes her mother hadn't asked for.

"There." She dropped the bag into the cart. "Happy? That didn't take long, did it?"

I had to laugh. "You're too much, you know that? You really are too much."

"And you sound like my mother." She smiled, but she wasn't laughing along. "You're way too young to be such a pole in the mud."

"Stick."

"Anyway, Gracie, I was only being friendly."

"Really? And what about Archie?"

Savanna's eyes widened. The only way she could have looked more innocent was if she'd had wings and a halo. "What about him?"

"You and Archie are practically going steady."

"*Practically* isn't the same as *are,* Gray. I mean, *practically* inheriting a million dollars isn't anything like *having* a million dollars, is it?"

"Well, no . . ." Besides selling ice to an Inuit, she could probably argue him out of his last blanket.

"And, anyway, I didn't do anything. All I did was talk to some other guy. Talking to some other guy is not, like, a criminal offense." She looked down at the list again and squidged up her nose as though the next item was something gross like the still-warm heart of a newborn lamb. "Cereal. Where's the cereal, Gracie?"

I could only hope that she knew what kind the Zindles ate for breakfast. There were a lot more cereals than oranges. I looked up at the signs that hung over the end of each aisle. "Aisle four." I pointed left. "Over there."

Savanna led the way. Grumbling. "I'd rather eat McDonald's every single day, no matter how fat it makes you, than have to do this. This is, like, totally my idea of hell."

"It can't be hell," I said as I followed her to the back of the store. "Hell has fire and brimstone, not lights fueled by mercury and energy-guzzling chill cabinets. This has to be purgatory."

Savanna honked with laughter. "You see? That's why I wanted you with me. You make even this bearable." She waved her arms. "But I'll tell you one thing—when we have our own place we're getting takeout on the nights we're not being wined and dined by gorgeous men with serious incomes. I'm not doing this every week."

Having our own place together was our big dream. When we got out of college, we were going to share an apartment in some major city—preferably one with easy access to The Great Outbores (as Savanna called it) for those of us who liked tramping through mud. We had it all planned. We'd talked about it so much that we knew what color we were painting each room. We were going to be sophisticated and cool and leave the dishes in the sink for as long as we liked. Savanna was going to get a job in TV and work her way up to being a news anchor, and I was going to be a wildlife biologist and work for some organization trying to save what's left of the planet. But, besides the hard work and professional dedication, there would be boyfriends. That's where the gorgeous men with serious incomes came in. Savanna was going to have tons of boyfriends, and they were all going to be disgustingly attractive and wealthy. I wasn't really into money. I was more of a realist; having more to be realistic about, all I wanted was one guy who was breathing, nice, smart, had a good sense of humor, and loved lizards.

"No takeout," I said. "We're going to be poor working girls on a budget, remember?"

"Only to begin with." Savanna said this with her usual certainty. Self-doubt wasn't in her makeup. Which was yet another thing I loved about her. Self-doubt was practically my middle name: Gracie Self-doubt Mooney. "Then we're going to be fantastically successful, and we'll move from our tiny little cramped but cozy apartment to a penthouse with a roof garden and a cleaning lady who comes in twice a week."

She edged between two carts coming from the other direction, knocking a box of cookies and a roll of paper towels to the floor.

I couldn't follow her until the women pushing the carts picked up the cookies and the paper towels.

By the time I caught up with Savanna, some guy with

a baby hanging off his back was handing her a box from the top shelf of aisle four, grinning as if she was the one who was doing him the favor.

"Thankyouthankyouthankyou," she gushed. There were curls and flashes all over the place. "I don't know what I would've done without you."

She would've gotten it herself. Mrs. Pontiac pretty much begged her to join the girls' basketball team.

"You see, that's where you leave the road when it comes to men," Savanna informed me as we watched her savior and his baby disappear around a corner. "You're way too self-sufficient, Gracie. You think men are the same as us, but they aren't."

"You mean because they have penises and facial hair?"

"No, Gray." Savanna started down the aisle. "Because they come from, like, a totally different planet. They're really put off by independent women. They want to feel needed and in control."

She stepped over a small child who was lying on the floor crying. I carefully pushed the cart around him.

"I thought this was the emancipated, non-sexist twenty-first century," I called after her.

"And that's another thing." She looked at me over her shoulder. With concern. "Did you know that lots of women who are lawyers and professors and stuff like that have to pretend to be waitresses and cabdrivers to get a boyfriend? Men don't like women who are too smart."

"Why not? They're afraid of getting a crick in their necks looking up to them?"

"Gracie . . ." Savanna sighed. "I get the equal-pay-and-any-fool-can-put-up-a-shelf thing, but the point is that you have to face facts. Men have very delicate egos. They have to be protected."

"Who told you a stupid thing like that?"

"It's not stupid. It's a genetic fact. Everybody knows it." Savanna turned right. "Except *you*."

"You're making it up."

She was always making things up. Like when she was trying to convince me to buy that sundress in the summer and she told me that orange makes you look taller. Or when she wanted me to take a day off from planting butterflies to go to the pool with her and she told me scientists had proved that swimming makes your breasts bigger. I couldn't decide if it was a gift or a syndrome.

Savanna was shaking her head. "No, Gracie, I am not making it up. And if you read a women's magazine for a change instead of always having your nose stuck in some depressing book about how the planet's dying, you'd know that." She came to a stop in front of the shelves of pasta. "Oh, God, another earth-shaking decision. What do you think? Spaghetti? Fusilli? Shells?"

"It's a three-for-one. Get one of each."

"What would I do without you?" Savanna beamed. "You're a genius."

A genius who'd never been kissed. And didn't look like she would be any time soon. I figured that at the rate I was going the only way I'd ever have a boyfriend was if I started writing to prisoners.

"So," I said. "You think that's the reason no one's ever asked me out? Because I can get the cereal off the shelf by myself and know what a partial differential equation is?"

She tossed the boxes into the cart. "Well, what do *you* think it is?"

My height, or lack of it. My body, or lack of it. My lack of flowing, tossable hair. The extra head.

"Oh, please, Gracie. I mean, sure, some guys get turned off by the second head, but it really is *not* your looks. If there's anybody should be worried about her looks, it's not *you*. I mean, like, omigod . . . If looks were money, Marilouise would be begging on the street with a used paper cup."

"That's not true, and you know it." Marilouise was cute, in a low-key kind of way.

"She has as much sex appeal as a potato," said Savanna.

"OK, but—"

"She's fat," filled in Savanna.

That wasn't what I was going to say.

"No, she isn't. I think she has a good figure." Marilouise had obvious breasts.

"OK, she's not fat; she's chubby. But she has those little eyes, like bird poo."

"They're nothing like bird poo. They're the most amazing shade of blue."

"Blue poo." Savanna laughed.

I laughed, too. "They're fantastic, and you know it."

"OK, so they're pretty amazing," Savanna conceded. "But you will agree that she's dull as flour and dresses like my grandmother."

I was still laughing. "I've never met your grand-mother."

"Consider yourself lucky," said Savanna. "And, any-way, you're sidetracking me. The point is that you're like that girl in *The Matrix*. . . . What's her name? Trixie."

"Trinity."

"Right. Trinity. Only shorter." She looked thoughtful. "The only thing wrong with you is your negative attitude."

"Which attitude is that? My psychotic work ethic or my pole-in-the-mudness?"

"Your insecurity. You are what you project, Gracie Mooney. All the magazines say so." She stopped to shake a finger at me. "And you project mega-self-doubt. I mean, not about saving the world or anything like that — you're very strong and clear about reptiles and pollution—I mean about your looks."

I didn't think it showed.

"Really?"

"Absolutely. I mean, for one thing, you have to stop, like, hiding your light under a rain forest. It's great that you know so much about elementary biology—"

"Evolutionary."

"Right. The point is, Gracie, that you have more to offer a guy than hours of information on global warming and lizards. You could look really great if you made an effort. It's time to let the world see the real you."

"But this *is* the real me." Jeans, hiking boots, gecko key ring, and all. "I'm not a bright-lights-and-high-heels kind of girl, Sav. I don't want someone to go out with me because of how I dress."

"I blame the Professor," said Savanna. "He's so old-fashioned."

Further examples of my father's "tetanus" grasp on the twenty-first century were the facts that he didn't own a cell phone, didn't drive a car, wouldn't go into (never mind shop in) a supermarket, and that the music he loved was pretty much all written before the 1960s.

"He's not old-fashioned," I explained. Again. "He's just historically, environmentally, and culturally aware."

"Yeah, maybe, but he's, like, you know . . . he's, like, sooo *male.*"

That wasn't a criticism I often heard about my dad. I said most fathers I'd met were pretty male. It was kind of a hazard of the occupation.

Savanna laughed. "You know what I mean, Gray. You can pitch a tent, but you can't put on eyeliner. You haven't had anyone to help you get in touch with your inner girl."

My *inner girl*? It was my outer girl who gave me all the trouble.

"That's not exactly my dad's fault, is it?" He wasn't the one who ran away.

Savanna sighed. "You don't have to get all defensive, Gray. I'm not criticizing the Professor. It's just that I think it's time you established your independence from him."

"But I am independent. You just said I was *too* independent."

"As a female person you are," said Savanna. "But not as a daughter. You haven't even started separating from him yet."

I didn't want to separate from him. I was all he had.

Savanna sighed. Sympathetically. "All I'm saying is that it's time you learned how to enjoy being a woman."

"Which part of being a woman?" I asked. "The cramps and bleeding every month, or the ripping the hair off your legs with wax?"

"The part that doesn't see herself as short, skinny, and flat-chested, so that's what everyone else sees, too."

34

"But I *am* short, skinny, and flat-chested."

"Yeah, but those are just tiny details, Gracie. You have to focus on the big picture."

"Savanna, no matter how big the picture is, I'm still short, skinny, and flat-chested."

"Oh, please . . . You're totally missing the point. And the point, Gracie Mooney, is that you have tons of potential. If you just took a little interest in makeup and stuff. . . . I mean, really, if you were just a couple of inches taller, you could be a model."

I said that I didn't want to be a model. I'd much rather be Charles Darwin.

"You see?" said Savanna. "That's, like, exactly what I mean."

It was raining when we came out of the store. People were running for their cars with their jackets pulled over their heads.

"Omigod. It never ends, does it?" moaned Savanna. She looked down at her feet. It was November, but she was still wearing her ballet slippers from the summer. "There is no way I'm walking home in these. They'll dissolve."

I didn't see that she had much choice. Since she couldn't fly and she didn't have a car. "It's not that far."

"It is if you're barefoot and carrying all these bags."

She had two.

"Why walk when you can ride?" Savanna put down the shopping and pulled her phone from her backpack.

"Who are you calling?" It could have been the marines for all I knew. She was capable of anything.

She grinned. "The cavalry. Who else?"

So, almost the marines.

She nodded her head back and forth impatiently while it rang. "Archie?" She gave the parking lot a big summer-day smile. Her voice got all warm and mushy. You know, as if she was talking to a small child. "Oh, Archie, I'm sooo glad I got you. What are you doing? Are you, like, reallyreally busy?"

"Savanna!" I hissed. "Savanna, you can't—"

She waved me silent. "Well, I reallyreally hate to bother you, but Gracie thought . . . We, like, have this mega-emergency? We're at Food First, you know, over by me? And we've got all these groceries and it's raining like in the Bible and— You will? Really? Oh, you are an absolute, total angel. Kisskisskisskisskiss. We'll see you soon." She snapped her phone shut and slipped it back into her pocket. "He's on his way." This time the big smile was for me. "What did I tell you? They *love* to help."

She was definitely one of Those Girls.

CHAPTER THREE

Why I Agree to Go to the Mall

I was late for lunch on Friday.

I hated being late for lunch. It wasn't as bad as being late for a class with everybody turning to stare at you, grinning snidely and snickering under their breath as if you'd done something a lot worse than overslept or missed the bus, but it was close. I couldn't stand making an entrance.

You might not think the Crow's Point High School cafeteria had anything in common with subantarctic islands, but as I opened the door to the lunchroom, I felt as if I was walking into a colony of king penguins. It was pretty much an endless mass of very similar-looking bodies and a relentless wall of noise. A king penguin can return to her colony after months away and go straight to her mate or her chick as if she has a map. Which, besides the beak and eating raw fish and stuff like that, is another thing I don't have in common with them. I kind of hovered in the doorway, looking for Savanna. There were a lot of kids walking around, and all of them were taller than I was, so it wasn't easy without X-ray vision. I was trying not to look right at anyone, but I was sure I could feel heads turn in my direction—their eyes on me like binoculars. I knew exactly what they saw. My sneakers had a hole in the left toe. My socks didn't match. My haircut was uneven. A button had come off my shirt. There was a pimple starting on my chin. And I wasn't any taller than I'd been the day before, either. I was just about to forget about lunch and slink off to the library to do some homework when I heard Savanna's let's-stop-every-cab-in-the-city whistle. It was one of the three sounds guaranteed to be heard above dozens of feeding teenagers.

"Gracie!" she shrieked. That would be the second sound. "Gracie! Over here!" The third sound would be an air-raid siren.

Savanna was at a table down at the front of the room, near the windows. She was waving Archie's baseball cap—just in case I was the only person in a ten-mile radius who hadn't heard her.

The year before, when Savanna and I first became friends, we always ate lunch with Marilouise and a couple of other girls she and Savanna knew from middle school. But now that Savanna was dating Archie, we ate with him and his friends—Pete, Leroy, and Cooper. Savanna called them "our boys," but they were only mine by default. You know, because I was Savanna's best friend.

Archie, Leroy, and Pete were kind of much of a muchness. They weren't exactly three peas in a pod, maybe, but they had definitely come off the same plant. They were all likable, pretty popular, regular white guys. They wore baseball caps and bought their clothes at the mall. And they were into all the usual, typical teenage boy things—like sports, cars, Xbox, and loud rock. Archie was the one with the looks, Leroy was the football player, and Pete was the clown.

That made Cooper the anomaly. He was about as popular as an elephant at a beach party and as regular as a Galapagos marine iguana. Cooper was sarcastic and argumentative, and was always going off on some tangent no one would have followed even if they could. No matter what everybody else thought, Cooper always thought something different. (Archie said that when Cooper died they were going to put just two words on his gravestone: Disagree strongly.) He was a boy of causes. Boycott this . . . Support that . . . He called himself an anarchist, which meant that his heroes were all people no one else had ever heard of. Cooper hated sports, he refused to learn to drive, he did his homework on an ancient manual typewriter, and he was into old movies and old music. He wore a brown fedora that looked as if it had come from a black-and-white gangster movie (he loved Jimmy

Cagney) and bought all his clothes secondhand (so somebody who wasn't a big corporation got his money). It wasn't so much that Cooper wasn't likable (I thought he was likable); it was just that not many people liked him. Because he was so weird. And because he acted like there was something really dumb and funny going on, but he was the only one who knew what it was. The only reason Cooper was part of the group was because he and Archie had been buddies since kindergarten. Which would be another pretty major example of opposites attracting.

As I walked toward the table, Savanna went back to whatever she'd been saying when she saw me hovering in the doorway.

To tell you the truth, I'd kind of liked it better when lunch was just us girls. The guys were OK, but they made it different. Except for Cooper (who had this running game with me that if one of us alluded to an old movie the other had to supply the title, the stars, or both), the things they were interested in didn't interest me. And vice versa. Which meant that I didn't have that much to say anymore. This wasn't a problem that afflicted Savanna. She always had something to say, whether she thought the boys wanted to hear it or not.

Archie was listening to Savanna while he ate, one arm draped across the back of her chair as if he was holding it down. Leroy, Cooper, and Pete all had their backs to me. Pete and Leroy had their heads bent over their trays.

Cooper was reading a book while he ate the salad he'd brought from home with miniature chopsticks. Savanna was the only one looking at me.

"Omigod, Gracie! Where have you been?" Savanna scooped up her bright red jacket and her backpack from the chair beside her and dumped them on the floor.

There was a monosyllabic rumble of greetings from the boys as I sat down.

"How could you leave me all alone with these guys?" demanded Savanna. "It's like talking to a wall." She made one of her long-suffering faces. "I had this, like, nuclear fight with my sister this morning, and not one of them was the teensiest little bit sympathetic. I don't think they were even listening."

Cooper looked up. "I was listening." He glanced over at me. "I told her she should've gone for the grapefruit-in-the-face routine."

"*Public Enemy.*" I answered automatically. "James Cagney and Jean Harlow, but it was Mae Clarke's face he squashed the grapefruit in."

That caught the attention of Leroy and Pete.

"Where are they?" Pete was looking around. "Are they still here?"

"Grapefruit?" said Leroy. "Cool. I can definitely dig that."

Savanna pulled on my arm. "So why are you so late, Gray? I was getting worried."

I opened my old Snoopy lunch box. Wearily. "I just had an encounter of the third kind with Señor Pérez."

Señor Pérez asked me to stay after class. "Please don't make a break for the border, Señorita Mooney," he said when the bell rang. "I'd like to have a word with you." You could tell it wasn't going to be a good word.

"Poor Gracie!" Savanna gave me a hug. "He didn't yell at you, did he?" She knew how much I hated being yelled at.

"No. He was just *muy* disappointed in my translation." I smiled. Sourly. "You know, as in: D for disappointed. He said it wasn't up to the high standards he's come to expect from me."

"Phew!" Savanna pretended to wipe sweat from her brow. "I am, like, sooo glad I didn't take Spanish. I mean, Pérez is such a hard-ass. Madame Bower is *never* disappointed. She's just grateful that we hand in anything."

Pete winked at me over a forkful of spaghetti. "Welcome to the wonderful world of underachievement."

Leroy grinned. "Trust me, you get used to it."

"Anyway, Gracie, it's not that bad, is it?" Archie leaned around Savanna's hair so he could see me. "You usually get As, so this isn't really going to wreck your average or anything. You'll make it up."

"I hope so." I took out my sandwich. "I need an A in Spanish if I'm going to get a scholarship for that project I'm applying for in the summer." It was an ecological project in Costa Rica. I'd be working with sea turtles, which was like a dream come true. I had my heart set on it. What I didn't have was the money to pay for it.

"Of course you'll make it up," said Savanna. "I mean, remember last year when I messed up in English because Genghis Coen got me so confused I, like, read the wrong book? But I made it up. It's no big deal."

She was supposed to read the play *Our Town,* but instead she'd watched the DVD of this old Gene Kelly movie *On the Town.* There wasn't any singing or dancing in *Our Town.*

I unwrapped my sandwich. "Señor Pérez wasn't exactly laughing the way Mr. Coen did." Reliable witnesses said that Mr. Coen had tears in his eyes, he was laughing so much. The only tears shed in my talk with Señor Pérez were mine.

Savanna grinned. "Yeah, old Genghis did think it was pretty funny. But let's not forget that I did get the flu right after that. I mean, obviously I was already coming down with it, so no wonder I didn't know what I was doing. And then I got, like, really way be —"

"So what did Pérez say?" Cooper had put down his book. "Why'd he give you a D?"

Señor Pérez had had a lot to say. That my translation lacked life and personality. That the syntax was awkward and the vocabulary was stilted. That if he didn't know better, he'd have thought it had been translated by a badly programmed robot and not one of his best students.

"He said I might as well have been translating a recipe for empanadas and not some of the finest Spanish prose of the twentieth century."

"Ouch," said Archie.

Pete made a dopey face. "I don't suppose that was a joke, right?"

"He expects you to know what *syntax* is?" asked Leroy.

"That's why I have so much trouble with Shakespeare," said Savanna. "I mean, not only is it, like, impossible to understand what he's—"

"Are you saying what I think you're saying?" asked Cooper. He was smirking. Which would be another thing people didn't like about him. He smirked a lot. "You shortcutted?"

That's correct, ladies and gentlemen. I took the shortcut straight from A to D.

I nodded. "I just—you know—I had a lot of stuff to do that night." I didn't get home till nearly six because I'd gone shopping with Savanna. And my bike wouldn't fit in Archie's car, so I had to ride home in the rain, which meant that I had to change and take a hot shower as soon as I got in to bring feeling back to my fingers and toes. And then it was time to fix supper. And then I had to do my other homework. "By the time I got to the translation, it was so late I could hardly keep my eyes open." So I decided to give myself a break, and instead

44

of sitting up half the night I used the resources available to a moron in the twenty-first century.

"Did you explain?" asked Savanna. "I mean, he's got to realize that you do have other classes—and other obligations. Your world isn't just about *adiós* and *mañana*, you know. This is a very stressful time in your life."

I snapped a carrot stick in half. "Señor Pérez isn't really interested in teenage angst and woe."

Cooper wasn't smirking anymore. He was shaking his head. In disbelief. "I can't believe you shortcutted, Gracie. You of all people. You've got to be one of the smartest kids in our class."

Only sometimes.

"I told you, I was really tired." I shrugged. "At midnight it seemed like a really good idea."

Cooper picked up his lunch container and read what was written on the lid. *"Feel of ease . . . enjoy a quiet lunchtime while feeling a season . . . nature put a person at his ease . . ."* He winked. *"That* could've been translated by one of those websites. They're only for the terminally lazy."

"I think they're pretty cool," said Leroy.

"They sure beat doing it yourself." Pete laughed.

Archie threw a balled-up napkin at Cooper. "Hey! Just who are you calling lazy?"

"Oh, come on, Mr. Holier-than-thou . . ." drawled Savanna. Mr. Holier-than-thou was only one of her names for Cooper. The others weren't so flattering. "Laziness has nothing to do with it. Everybody uses those sites. I've done it a couple of times myself—like when I was even more desperate than Gracie was—and Madame Bower has never said a word about it. She always gives me at least a B."

"Yeah, but Señor Pérez isn't Madame Bower. Pérez would spot it before he finished reading the first sentence." Cooper was still looking at me. "Especially from *you*. Really, Gracie. It's like Ry Cooder picking up a guitar and only playing one chord. Badly."

You could tell from the sneers and rolling eyes that I was the only one who'd ever heard of Ry Cooder. Ry Cooder was my dad's all-time favorite guitarist.

"You leave Gracie alone," ordered Savanna. "Archie's right. It's not like it's this mega-big deal. It's like getting this teensy-tiny drop of nail polish on a patchwork quilt. Like, who's ever going to notice?"

I said, "Zelda Zindle." It had been her nail polish and her patchwork quilt.

Savanna honked. "OK, Gray. So maybe that wasn't the best example. But you know what I mean. You've got an A average. What's one little D in a solid A average?" She helped herself to one of the pickles I'd packed with my lunch. "And, anyway, you've had enough trauma for one day. I think we should talk about something else."

Cooper smirked again. "You mean like *you*?"

Savanna didn't like to scowl in case it made her look

like her mother when she got older, but she always made an exception for Cooper. "No, oh Great One, I don't mean like me. I mean like thinking of something to do on the weekend to cheer poor Gracie up."

"Well, why doesn't she come to the game with us tomorrow?" Archie was pretty easy to make happy. "We could all go for burgers afterward."

"I can't go to the game when Gracie needs me." Savanna jabbed him in the ribs. "You know she doesn't like football." I wasn't the only one. "And, anyway, Gracie doesn't eat burgers." She put her arm around my shoulders. "We're going to do something that *she* thinks is fun."

Cooper looked like he was trying not to laugh. "I thought you didn't like hiking, Savanna." Which would have been my first choice.

Savanna ignored him. "I know!" She squeezed my arm. "We'll go to the mall! I have to get a birthday present for Marilouise anyway. We can spend the whole afternoon there." She took my last pickle. "It'll be more fun than monkeys in a barrel."

"I don't know, Savanna." I'd already gotten Marilouise something in the little craft store in town. It was a pair of turquoise earrings almost the same color as her eyes. "I don't really need any—"

"Gracie, how many times do I have to tell you? Going to the mall isn't about *need*—"

Cooper sniggered. "It's about taking away our

manufacturing jobs for bigger profits and then selling us all the useless junk that's been made in China, that's what it's about."

"No, it isn't," said Savanna. It was just as well that looks can't kill. "It's about having a good time."

I went to the mall with Savanna—you know, because she was my soul sister and cosmic twin—but I didn't really consider malling a recreational activity. To tell you the truth, I found it kind of depressing. Ignoring the fact that most of the clothes for sale were made by women and children who might as well be slaves, it all looked pretty much the same, too. Except for the different labels. Besides, I always got a headache when I went to the mall.

"I'm supposed to clear up the yard. And I really should—"

"Oh, come on. You're not going to stay home and do *chores* when you could be enjoying some retail therapy," Savanna pleaded. "I guarantee it'll make you forget all about Pérez and his unreasonable standards."

Cooper sniggered again. "Yeah, because you'll be brain-dead within an hour."

Savanna's mouth scrunched together. I figured he'd hurt her feelings.

"All right," I said to Savanna. "But you're buying lunch."

CHAPTER FOUR

Waiting for Savanna — Part Two

Savanna and I arranged to meet in Java, the new coffee bar in town, to take the bus to the mall on Saturday afternoon. I was ten minutes early. I got myself a drink and sat down by the window so she would see me right away.

It was a perfect autumn day — all crisp and blue-skied. If I had been going for a hike, I would have followed the river out of town to the waterfall deep in the woods. Hardly anybody ever went there. Which meant it had a timeless quality that I loved. I liked to just sit by the falls, watching for deer or wild turkeys and listening to the leaves drift to the ground, and after a while I wouldn't know what century — or even what millennium — I was in. All I'd know was that I was alive, and on this amazing and beautiful planet. But since I wasn't at the waterfall, I watched the street outside instead, trying to imagine what Crow's Point looked like before the town was built, way before any white people decided this was a good place to settle—when there was a village by the river, and it was just trees and mountains and hunters and gatherers and the stuff they hunted and gathered.

When I finished my tea I checked the time. I'd been sitting there imagining bears lumbering through the traffic and mountain lions sunning themselves on the roof of the bank for half an hour. *She'll be here any minute,* I told myself. I picked up the sugar wrapper and folded it into a teeny tiny rectangle. I took out my phone to check that I hadn't turned it off by accident. I called Savanna and left a message. "Hi!" I said. "It's me. Just so you know, I'm at Java. See you soon." I slurped the last couple of drops from my cup, and then I made an origami duck from my napkin. After that, I got myself another tea. When I finished drinking that, I texted Savanna: WH R U? The next time I called I said, "Hi, it's me again. Are you OK? Phone me when you get this." The time after that I texted again: STL @ J. & U?

I did that for over an hour, but since she never answered or phoned or texted back, eventually I gave up and got one of the newspapers from the rack by the door. You know, so everyone would think I was there to catch up on current events and wasn't just some short, loser dweeble who had nothing to do on a Saturday afternoon but sit by herself in a busy café, checking her phone.

I wasn't really worried. To be honest, Savanna was

late on a pretty regular basis. The sun rose, the clouds drifted by, cows mooed, and Savanna Zindle was late. As Marilouise said, Savanna was easily distracted. She might be an expert on her inner girl, but she didn't really have what you'd call a highly developed sense of time. So, because Savanna was always late, if I wanted to meet her at five I'd usually tell her to meet me at four — and I usually brought a book with me. But today I hadn't done either of those things because she had an appointment with her dentist at ten and I figured I was safe. If she'd been coming from home she might have been delayed because she had to spend a couple of extra hours looking for something to wear that matched her mood or her horoscope or something like that, but, since she was coming from Dentist Tim, that stuff would all have happened before nine thirty.

I turned one page of the paper after another, slowly, reading the words without taking them in and looking at the pictures.

She's on her way. . . . I told myself. *The dentist is on the other side of town. . . . Maybe it took longer than she thought. . . . Maybe she was confused because she was coming from his office and got lost. . . . Maybe she has a blister on her foot from her new shoes so she's walking really slowly. . . . Maybe she left her bag at Dentist Tim's and had to go back for it. . . . Maybe she left her bag at home and had to go all the way back there. . . . Maybe she had to run an errand for her mom before she met me. . . . Maybe there was an accident or a fire or something like that and the road was closed off. . . .* I looked at my phone, sitting on the table like a dead mouse. *Maybe she ran into someone she knows. . . . Maybe she ran into someone she doesn't know. . . .*

As the clock on my phone crawled past hour two I started worrying that maybe I was wrong not to worry about Savanna. Something could have happened to her. It could have been something bad—she could have been hit by a car or her appendix could have burst—but I didn't want to get started on that. I figure that fear is like a bag of potato chips. Experience suggested that once you open the bag and eat that first chip, you don't stop until you've eaten them all. If I started thinking about all the really awful things that could have happened to make Savanna so late, I'd wind up calling Mrs. Zindle and maybe upsetting her. So I decided that if something had happened to her it was probably something extraordinary. That was more likely anyway. Extraordinary things never happened to me, of course, but they happened to Savanna a lot. Like the time she had to run out of the store practically in her underwear because there was a bomb scare. And the time she set the dryer on fire with her synthetic bra. And the time she was putting money in her Christmas Club and someone robbed the bank. And the time she found the ferret in the garage. And who could forget the runaway sheep? It was like she was some kind of magnet for chaos, excitement, and weird events. Which was one more thing I loved about her. Being so predictable and dull myself.

I stared down at a photograph of some celebrity getting out of rehab again.

Maybe drug addicts broke into the office and took Dentist Tim and his patients prisoner. . . . Maybe there were unexpected complications. . . . Dentist Tim had to knock Savanna out to do some major emergency surgery. . . . Or she passed out from the pain. . . .

Any of those options would explain why she wasn't answering. The thieves would have taken everyone's phones and now Savanna would be locked in the bathroom with Dentist Tim and the others while they made their escape. Or she would have turned off her ring tone when she got to the office—you couldn't have this bored voice inside your bag saying, *Your phone is so ringing. . . . Yo, like, answer the phone, girl . . .* in the middle of the waiting room—and now Savanna would be unconscious in the chair and couldn't put it back on. Maybe I should have gone with her or met her at Dentist Tim's. So I'd know she was all right.

I started playing a game with myself to occupy my mind and pass the time. After five girls with dark hair had gone by the window, Savanna would be the sixth. After seven women with screaming children had passed, Savanna would appear from the dark blob of shoppers like the sun coming out from the clouds. After ten boys wearing baseball caps had slouched past, Savanna would suddenly burst through the door and everybody would turn to look at her the way they did—but I'd be the only one who waved.

I was watching the fifteenth baseball-cap-wearing boy shamble past Java when someone shouted, "Hey, Gracie!" I didn't know anyone else with that name. So I looked over.

Some weirdo was standing in the doorway. He was wearing a tweed suit, a green hat with a crow's feather stuck in the brim, and yellow-framed shades. He looked like he'd just stepped out of his time machine. You could tell from the way the other customers were eyeing him that they thought so, too.

"Hi, Gracie." He smiled.

I peered over the tops of my reading glasses. "Cooper? Is that you?" He looked different. This may sound strange, but I'd never really seen him away from the others before. Or outside school. The rest of us sometimes did things together, but Cooper never joined in. And the shades kind of made him look like an owl.

He came over to my table. "You didn't recognize me because I don't really dress up for school. You've never seen me at my sartorial best." You didn't want to imagine what his sartorial worst could be. "And, anyway, that makes us even," said Cooper. "I almost didn't recognize you because I've never really seen you without Savanna before. Where is she?" He pretended to look under the table. "Don't tell me you're traveling solo today — striding out to explore the rich tapestry that is life with only a backpack and a cell phone."

"Excuse me . . ." I was still coming to terms with Cooper being in Java. It wasn't exactly his kind of place. Unless, of course, he was staging a one-man picket because they didn't serve fair-trade coffee, or something like that. "What are *you* doing here?"

"I'm on my way to the Meeting House to improve my teaching skills." That would be the Neighbors' Project. Another of Cooper's causes. The local churches had all banded together to run a community-action volunteer program that taught English as a second language and reading and stuff like that at the Quaker Meeting House. Cooper had been involved in the program since the summer. "I saw you in the window as I was walking past. In a trance of terminal boredom. So I thought I'd come in and say hello. You know, brighten up your dismal day."

I thanked him for his concern. "Only I'm not going to be here too long. I'm waiting for Savanna."

"You see?" He pulled out a chair and sat down. "I knew she had to be lurking in the shadows somewhere nearby. The whole state would've known if she wasn't. We would've felt the world come to a sudden stop and the heavens quake." Cooper laughed. "Rogers and Astaire, Tracy and Hepburn, Zindle and Mooney."

Or, to put it another way, bread and jam. That would be me with the crust.

Cooper took off his glasses and laid them on the table. "So where is Princess Zindle on this glorious afternoon?"

"She's on her way. We have a date to go to the mall, remember?"

"Of course! To cheer you up from yesterday's defeat and disappointment!" He gave me a crooked, cocky kind of smile. "So, where is she?"

"I don't know." I started folding up the newspaper.

"I take it you've tried calling."

"She's not answering her phone."

"Now there's another first." Cooper laughed. "I always figured Savanna would answer her phone even if she was in the middle of being interviewed on TV." He gave me another smile. "And you've been sitting here waiting for how long?"

I acted like I had to think about that question for a couple of seconds. Because it wasn't that long and the time had gone by so quickly. "I'm not sure . . . An hour or so."

"*Or so?* An hour or two? Or an hour or three?"

Savanna's lateness was pretty legendary. Archie always joked that Savanna would be late for her own funeral, but Pete said she probably wouldn't show up at all.

"Maybe an hour and a half." Or maybe a little more. "I guess she's been held up."

"Who by?" asked Cooper. "Bonnie and Clyde?"

"Warren Beatty and Faye Dunaway."

We both laughed.

Cooper tipped his chair back. "I suppose she could've fallen into a time warp," he suggested. "Right this minute, Savanna Zindle is wandering through first-century Rome, trying to make her cell phone work."

"Or maybe she was abducted by aliens."

Cooper nodded. Thoughtfully. "That could be it. She could be sitting in a zoo on Tralfamadore right this minute." He held up his hands as though he was reading a newspaper. *"Local girl beamed into deepest space while friend drinks enough tea to drown the whole town."*

"Slaughterhouse-Five, Michael Sacks, Ron Leibman, and Valerie Perrine." I raised my empty cup to him. "She'll show up before my second gallon."

"Sure she will." He raised one eyebrow. Inquisitively. "But what if she doesn't?"

It wasn't often that Savanna never showed up at all, but it had been known to happen. And not just to Marilouise. There was always a really good reason, though. Like the time the sheep escaped from the truck and blocked the road.

"She'll show."

He leaned forward. "But what if she doesn't?"

I made a well-what-can-you-do? kind of face. "Then I guess I'll go home."

He was tapping his shades against the table. "I have a better idea."

If we'd been at lunch and he'd said something like that, the others would have exchanged looks and groaned. Cooper's ideas *never* involved anything like ball games or burgers or getting a pizza like theirs.

"What is it?"

He gave me a big grin. If you ignored the hat and the feather and the suit, the grin made him look almost normal. "Why don't you come with me?"

The last time he'd asked Archie to go somewhere with him it was to a demonstration.

"Come with you where?"

"To the Meeting House." He sat back. "I know some of us have a skeptical attitude toward the Neighbors' Project. . . ." That would be Savanna. She wanted to know what Cooper was trying to prove. The boys just thought it was a joke. The only extracurricular activities they took seriously involved sweat and jock straps. "But it's actually a lot of fun," Cooper continued. "Makes you feel like more than a ball of fluff on the carpet of time."

"Yeah, it sounds like it's cool and everything. . . ." I was the only one who'd given any real thought to joining, but Savanna had laughed so much when I told her that I kind of chickened out. "It's just that, you know . . ."

"What?" He cocked an eyebrow. "You're too busy?"

"That wasn't what I was going to say. I was going to say that I don't exactly belong to a church."

"Me, neither." The smile came back. "The only faith I have is in doom."

I laughed. I was also the only one in our group who found Cooper funny ha-ha—instead of funny peculiar. "Which means you're never going to be disappointed."

He picked up his glasses and shook them at me. "You see . . . you're like me—you're a realist. On whom the fate of our troubled world depends."

"I thought you were a pessimist." Another of Savanna's names for him was Mr. Negativity. She said he was the guy who looked at a silver lining and saw a cloud.

Cooper laughed. "You mean because I'm supposed to be anti-everything?"

"You do have a reputation."

"So do you. You want to save everything."

"Not *everything*." I had a long list of things I thought the planet could do without. "If every golf course on the planet was turned into a primeval swamp, I'd jump for joy." To give you just one example.

"You see?" Cooper laughed. "You *are* like me." He gave me a thumbs-up. "And like the good folks at Neighbors'. Pessimism is thinking you can't change any-thing—ever—and none of us thinks that." He gave me a wink. "You're just the kind of person we need."

"I don't know . . . I'm really better with other species. . . ." You know where you are with whales.

"Look, I'm not trying to pressure you." Cooper tilted his hat back on his head. "Not too much, anyway. I'm just saying you should come along and see what it's like. You don't have to commit yourself to anything. Just check it out. They can always use another volunteer. And, despite your intense love of poikilothermic herptiles, you have had dealings with human children, right? Didn't you do some teaching in the summer? So you're not unfamiliar with the concept."

"Well . . . sort of . . ." *This is a tree. This is a bat roost. Those are deer droppings. Here's how you plant a seedling. . . .* "But those were little kids." I was OK with little kids — they were close to my height.

"We have little kids!" He clapped his hands together. "We have lots of little kids, Gracie. Really cute little kids. And you have experience. Mrs. Darling — she runs the program — she'll be really excited to get somebody with experience."

"Yeah, but you know . . . I'm really more into the environment than little kids."

Cooper was amused. "I hate to be the one to point this out, Ms. Mooney, but little kids are part of the environment. Besides, this is a good chance for you to spread the word. Inspire them. Convert them to the cause. Not every book for little kids is about teddy bears and talking giraffes. It's more *Good-Bye Moon* than *Goodnight Moon* nowadays, isn't it? I bet you could get some stories from the library about the stuff you're into." I'd never really noticed before, but he actually had a really nice smile. "You know, iguanas and trees and the collapse of civilization as we know it."

"You could be right. . . ." Mr. McGregor had been using toxic pesticides in his garden for decades—Peter Rabbit had to be in really big trouble by now. Maybe Cooper's ideas weren't as bad as everybody thought. "But I don't really know very much about real teaching."

"And *I* do?" asked Cooper. "I never even taught my dog to bring the ball back. He goes after it all right, but then he looks around for anyone who isn't me and gives it to them."

Maybe he was even funnier than I'd thought. "Yeah, but I'm kind of shy."

"You should've seen how nervous I was at first, Gracie." He was leaning forward again. "I thought I was going to be the youngest person in Crow's Point ever to go into cardiac arrest. But now I really enjoy it. We laugh a lot. Mainly at me, it may be true, but we do laugh."

I was weakening. I'd had a good time pointing out bat roosts and planting butterflies. "I'll admit that I'm tempted. . . . But, you know, I can't. Not today." I couldn't. Savanna joked that there were only three things you could really depend on in life: death, taxes, and Gracie

Mooney. She expected me to be in Java like I'd said. And so did I. "I have to wait for Savanna. Something must have happened to her phone so she can't call me, but I know she'll show."

"Doesn't your dad teach history?" said Cooper. "Didn't he ever tell you how we're supposed to learn things from the past?"

"Meaning?"

"Meaning Savanna is always late. Archie says she's even late when he picks her up later than the time they agreed on. And she's always got some really terrific, not to say inspired, excuse. You know, like today it'll turn out there was a herd of elephants that escaped from a traveling circus who were blocking her way."

I laughed. Uneasily. It had never occurred to me before that the runaway sheep story might not be true.

"I just think it's stupid for you to sit here all afternoon when you could be doing something really interesting."

"I can't. I really can't." Five minutes after I walked out of Java, Savanna would arrive, shaken and upset because she was so late and needed to tell me what had happened—but all she'd find would be an empty table and a half-drank cup of peppermint tea.

Cooper snapped his fingers. "OK, I have an idea."

Another one?

"Why don't you leave a note for her at the counter? Since her phone isn't working. Then if she does show up, she'll know where you are. She can come after you if she wants."

"I don't know . . ." Friends don't desert their post. What if there really had been a robbery or she'd had to have emergency surgery? How bad was I going to feel then?

"Look, you're not abandoning Savanna, Gracie. You're just waiting for her somewhere else."

That was true. It wasn't as if I was going to be a million miles away. I'd be just up the road, at the other end of town. If Savanna called from Java, I could be back in no time. "Well . . . OK, but I'm probably not going to stay long. I'm just going to check it out."

"Great." You'd think he'd won the lottery or something. I'd never seen Cooper look so pleased. "I guarantee that you're going to like Neighbors', Gracie. It's cool." He pulled a notebook and pen from the pocket of his jacket and handed them to me. "Come on, be daring. Seize this moment of opportunity the way a dolphin rides a wave. Write her a note. Just tell the cashier it's for the girl with all the hair who sounds like she's herding a flock of geese."

CHAPTER FIVE

Why I Never Got to the Mall

As soon as I stepped through the door of Neighbors', I liked it. It had a really easygoing, friendly kind of atmosphere. You could hear people laughing. Every person we passed said "hi." And Mrs. Darling couldn't have been happier to see me if I'd been teaching English for the last fifty years. "If Zebediah recommends you, then that's good enough for me," said Mrs. Darling. It took me a second to realize she meant Cooper. Nobody I knew called him Zebediah. And nobody I knew paid any attention to his opinions — not in a positive way, at least. Mrs. Darling said that, if I did decide to join, there was a workshop where I could learn the basics, but for now I could just sit in on a class and see what I thought. I explained that I probably wouldn't be able to stay too long because my friend was coming for me. I stayed all afternoon.

I sat in with the youngest class, which was taught by Mrs. Hendricks from the hardware store. It was the second time since elementary school that I'd been in a group where everyone else wasn't taller than I was. The other cool thing was that, unlike the kids I'd worked with in the summer who often had limited attention spans when it came to nature, these kids were endlessly enthusiastic. They didn't fidget, or complain that they were tired or thirsty, or wander off to stomp on some unwary insect the minute you turned your back. They were all systems go right to the very end. The person who had trouble concentrating was me. I'd get involved with the class for a while, but then I'd suddenly remember Savanna and start worrying about her again. Where was she? Was she all right?

I'd had to leave my phone in my backpack because they weren't allowed in the classrooms. Had she made it to Java? Was she trying to call me? Was she mad at me for deserting my post? Or was she striding up Main Street, punching ON MY WAY into her phone? Every time I heard someone in the hall I looked up, half expecting to see Savanna peering through the window in the door, rolling her eyes and sighing. I kept trying to read Mrs. Hendricks's watch upside down.

When we finally took a break, I went into the hall to check my phone (there weren't any messages) and Mrs. Hendricks came after me. She wanted to know if I'd mind if next week we split the class into two groups. "That's only five each," said Mrs. Hendricks. "They'd get so much more out of it." I hemmed and hawed. *Well . . . you know . . . I'm not really sure. . . .* "Oh, but you have to come back," said Mrs. Hendricks. "They really like you. You have so much charisma." I did? That didn't sound like me. "Of course you do," said Mrs. Hendricks. "You're terrific with them. You're a natural teacher." She gave me a big smile. "You must take after your dad."

So that would be the point where I finally stopped thinking about Savanna Zindle, what she was doing, and what kind of mood she was in. I had charisma . . . I was a natural teacher . . . I took after my dad. . . . I got into the rest of the afternoon with a vengeance. And I didn't remember Savanna when the class was over, either. I was too excited. So instead of remembering Savanna, I hung out in the café in the basement with Cooper and a couple of the other volunteers for nearly an hour. They called him Zebediah and acted like he wasn't even a little bit weird. I had such a great time that I was still buzzing when I got back home. I couldn't wait to tell my dad all about it.

It was starting to get dark, but he was still out in the yard, raking up the leaves. He was wearing his old plaid jacket and singing "I Dreamed I Saw Joe Hill Last Night" while he worked, but he broke off when he saw me turn up the front path.

"You're so quiet, I didn't hear you coming," said Dad. "Where's your early warning system?"

That would be Savanna Zindle.

So this would be the point where I finally remembered her again. I stopped like a polar bear who's just noticed that the ice has melted all around her. How could I have totally forgotten about Savanna? OK, I'd had a busy afternoon, but it wasn't *that* busy. It wasn't as if I'd been fighting off The Forces of Darkness by myself armed only with my Swiss Army knife or anything like that. Which is the kind of thing that would pretty much put everything else out of your mind. I was doing words-that-sound-alike exercises with six-year-olds. Which isn't. It was pretty much beyond belief. From practically the moment we met, I'd thought about Savanna all the time.

"Gracie?" My dad was giving me a puzzled kind of smile. "Where's Savanna? I thought you two were going shopping."

Now was not the time for in-depth explanations. I had to get to the phone.

"She has a date with Archie tonight." As answers go, this one was evasive, but it was also true. "You know, so she decided not to come back with me after all — she has things to do."

He leaned on his rake. He was still looking puzzled. "What happened? You look a little tense. Black day at the mall?" He chuckled the way he does when he thinks he's about to say something really funny. "Don't tell me they ran out of clothes."

"We didn't go." I didn't want to tell him that she

never showed. "She couldn't make it after all. Something came up." My dad never said he didn't like Savanna or anything like that, but he teased her and joked about her a lot—about how she took up more space than the Philharmonic Orchestra and talked more than the UN General Assembly and spent so much time on the phone with me it'd be cheaper if she moved in—that kind of thing. And sometimes I'd catch him eyeing Savanna the way you'd eye a Komodo dragon that suddenly appeared in your kitchen. Very suspiciously. Which was pretty much the way he was looking at me.

"Really?" He and the rake swayed back and forth. "What did you do instead?"

A minute ago, I'd been ready to tell him all about Neighbors'—but that minute was *before* I remembered that my best friend was still missing in action. The only thing making me buzz now was the swarm of guilt in my stomach. All I wanted to do was get into the house and phone her. "Oh, you know . . . Nothing much . . . I'll tell you later. There's something I have to do first."

My dad nodded as I turned away. "So who was that boy you were with?"

That would be Cooper.

I blinked in surprise. "I thought you didn't hear me coming."

"I didn't." He laughed. "But you couldn't miss that hat."

I said he wasn't anybody. I didn't have time to explain about Cooper, either. I really needed to call Savanna. What if she really was mad at me for leaving Java like that? That would be why she'd never come after me. She'd expected me to be waiting for her and I wasn't. I'd let her down. I was a bad friend. If she found out that I'd actually forgotten about her she might never speak to me again. And I wouldn't blame her.

"Not anybody?" I could tell that he was hoping that Cooper was somebody. You know, somebody who was interested in me. My father is pretty optimistic for a historian. Unlike some of us, he didn't think my only hope was a boyfriend on Death Row. He was always telling me how much I had going for me. You know, like I was smart and loyal and loved iguanas and could stand on my head. "You looked like you were enjoying yourselves."

"He's Archie's friend, Dad." I started sidling toward the house. "He hangs out with us at school. I—You know, I bumped into him in town and he walked me home, that's all."

My father nodded. "He looks like a nice kid."

He was a nice kid, but that wasn't what he looked like. What he looked like was an advance scout from Planet Bizarro.

"I'm kind of in a hurry, Dad." I took the front steps two at a time. "I have to call Savanna."

My father shifted his rake. "Of course you do."

By the time I got into the house I was in mega-anxiety mode, all damp palms and thudding heart. I raced up the stairs. What had I been thinking? Or, more accurately, why *hadn't* I been thinking? No wonder Savanna hadn't come by the Meeting House. She must be devastated that I'd just go off and leave her like that. Maybe she'd been so upset when she saw that I wasn't waiting at Java that she hadn't even gone inside. So of course she never got my note. Why didn't I leave another message on her phone instead? Like a good friend would do. I slammed the door of my bedroom behind me. My hands were shaking so much I had trouble turning my phone on. Thank God for speed dial, that's all I can say. If I'd had to hit every digit of her number, I'd have been there half the night.

Savanna answered on the first ring. I collapsed on my bed with relief. At least she was still on the Earth in the twenty-first century and probably not in traction. And she was taking my calls. I knew what Savanna was like. If she was really mad at me she wouldn't answer the phone.

"Gracie!" shrieked Savanna. Music was blaring behind her. "I Will Always Love You." Radio Romance, 98.6 on your dial. "Gracie, where were you? I've been calling you for, like, hours on both your phones. . . . I must've left, like, a hundred messages — I was sooo worried. I couldn't imagine what happened to you."

"I'm really, really sorry, Savanna. I—I just got home." Turning my phone back on after I left Neighbors' was another thing I'd forgotten. "Didn't you get my note?"

"What note?"

"The one I left at Java." I should have known the girl would forget to give it to her. It wasn't as if she had nothing else to do. "You know, to tell you where I was so you could come after me. Because you weren't answering your phone."

"Omigod, Gracie . . ." Savanna's laugh didn't always sound like a honking goose. "You left me a note?" Sometimes it sounded like beads bouncing on the floor. "But I never made it to Java."

"Really? You didn't show up at all?" That would be one scenario I hadn't actually thought of.

"Well, I didn't see any point." Savanna's voice kind of shrugged. "I mean, it got pretty late so I figured you'd have given up and gone home."

Maybe I didn't give Savanna enough credit for being practical.

"You did?" It was just as well Cooper turned up or I might still be there, on my hundredth cup of tea.

"Well, it's not like it matters, is it?" asked Savanna. Another handful of beads clattered to the floor. "I mean, Gracie, *you weren't there*. It really would've been, like, a total waste of my time if I'd gone to Java. And I called you as soon as I got home. I mean, I didn't think you were going to go all incognito on me."

"*Incommunicado.*"

"I've been calling you for hours, Gracie. Hours and hours. Why didn't you answer your phone? You knew I'd be trying to get you."

"I'm sorry, Sav. I had to turn it off. And, anyway, what about you? I tried to get you for hours and hours, too. Why didn't you answer *your* phone?"

"Because I couldn't." Savanna opened something that crackled.

"What's that?" I asked. "Mesquite potato chips?" Those were her favorite.

"I know, I know . . . Too much salt and fat. But I'm, like, starving, Gray. I didn't have any lunch." She bit into a chip. "Anyway, I couldn't answer my phone because I didn't have it with me. The Crow's Point Cuckoo hid it again." The Crow's Point Cuckoo was Savanna's little sister, Sofia. Sofia was always finding new and imaginative places to hide Savanna's phone. When I'd longed for a sister, it wasn't one like her.

I kicked off my shoes and leaned back against my pillows. "Where was it this time?" Everything was back to normal.

"The mother found it in the hamper."

"But couldn't you have called on—"

"Gracie," interrupted Savanna. "Gracie, stop nudging

me. There were really seriously extended circumstances working here."

"*Extenuating.*"

"I mean, I have, like, the most awesome reason for not showing up today."

"Duh . . . I know that, Savanna." Maybe it wasn't alien abduction, but it had to be something bigger than getting a run in her tights. "What is it?"

"I mean, like, really, Gray, you are *not* going to believe it! I almost can't believe it myself." Savanna's voice rose with excitement.

"Don't keep me in suspense!" I laughed. "What happened?"

"Oh, for God's sake. Wait a second, will you? The Queen of the Nags is bellowing for me. I really don't know why I couldn't have been born to a normal family." I heard her thump across her room and open the door. "Now what?" she bawled. "Can't I even just talk on the phone in my own room without you getting on my case?" I moved my phone away from my ear. "All right . . . all right . . . I'll turn it down. And then I'll sit in the closet and whisper, shall I? Will that make you happy?" The door banged shut again. "Really, I'd be better off if I was being raised by wolves. She doesn't let up on me for one teensy-tiny fraction of a nanosecond. I swear she was on me as soon as I walked through the door."

"Savanna!" I begged. "Just tell me what happened!"

"Are you sitting down? You have to be sitting down."

"I'm sitting down. Are you all right?"

"All right? I'm like ten zillion times better than all right. I'm, like, excellently fabulous. I've never been so happy to be me in my whole life."

Since, unlike some of us, Savanna was always really happy to be herself, this was definitely something way more awesome, fantastic, and phenomenal than mere time warps or alien abductions.

"What, Savanna? What happened?"

"It was incredible, Gray. It was, like, the last thing I expected. I mean, you wouldn't. You couldn't. It was like a boat from the blue."

I was so caught up in her excitement by then that I didn't even correct her.

"Savanna, for Pete's sake! What happened? What was on the boat?"

"You're really sitting down, right?"

"Savanna!"

"And you understand that this is, like, totally and completely top secret, right? I mean, you have to promise and solemnly swear not to tell anyone, Gracie. Not even if they bribe you with a billion dollars or threaten to harm every iguana on the planet. Understood? It's so top secret you can't even tell yourself."

"Of course I promise."

"Reallyreallyreally?"

"Savanna!"

She took a big breath. "Gracie . . ." She paused. Dramatically. "Gracie, hold on to your socks!"

"Savanna, I'm really begging you, just tell me what happened."

"I met someone!"

That was so not what I was expecting to hear that I didn't understand what she meant.

"You what?"

"I met someone! I met someone!" Now her voice was hitting heights usually only reached by panicked rabbits.

"What do you mean, *you met someone*?" What kind of someone? An elephant herder? A camel driver? The president? Or did she mean like a hypnotist who made her forget she was going to the mall?

"Oh, Gracie . . ." She laughed. "I mean, *I met someone. You know. I met a guy!* This fantastic, incredible guy. I mean, like really, Gray, he's totally awesome."

"You met a guy?" I knew I sounded like an echo, but I couldn't help myself. How could meeting a guy take half the day?

"You can't believe it either, can you? I mean, it is, like, so awesomely amazing how your whole life can change in just a few minutes."

I could have walked into town for the next hundred years and the only way my whole life would change was if a car hit me.

"So you—"

Savanna cut me off. "Omigod, he's calling me! He's calling me now! This is like so not typical guy behavior. I mean, like, he only— Gracie, I have to go. I'll talk to you later. Kisskiss, byebye."

I shut my phone with a sigh.

It was only then that I realized I never told Savanna what had happened to me.

CHAPTER SIX

More than One Surprise

After Savanna hung up I sat down at my desk to do some homework while I waited for her to call back. I opened my math book. I got out a pad of paper. I sharpened a pencil. I turned to the first question. It might as well have been written in Urdu. I leaned back in my chair and stared at the photograph of a Jackson's chameleon that I'd taped to the wall. He was hanging upside down on a piece of string.

It was definitely my day for not being able to concentrate. I guess meeting someone is a lot more glamorous than discovering a talent for teaching, because all I could think about was Savanna. Who was this guy? What was his name? What did he look like? How did they meet? Where? Did she bump into him because she wasn't looking where she was going? Did he drop something and she picked it up? Did he stop her to ask for directions? Did she stop him to pet his dog? The more I thought about Savanna's day, the more my own seemed to pale into insignificance.

I doodled in one corner of my pad. When I was younger and we still had a car, my dad and I used to go on camping trips in the summer. This one time we got to the campsite really late in a storm, and we pitched our tent in the dark without really knowing where we were. When I woke up in the morning, my dad was outside, calling me. "Gracie, come here!" he was shouting. "Hurry up!" I thought the car had been stolen. I hurried up. We were camped beside a swamp. Mist was wrapped around it like a veil. Cranes and herons skimmed over the green water. An otter swam past as though we weren't there. It was the most perfect thing I'd ever seen. That was the moment when I knew that I wanted to be a wildlife biologist. It was so beautiful it practically broke my heart. I burst into tears. But aside from that and stuff like getting choked up over sunrises and sunsets, I didn't really have what you'd call a romantic nature. I preferred documentaries to love stories. Savanna liked love stories.

I was still gazing at the wall behind my desk, but I wasn't seeing the dangling chameleon with his three tiny horns; I was seeing Savanna. She was pulling her phone out of her bag as she left the dentist's. With her dark hair and her red jacket and her nails decorated with tiny gold stars, she looked like a gypsy princess — one who happened to be standing by a sign that said T. L. Moreau,

DDS. She flipped open her phone. She was about to call and tell me she was out of the chair and on her way. But just as she was about to hit *Contacts,* she looked up. This fantastic, incredible guy was coming toward her. She caught his eye. He stopped. He smiled. And then . . .

And then what? Was it like that scene in *The Godfather* where Michael Corleone first sees Apollonia and is hit by the thunderbolt? Did he shout out loud? Did he run after her? Or maybe it was more like *Seven Brides for Seven Brothers.* He slung her over his shoulder and ran out of town.

I was so lost in my thoughts that when my dad called me for supper I nearly jumped out of my chair.

"Sanctuary!" cried Savanna. "A safe harbor in the storm-tossed seas of life!" She pushed open my bedroom door and strode through.

I followed her into the room with the tray and shut the door with my foot.

"Omigod, Gracie . . . Omigod . . ." Savanna dropped her bag on the floor and flung herself on my bed as though instead of getting a ride from her mother, she'd run all the way and couldn't stand up anymore. "What would I have done if you weren't home? I am, like, sooo glad you're here."

And I was surprised that she was. I thought she had a date.

Savanna's shoes dropped to the floor. "And I know I'm, like, truly terrible, ditching Arch at the last minute like that. . . . But I just couldn't deal with the Planet Archibald Snell tonight, Gray. Really and truly. I'd rather be plucking chickens. I mean, he *eats* through the whole movie, and then afterward he spends, like, hours explaining the plot to me. The plot! Of a thriller! I mean, what's to explain? They're all the same." She plumped a pillow and stuck it behind her. "Anyway, all I wanted to do tonight was talk to you."

I put the snacks down on the table next to the bed. "Are you sure you don't want something else? I could heat up some soup." Savanna hadn't had any supper.

"No, this is great." She reached for a pickle. "I mean, frankly, I'm amazed I can eat *anything*. My stomach has more knots in it than a noose."

I sat down across from her. "Tell me everything," I ordered. "Every single detail. I can't stand the suspense any longer." I couldn't. When the bell rang and my dad said it was either the police or Savanna Zindle, I was at the door before he finished his sentence.

"Omigod . . ." Savanna leaned back with a sigh. "It's been such an awesome day. . . . I don't think I know where to start."

"Start at the beginning."

"Well . . ." She looked as if there was a really high probability that she would never stop smiling. "His name's

Morgan—Morgan Scheck—and he's, like, six foot two, and he's got blond hair and the most awesome eyes, and he's really well built, but not all muscles like he's diseased or something, and when he smiles it's like someone just turned on the lights, and—"

"Savanna, that's not what I meant." I nudged her foot with mine. "I meant, how did you meet him? Were you strolling down the street and he just came up to you and said, 'Hi, my name's Morgan Scheck, and I'd like to change your life'?"

"Oh, Gracie, you are, like, sooo funny. . . ." crowed Savanna. "Of course it wasn't like that!" She bit into a chunk of cheese. "I met him at Dentist Tim's."

I hadn't thought of that possibility. "What?"

"I know . . . I know . . . It is like so totally incredible." She took another bite. "Usually the only people in the waiting room are either under twelve or over thirty. But there he was, just sitting there, suffering in manful silence and checking his e-mails."

"Are you saying you met a boy at the dentist's?" The only thing that ever happened to me at the dentist's was a shot of Novocain and a filling. And, sometimes, I had my teeth cleaned.

"Not just a *boy*, Gray." Savanna hugged herself. "This one's really, really special. I just know he is. I mean, like, how incredible *is* that? What are the chances? Like twenty trillion to one? There has to be, like, more chance of a blizzard in July. And get this—he was only there because he had a toothache and his regular dentist doesn't work on Saturday so he was seeing Mrs. Dentist Tim as an emergency. Isn't that, like, too awesome? I mean, what if he'd gone to someone else? Or his tooth didn't start throbbing till Sunday?"

If may be a small word, but it takes up a lot of space.

"Then you wouldn't've met him." I told you I wasn't naturally romantic.

"Exactly! We would've been like sheep that pass in the night."

"Ships."

"And you know what else is incredible?" She picked up another chunk of cheese. "He's a Cancerian. Isn't that amazing, Gracie? A Cancerian. I mean, that's like my romantic ideal." She paused to let her breath catch up with her. "It's destiny, Gray, that's what it is. It's like Fate brought us together." This time she wrapped a piece of bread around the cheese. "It can't be anything else."

"Are you sure it wasn't the Tooth Fairy?"

Savanna laughed. "Scoff all you want, Gracie Mooney, but it has to be Fate. I mean, what else could it be?"

Dumb luck?

Savanna made one of her Oh-Gracie faces. "I know you're not into astrology and stuff like that," Savanna went on, "but my horoscope *did* say something totally overwhelming and unexpected was going to happen today!" She waved her mini-sandwich at me. "And it did! Just like the stars predicted! I mean, how glad am I that I wore red?" Red was Savanna's color—the brighter the better. Mine was brown. "And I almost didn't! I almost wore my blue turtleneck because it was already ironed and I was running really late. I mean, omigod, Gracie, I would've like blended right into the wall and he wouldn't've known I was there and my life would've been ruined forever."

It was a miracle the entire human species didn't just stay in bed, paralyzed by the fear of wearing the wrong color and nuking their lives.

"Oh, don't be unkind, Gracie. I know you're an unbeliever, but I thought you'd be happy for me."

"I'm just teasing you, Sav. Of course I'm happy for you." I was. But though I don't have a romantic nature, I do have a cautious one. "I just don't understand how you can be so stoked about someone you only talked to for a couple of minutes."

She bit into her bread and cheese. "But I didn't. We talked for, like, hours. I don't think I've ever talked so much in my life. The words just flowed from me like water down a drain."

In Dentist Tim's waiting room? How was that possible? He didn't open till nine, and he closed at noon on Saturdays. They'd have had to get there the night before.

"Oh, Gracie . . ." honked Savanna. "Obviously we

didn't *stay* in the waiting room. I mean, it looks like an airport lounge—except for the old magazines and not being able to get a snack and stuff like that. You can't have a real conversation in that kind of atmosphere. He was still hanging around when I came out and he asked if I wanted to get a coffee. So of course I said sure."

"You said *sure*?" People besides my dad thought I was pretty smart, but sometimes I was so slow to get things I might as well have been in another country. If I hadn't figured out that she'd spent the afternoon with him, what had I thought happened? That he really had hypnotized her or carried her off? "You mean *that's* why you never made it to Java? Because you went for coffee with *him*?"

"Morgan. And I know . . . I know . . ." She took another pickle. "You're right. I'm, like, totally impossible. But you know me. I just don't seem to be able to stop myself. I'm very impetuous. You're really balanced—you always think things through—but I just kind of jump into the pool with my shoes on. I mean, I, like, had to say yes, Gray. You do understand, don't you? My heart wouldn't let me say no."

Of course I understood. I was her best friend. That was what Savanna was like. Passionate. Spontaneous. Swimming around in a pool with her shoes on. While I stood on the side, wondering how much chlorine was in the water.

"It's kind of too bad your heart didn't tell you to borrow his phone so you could call me," I joked.

Savanna laughed. "I would have, Gray, I really would have. But you know what it's like. I was swept away. I lost all sense of time."

I didn't want to sound a sour note here or anything, but it did strike me that that wasn't the only sense she'd lost.

"I just have one question, Savanna."

"What?" She picked up a drink from the tray. "You want to know when I'm going to see him again?"

That wasn't it.

"What about Archie?"

She looked at me over her glass. "Archie?"

"Yeah, you know, tall guy . . . dark hair . . . strong jaw . . . heavy earlobes—you know, the guy you already have."

She shrugged. "I think Archie's great, Gracie, you know that." She took a sip. "But it isn't all beds and roses, is it? I mean, I was thinking just the other day that maybe Archie was just one of those summer things."

"You mean like sunburn or poison ivy?"

"More like lemonade. You don't want lemonade in the fall, do you?" She raised her glass. "You want cider."

"But don't you have to put the lemonade back in the fridge, first?"

"Meaning?"

"You know . . . Meaning, you can't date two boys at the same time, Savanna."

"But I'm not dating two boys. I haven't exactly had a date with Morgan yet, have I? We, like, only just met."

"Yeah, but you said he's really special and—"

"You're worrying about nothing as usual, Gray. The point is that until I do have a date with Morgan, I'm not dating two boys, am I?"

"Well, no—not technically."

Savanna patted my foot. "You're, like, hitching up the cart before I even have a horse."

"I just—"

"So what happened to you this afternoon?" asked Savanna. "You never told me why you left a note for me at Java. Where'd you go?"

"Me?" By then I'd almost forgotten that I'd gone anywhere. "Oh, I kind of ran into—"

"Omigod!" Savanna put her glass back on the tray. "Don't tell me you got snared by Marilouise." Hair swished and eyes rolled. "I mean, is she like Crow's Point's answer to death squads or what? I forgot how she wanders around town on the weekends because she has nothing to do. Oh, poor you, Gracie. I am, like, sooo sorry. No wonder you weren't answering your phone. You were probably too numb with boredom to even pick it up."

I shook my head. "No, I didn't see Marilouise. I went with Cooper—"

"Cooper?" Savanna laughed. "You don't mean Zebediah Cooper, geek extraordinaire, do you?"

"He saw me in Java and—"

"But why would you go somewhere with *him*? What did he do? Threaten to kill the last chinchilla?"

"No, he just asked me if—"

"Cooper asked *you* to go somewhere with him?" She was still laughing, but she was looking at me now in a serious, what's-in-that-suitcase-that's-been-left-behind-on-the-train kind of way. "Why? He saw you sitting all by yourself waiting for stupid Savanna and he felt sorry for you?"

"Of course not." I hadn't thought of that before—that the real reason he came in was because he thought I was some short, loser dweeble who had nothing to do on a Saturday afternoon but sit by herself in a busy café and pretend to read a newspaper. "And Cooper doesn't think you're stupid, Sav." He just liked to tease her.

She bit into another piece of bread and cheese. Dubiously. "Really? He acts like he does. I can't buy a new blouse without him telling me how it's seeping toxins and made by blind orphans in some sweatshop somewhere."

"That doesn't mean he thinks you're stupid. You know Cooper—he thinks it's his job to educate everyone."

Savanna smiled. Sourly. "So where did he take you? I bet it was someplace really fun like a convention of fruit pickers."

"To tell you the truth, it was fun. He was on his way to the Meeting House, so he suggested I go with him. You know, since I was starting to get worried about you. He figured it would give me something to do besides wonder which hospital you were in."

"Meetinghouse?" Savanna brushed some crumbs onto the spread. "What meetinghouse?"

"You know, the Quaker Meeting House? Up by the library? You know, where they run that literacy program."

"Omigod! He took you *there*? To that good-neighbor thing he belongs to?" Savanna was looking at me with concern. "What for? To have you brainwashed?"

"Of course not." I laughed. "And it's called Neighbors'. I just went to see what it was like."

"You know what it's like." Savanna wrinkled her nose. "It's full of missionaries thumping their Bibles and telling everybody not to wear makeup or listen to pop music."

"It's nothing like that." I was still laughing. "It was really interesting. The kids were —"

"Oh, you can't be serious. . . ." She'd been leaning back against the pillow, but now she sat up so sharply that the bed rocked. "Don't tell me you actually joined up."

"No, I . . . You know, I was thinking about it. Mrs. Hen —"

"See? Didn't I say he wanted to brainwash you?"

"Oh, Savanna, please . . . It's not a cult; it's a literacy program."

"Just promise me you won't do it, Gracie. I mean, it's, like, so major God squad."

"No, it isn't." She was the first person to mention God all day. "And the people I met were —"

"OK, like maybe I'm wrong about the God-squad thing. I mean, I'm sure they're doing great stuff. Like the Statue of Liberty. But you're already so busy, Gracie. I mean, like, when am I going to see you if you spend your weekends doing that?"

"It's not the whole weekend, Sav, it's —"

From somewhere on the floor someone started singing that song from *Dirty Dancing* about having the time of her life.

"Omigod!" shrieked Savanna. "That could be Morgan!"

She threw herself across my legs and hung over the bed, reaching for her bag.

I had to laugh. She'd just met him and she'd already put a new ring tone on her phone. She'd been going out with Archie for weeks before she put on "My Guy."

Talk about changing your life.

CHAPTER SEVEN

Savanna Starts Rewriting My Life

Savanna said that the social side of school is just as important as the academic, so we always got there a little early to hang out together in the Student Lounge before homeroom. That would be all of us except for Zebediah Cooper. Cooper never arrived on campus more than a minute before the first bell and—since, unlike some of us, he didn't mind making an entrance—usually more like several minutes after. Cooper had a pretty firm policy of not spending any more time at school than was absolutely necessary.

On that Monday, Pete and Leroy were in one corner of the sofa halfheartedly trying to come to grips with their math homework while they socialized and Savanna and Archie were sitting hip to hip in a we're-so-going-out kind of way in the other. I was on a chair across from them. Archie was telling us about some movie he'd seen. As Savanna said, Archie's movies were kind of interchangeable. They had different settings, different characters, and different body counts, but otherwise they were more or less the same story. Not that you could tell that she'd heard it all before by looking at Savanna. She was listening to him as if he was Franklin Roosevelt giving his famous "The only thing we have to fear is fear itself" speech and she was a grateful nation.

I was smiling and nodding, but to tell you the truth, I'd pretty much stopped listening to Archie after the first major shoot-out. I was keeping myself awake by conjugating the Spanish verb *aburrir* in my head (*yo me aburro, ella se aburre, nosotras nos aburrimos* — meaning: I'm bored, she's bored, we're bored out of our gourds) when my unspoken prayers were answered by a merciful God and Archie suddenly broke off mid-bloodbath. "Oh, dude . . . !" he shouted. He pointed across the room. "Am I seeing what I'm seeing, or am I having some kind of massive hallucination?"

The rest of us all looked to the door. Cooper was sauntering toward us, wearing his normal wise-guy grin. He was back to his sartorial not-so-good — a striped collarless shirt, baggy corduroys, black-and-white polka dot suspenders, and his beat-up brown fedora — and had the old mailbag he carried his books in slung over his shoulder. Nonchalantly. (Just in case you wondered why people thought he was strange.)

"I don't believe it!" Archie had taken his arm from

91

around Savanna and was leaning forward, waving a hand at Cooper. "Get out of here, you evil impostor!" he laughed. "I know your game! What have you done with my friend?"

"Omigod! Isn't it illegal for you to get here before the bell?" screeched Savanna. "I mean, like, to what do we owe this great honor? Is the world about to come to an end, and you wanted a chance to say '*I told you so*' before we're all blown up?"

Cooper swung his bag to the floor. "I woke up early, so I figured I might as well come in." He didn't bother looking for somewhere to sit, he just dropped down next to my chair. "See what you guys get up to when I'm not around."

"I told you that you were missing out," said Archie. He put his arm around Savanna's shoulders again. "I was telling everybody about this movie I saw on cable last night. It was pretty cool." And, making a quick recovery from the unexpected interruption, Archie effortlessly picked up where he'd left off. "So, anyway, the dude's lost his gun and he's wounded and . . ."

But Zebediah Cooper wasn't the kind of person to pretend to be into something when he wasn't—and he probably hadn't been into the same movies as Archie since second grade. He looked up at me. "So, Gracie . . ." He wasn't whispering, but he was definitely only talking to me. "What did you decide? You going to join us on the front lines of the war against illiteracy?"

"Well, I—" Hadn't really thought any more about it after Savanna pretty much begged me not to join, to tell the truth. Not because of what she'd said—it was just that, what with the whole Morgan saga and everything, I'd kind of put it out of my mind.

"It's a yes-or-no question," said Cooper.

I could feel Savanna's eyes on me. For some reason it made me feel as nervous as standing up in front of the class giving a speech always made me feel. "Well, I—"

I don't really know what I was about to say, because I never had a chance to say it. And Archie never had a chance to finish the sentence he was in the middle of, either.

Which would be because Savanna suddenly wailed, "Omigod . . . Gracie, I can't believe it! You never told Archie about your awesome weekend!"

You'd think from the way she said it that I was in the habit of telling Archie about my weekends. As if his Monday wasn't complete unless he'd heard that I'd watched the 1935 version of *The 39 Steps* or helped my dad clean the gutters on Sunday afternoon.

Archie's head swung from her to me and back again. "What?" He looked like a dog who doesn't know which hand the ball is in.

I, however, did know which hand it was in. Because I knew Savanna so well, I knew exactly what she was doing. Even though Archie had been letting loose his catalog of movie mayhem pretty much in her ear, she'd heard what Cooper had said to me. She was putting me on the spot, that's what she was doing. She figured if the others all heard I'd gone to Neighbors', their general ridicule and hilarity would discourage me from deciding to join. She knew me pretty well, too.

"Savanna, please . . ." I laughed. "I'm sure Archie hasn't felt there was this major hole in his life because—"

"No, I'm really interested, Gracie." Poor Archie. Savanna was snuggled against him so closely now that I figured she must have her nails dug into his ribs. "I can't believe I forgot to ask you." He gave me a big, enthusiastic smile. "So, Savanna said you two went to see your dad in that play yesterday. How was it?"

This, of course, was not what I thought he was going to ask. But it was a pretty interesting question, as questions go. Mainly because my dad has never been in a play in his life, and because Savanna and I hadn't gone to see it. I really had helped my dad clean the gutters on Sunday. And, up until that moment, I'd been under the impression that Savanna had hung out with Archie. Since she'd told me that was what she was going to do—to make up for breaking their Saturday date.

I glanced over at Savanna. Her smile had more or less frozen and her eyes were locked on mine. Some people can read lips. Some people can read sign language. Some people can read smoke signals. I could read Savanna.

This wasn't the question she thought Archie was going to ask, either, but it was as clear as a mountain spring what my answer should be.

I smiled back at Archie. I could feel myself blushing. Which would be one of the reasons I really don't like to lie. I'm not exactly convincing. "Yeah, it was . . . You know, it was good. It was pretty good. I mean, even though I'm, you know, biased—because of my dad."

Savanna's smile melted into an um-duh-I-am-such-a-dummy kind of face. "And can you believe I, like, totally forgot we were going?" she shrieked. "I mean I, like, completely wiped it from my memory when I talked to Arch on Saturday." Her eyes looked into mine. "I mean, I was actually, like, getting ready to hang out with him yesterday when you called and reminded me." Savanna honked. "I guess I blanked it out because I was afraid, you know, that if your dad wasn't any good, it'd be, like, really cringe making and humiliating. I mean, what would I say to *you*? How could I ever face your dad again?" She leaned back, beaming. "But like I told Arch, the Professor was totally great. I mean, like, really, I was sooo surprised. I didn't know he could act."

So that made three of us, since I was pretty sure my dad didn't know he could act, either.

Savanna steamed on like a missile. "I mean, usually these amateur groups are, like, so amateur. . . . But your dad's group is really good. And that woman who played the lead—You know, the blonde? I mean, she could be on Broadway or something."

She wasn't the only one.

"Yeah," I agreed. "She's terrific."

"I didn't know your father was into amateur dramatics," said Cooper. "I thought he was a musician in his spare time."

"That, too." Hahaha. "He's a man of many talents."

"I can dig that. That's cool." Cooper nodded. "So what was the play?"

"Huh?"

"What play was it?"

"Yeah, what was it?" Archie gave Savanna a playful poke. "You know Savanna, she can never remember the name of anything."

I glanced at Savanna. She was examining her nails—you know, for microscopic chips or cracks or a patch where the color wasn't even. All of a sudden she had nothing to say.

I watched a lot of documentaries where CEOs of mega-corporations and politicians are interviewed about climate change and the environment and stuff like that. So I knew that the way of avoiding answering a question you'd been asked was just to answer some other question. I turned to Cooper. "About Neighbors'," I said. "Yeah, I've decided to join."

CHAPTER EIGHT

I'm Determined to Give Savanna at Least a Very Small Piece of My Mind

Because Savanna and I didn't have any classes together and lunch was always a group affair (and because every time I saw her between periods that day Archie was pretty much glued to her side), I didn't have a chance to see her alone until school was over. Which gave me plenty of time to think about what had happened in the lounge. At first I was surprised and shocked, but a part of me was also kind of admiring of Savanna. It isn't everybody who would not only make up a lie like that, but also involve someone else in the lie without even telling her. That took real chutzpah. I mean, really. You had to hand it to her, the girl had nerves of steel. But as the day wore on, surprise and shock started to change into something more like horror, and the admiring part more or less faded out. *How could she do a thing like that?* I fumed. *Isn't there the slightest connection between her brain and her mouth? Is she out of her mind?* It really wasn't fair. She'd dropped me into her lie to Archie like someone throwing an empty can into a river. *Plop.* And, like someone throwing a can into a river, she hadn't given me another thought or wondered how I'd feel about it. Not for a second. Not for as long as it takes a hummingbird to beat its wings once. For Pete's sake, she didn't even think to *warn* me! It would have served her right if when Archie asked me how I'd liked the play, instead of saying it was good, I'd said, *What play?* or, *Play? Did I go to a play?*

By now you know that I wasn't exactly a confrontational kind of person. The closest I usually got to confrontational was two rooms away with the door closed. If I saw somebody being mean to an animal I'd say something, but when it came to me, personally, I pretty much kept my mouth shut. I figured that the less you said, the less you had to wish you hadn't said. I really didn't like scenes or anyone yelling at me. But the other thing I really didn't like was lying. My dad's so old-fashioned he doesn't think honesty is just the best policy; he thinks it's the *only* policy.

By the end of that Monday, I'd thought so much about Savanna getting me to lie for her and everything that I'd actually decided to say something to her about it. *It really wasn't on,* I'd tell her. *You really dropped me in it.* As soon as the bell rang in English I was out of my seat and through the door like a tiger with a pack of poachers after her. *Come on, Savanna, get real . . .* I'd say. *You can't just make things up like that. . . . You can't tell lies that involve me and not even tell me you've told them. . . .* I knew that if I didn't say all this in the next ten minutes, it would probably never get said at all. That's what I was like. I got mad for a while, but then it passed. Or I just lost my nerve. Losing my nerve was something I was really good at.

I hurried down the corridor, marched out of the building, and strode across the quad. Savanna was standing by the bike rack, looking bored. I took a deep breath and kept walking.

Savanna, you know how much I hate lying. . . . Savanna, at least you could've warned me. . . . Savanna, I really don't like being treated like that.

"Gracie!" She was on me so fast I almost didn't even see her coming. "Gracie, I am, like, sooo glad to see you." She threw her arms around me, banging my butt with her bag.

"I just haven't had a second to myself, and I've been *dying* to talk to you since this morning."

I practically laughed out loud with relief. Savanna knew she'd messed up. I didn't have to confront her — she'd been waiting all day to apologize and beg my forgiveness.

"Really?" I hugged her back. "I was kind of worri—"

"Oh, Gracie, I am sooo happy. I can't tell you how happy I am!" Savanna was the only girl I knew who could clap her hands together like that and not look like she was two years old. "Guess what I did yesterday? Guessguessguess!"

This time, it was surprise that made me laugh. "Well, I know what you *didn't* do—" I began. And then I realized why she'd wanted to talk to me—and it wasn't because she was desperate to apologize. "You had a date with Morgan."

"You guessed!" Savanna jumped up and down. "I knew you'd guessed. I could tell this morning when you covered for me with Archie like that. You couldn't have been better if we'd planned it. You are, like, so awesome. You really can read my mind, can't you?"

This was my chance to go back to Plan A. *Savanna, you can't just tell lies. . . . You should have warned me. . . . Savanna—*

But what I said was, "Not as much as I'd like to."

She jumped some more. "Oh, Gracie, it was just so awesome. I mean, to start with, Morgan is, hands down, one of the most gorgeous guys I've ever seen in real life. It's true, Gray, he's just unbelievable looking. His eyes actually have little flecks of gold in them. And his smile . . . It practically glows like a lightbulb. Really. You can laugh, Gracie, but I'm totally serious. I think he's possibly perfect." Smart . . . funny . . . a great conversationalist . . . "I've never known any guy who's sooo phenomenally interesting. He knows so much about politics and music and books and art. . . . And he's got, like, tons of interests. I mean, he's practically one of those Resonance men."

"Renaissance."

"Exactly. I mean, it's like an education just hanging out with him." She looked as if she didn't know whether to hug me or hug herself. "And you'd love him, Gray. He's, like, totally into the environment. He was mega-impressed that I knew so much about climate change and sea turtles and everything."

And I thought she never listened to me.

"That's great," I said. It was great. She was so happy it had to be great. I bent down to unlock my bike. "But I really wish you'd —"

"Told you right away. I know. I know." So Savanna could read my mind, too. She stood beside me, shimmering with happiness. "I, like, sooo wanted to call you last night to tell you all about it — I mean, you know I did. Nothing seems really real until I've told you. It's all I could think of on the way home. *I can't wait to tell Gracie. . . .* I was, like, sooo far over the moon I was practically in another galaxy. Only Mother Zindle started yelling as soon as I got in the house, of course. Blahblahblah. God knows what she'd do with herself if I'd never been born. And then Marilouise called to test the outer limits of boredom by going on and on about eggplant parmigiana for, like, hours. And then Archie called to say good night and everything, and by the time all that was over I was, like, so emotionally drained I just went to bed."

I stared at the shadow my bike made on the ground.

Savanna, you can't just tell lies. . . . Savanna, it's not fair to Archie. . . . You're treating him like he's a fool. . . . Savanna, you should at least have warned me. . . . "I have a question." I straightened up again, tossing the lock in the basket. "Why did you tell Archie we went to see my dad in a *play*?"

"What?" She looked as if she wasn't sure she understood what I was asking. "But I had to tell him something, didn't I?" The truth obviously being out of the question. "I couldn't, like, break our date at the last minute without an excuse."

"Yeah, but you didn't tell *me* that's what you told him. I—"

"Oh, *that*. I'm really sorry, Gracie. I mean, if I'd known Archie was going to put you on the spot like that, of course I would've warned you. But I figured he'd forgotten about the play. I thought he was going to ask you about that house-meeting thing. He thought it was hilarious that Cooper got you to go."

"Meeting House."

"Anyway, it was OK in the end, wasn't it? You did great. Soul sister to the rescue! But now you've got to come home with me, Gracie." She linked her arm through mine as we started down the drive. "So I can tell you everything about my date. I mean, you are not, like, going to believe how totally awesome it was." She squeezed my arm. "It wasn't like any other date I've ever had. I mean, really. The difference between last night and a regular date was like the difference between kissing a guy and kissing the back of your hand."

And I would know?

I could feel my determination and resolve sort of drifting away on the tide of Savanna's happiness. I grabbed hold of as much of it as I could. "Yeah, but, Savanna—" I managed to choke out. "Savanna, what about Archie?"

She smiled. "What about him?"

"It's just that . . . You can't just keep on lying to him. . . . Isn't it time you told him about Morgan?"

She blinked. "Why would I do that?"

"You know, because now you *are* dating someone else." I shrugged. "I just think that if you're going to break up with Archie, it might be a good idea to let him know."

She was still smiling, but it was a baffled kind of smile. "I'm not breaking up with Archie, Gray. Not yet, anyway."

"Not yet?" If not yet—when? At her wedding to Morgan Scheck?

"I don't know why you worry so much, Gracie," said Savanna. "I mean, it's like you're turning into my mother."

"But if you're dating Morgan now—"

"Starting to date," she corrected. "One date doesn't exactly make a relationship. And, anyway, I don't want to jump on the gun here."

"*You* don't want to jump the gun?" That didn't sound

like the Savanna I knew and loved. My Savanna was usually running before the starter pistol was even in the air.

"I mean, yeah, Morgan and I had one awesome, unforgettable date that will live in my heart forever and ever, but who knows what's going to happen next?" She was all big eyed like Bambi. "I have to see how things go, Gracie. It might not be a really great idea to dump Archie before I get to know Morgan a little more. I mean, what if it doesn't work out with him after all? What if after a couple of dates I find out he eats his toe jam or something? Archie may not be perfect, but I don't want to dump him for no reason. You know what they say about having a bird. And he is, like, a really nice guy."

"Yeah, but that's the point, Savanna. Don't you think you should be straight with Archie *because* he is a really nice guy? He's going to feel like a total jerk when he finds out the truth."

"Ummm." She was looking at the pavement. "The thing is, Gracie, there is this little complication."

That would be aside from the fact that she was already going out with someone else.

"You don't understand . . ." She was chewing on her bottom lip. Which meant it was something serious. "There's, like, a little problem with Morgan."

"Don't tell me—he's got a tattoo of Washington crossing the Delaware across his face?"

She didn't laugh. "It's kind of really important that my parents don't find out about him yet."

"Why not?"

She moved her eyes from the sidewalk to me. "You know you're still under oath, right? You can't reveal what I'm going to tell you to a single living soul."

"Who is this guy? Is his father a Mafia don?"

"Oh, Gracie . . ." She still wasn't laughing. "His father sells insurance." She twiddled with her hair some more. It wasn't just serious; it was really serious. "It's just that Morgan's . . . you know, he's, like, kind of not in high school anymore."

"You mean he, like, kind of dropped out?" I could see that could be a problem. The Zindles had always been very supportive of Savanna's desire to have really rich boyfriends. "Or you mean he kind of got expelled?"

"He kind of goes to State."

"He's in *college*?"

"Isn't that too much?" She was smiling and looking above ground level again. "I'm going out with a college man!"

"So what is he—a freshman?"

She shook her head. "Uh-uh."

"Sophomore?"

"No!" By now we'd left the school grounds and had stopped at the top of someone's driveway. Savanna was more or less bouncing in place. "He's a junior, Gracie! Pre-law! Isn't that totally awesome?"

Awesome was one way of putting it.

"And he knows how old *you* are?"

She stopped bouncing and flicked her hair over her shoulder. "Sure."

I nodded. "So how old does he *think* you are?"

Now Savanna was gazing at her shoes in a critical way. "He thinks I'm eighteen."

"Eighteen? You told him you're eighteen?" I laughed. But it was more with admiration than with sarcasm. She had more balls than the World Series. "You really are too much."

"I know." Savanna's smile was pleased. "*And* he thinks I'm very mature for my age."

"So he's in for more than one surprise."

"Oh, don't . . ." Savanna gave me a playful push. "I am very mature for my age."

"Which one? In case you forgot, you're sixteen, not eighteen."

"Yeah, but I won't be sixteen forever, will I, Gray? And, anyway, I couldn't tell him the truth. I didn't want him to, like, get all warped out of shape because of the age difference. It's not a big deal."

"Maybe not to you." But I could think of two people who would think it was a really big deal. The Zindles were super-aware of all the things that could lead their children astray—and pretty determined that it was never going to happen. I figured Older Men had to be somewhere on that list.

"Exactly. You know how overprotective the parents are. They'd go into meltdown. That's why I said they were missionaries."

"Missionaries? Gus and Zelda?" Gus owned a couple of liquor stores and Zelda sold houses. The only time they went to church was Christmas. "You told him Gus and Zelda are *missionaries*?"

She joined in my laughter. "In Africa. Really strict Evangelicals."

"But why would you tell him that? What happens when he asks them about their mission and whether they ever met any lions or saved any heathen souls?"

"Um, duh . . ." Savanna was rolling her eyes. "That's the whole point, isn't it, Gracie? I mean, he can't possibly meet them, can he? Or he'll find out how old I am."

"And they'd find out how old he is."

"Right. So I had to come up with a really good reason why that'll never happen. You know, because they're so strict and won't let me go out with boys until I'm twenty-one and stuff like that."

"I don't see why they had to leave the country for that. You could just—"

"Because it also explains why I'm still in high school. You know, because I started school late because we were living in the bushes."

"*Bush.*"

She hugged her bag against her. "I thought it was like a stroke of genius. I mean, he wears a crucifix, so besides keeping him away from the 'rents, I figured it would impress him."

It impressed me. I couldn't have come up with something like that in a million years.

"So, anyway, the point is that I can't break up with Archie. The 'rents have to think that I'm still seeing him." She gave me a what-can-I-do? kind of smile. "You know, especially if I'm seeing someone else. I mean, if they think I'm seeing someone else, they're, like, going to insist on meeting him, aren't they? You know how nosy Mother Zindle is."

"So you're definitely going to see Morgan again."

"Of course I am. I mean, we didn't make another date — you know, because he's really busy with his classes and tests and stuff like that, and he shares a car with two other guys, so he can't get it whenever he wants it — but I'm definitely going to see him again. He said so. He said, 'I'll call you.' And then he made this seriously cute smile and said he wouldn't be able to help himself."

"Savanna," I said. "Savanna, you really can't date two boys at once."

She didn't blink. "Why not?"

"Because it isn't right, that's why not. It's called cheating, remember?"

"Oh, please . . . It's only cheating if you're married or engaged or something like that. It's not cheating if you just go to the movies or get a pizza together now and then."

"But what if Archie finds out?"

"And how would he do that?" She tilted her head as if the sun was in her eyes. "The only way he'd find out is if someone tells him, Gracie. And I'm not going to tell him. . . ."

And neither was I.

"You see? So everything's, like, totally great."

She slipped her arm through mine again. "Oh and, Gracie," she added, "if Mother Zindle asks you anything about your dad's play, you'll tell her it started late, OK?"

CHAPTER NINE

A Bad Week for Love

So what do you think, Savanna?" Archie's smile was patient. This was a question he'd already asked.

I was helping Pete and Leroy with their chemistry homework, but I glanced over at Savanna. She'd scraped off all the whipped topping and was now scooping up spoonfuls of chocolate pudding and watching them fall back into the bowl.

"Savanna!" Archie helped himself to the salad she hadn't touched. "What do you think?"

Savanna blinked, glancing over at him as if she hadn't realized he was there. "About what?"

She'd been like this for the last couple of days when we were with the others. Zombie-girl mode—with us in body but not in spirit or mind. In the mornings she'd sit next to Archie as usual, smiling and acting as if she was listening, but her thoughts were somewhere else—somewhere approximately twenty miles away. At lunch she was distracted and so quiet you'd think she was someone else, playing with her food and staring into space. Which would be why I was helping Leroy and Pete. It gave me something to do. The day before, I'd helped them with their math.

Archie's smile became beatific. "About the Christmas dance." The Christmas dance was a Crow's Point High tradition. It was almost as big a deal as the prom, but with snow. The posters had gone up that morning. "Do you want to go?"

Because I was standing behind Leroy and Pete, I could see the expression on Savanna's face change from the blank one you have when you're watching pudding plop into a bowl to the blank one of complete disbelief. I half expected her to shriek in horror, "You mean with *you*?"

Instead, she shrugged. "I don't know . . . high school dances are kind of childish, aren't they?"

This was news to Archie.

"They are?" He looked like a little kid who's just been laughed at because his Superman outfit is nothing but a dish towel and a pair of his mother's old tights. "I thought you liked them."

"I guess I used to. . . ." Savanna shrugged again. "But now I feel that I've, like, outgrown them."

Archie, however, was dogged. Or maybe just doglike. "But this is really mega, Sav. Suits and ties and formals. You know how you love to dress up." His smile was making my jaw hurt. "It's going to be a Winter Wonderland."

He might as well have said it was going to be a Winter Wonder bread for all the enthusiasm that got him.

"All right, all right . . . I'll think about it, OK?" She pushed back her chair and stood up. "I'll let you know."

"Now where are you going?" asked Archie.

She leaned her head toward his. "Kisskiss. I've got to go to the ladies room. Girl things."

"Oh, right . . ." Archie nodded. "See you later."

Savanna looked over at me. "You coming, Gracie?"

I know how horrible and disloyal this sounds, but my heart dropped like a white rhino shot at close range. Girl things didn't mean what Archie thought it meant. Girl things meant Morgan Scheck. She might be quiet when we were with the boys, but when we were alone she didn't shut up. At first it was all about how awesome Morgan was. Savanna might have trouble remembering to let me know when I was supposed to be lying for her, but she had total recall when it came to every single thing Morgan Scheck said or did—from the way he laughed to the way he tied his shoes. About the only things she hadn't told me about him was whether he preferred Pepsi to Coke and if he'd ever been inoculated against malaria. I almost felt as if I actually knew Morgan. Personally. That, if he suddenly came walking down the street, I'd know who he was—because of the way his laces wrapped around his ankles, or because of the scar over his left eyebrow (caused by his brother harpooning him with a knitting needle when he was six), or because of those little gold flecks in his eyes. But over the last couple of days her conversation had pretty much narrowed down to how depressed she was that he hadn't called her since Sunday. I was starting to feel a little compassion fatigue. I didn't want to be a bad friend, but how many times can you say, *Gee, I don't know,* or, *Gee, that's awful?*

I nodded. "Yeah, sure."

Which was when Cooper suddenly looked up from his book. "Hey, Gracie. I almost forgot . . ." He'd run into Mrs. Hendricks the night before and he'd mentioned my idea to her. "She said it sounded terrific," said Cooper.

Now everybody was looking at me.

I could feel myself blush. "What idea?"

Cooper said the one about using books about things I was interested in like the environment and disappearing reptiles for the class. I said I thought it was his idea, not mine. He said we'd had it together. "Anyway, I figured we could go to the library after school today. See what we can find."

Savanna was standing beside me, holding my jacket and lunch box.

I knew I should say I was busy. Which I should be. I should be listening to Savanna wondering why Morgan hadn't called her. "Yeah," I said, quick as the flick of a chameleon's tongue. "That'd be cool." It would also be a Morgan Scheck–free zone.

As an example of how depressed she really was, Savanna didn't say anything about me going with Cooper after school when I knew she was expecting me to hang out with her—or at least be on the phone. As soon as we were away from the boys, she started talking about Morgan and going through all the reasons why he hadn't called her and deciding in the end that he was definitely going to call her today. Probably as soon as she got home.

Not that I needed Savanna to say anything for me to feel guilty. I felt like a creep. A friend's supposed to be there for you when you're feeling bad—not run away the first chance she gets. All through my afternoon classes, I debated changing my mind. *It's not too late,* I told myself. *You can still say no. Tell him you forgot you had something to do at home. He won't care.* The minute English was over, I pulled my phone out of my bag so as soon as I got outside I could call him and tell him I couldn't go.

Cooper was waiting by the door as I stepped through it. I'd never had a boy wait outside a class for me before. Even though it was Zebediah Cooper and not someone normal—and even though it wasn't a date or anything—I couldn't help feeling kind of pleased. You know, like I was the kind of girl boys waited for in corridors.

"You all set?" asked Cooper.

I said I was all set.

I don't know if it was because I didn't want to hear myself thinking about how I'd abandoned Savanna, or what, but I did most of the talking on the way to the library. About how I felt about all the other earthlings on the planet and how badly we treated them, and the fragility of the ecosystem, and how we were destroying our land base, and why I loved iguanas and stuff like that. The only time Cooper laughed at me was when I made a joke. By the time we got to library, I was feeling really glad I hadn't changed my mind after all.

"Look at this, Gracie!" Cooper handed me a book he'd just pulled from the shelf. "Iguanas! A whole picture book about iguanas!"

"Oh, wow." I flicked through the pages. Iguanas on rocks. Iguanas on trees. Iguanas all piled up on one another like acrobats showing off. Who could not love them? "This is really excellent." I held it up. "Aren't they beautiful?"

"In a prehistoric kind of way," agreed Cooper. "But I have to confess that I'm more a dog man myself. They're cuddlier." He sat down on the chair next to mine. Which, since we were in the children's section of the library, meant that his knees were more or less level with his chin. "What do you think?" Cooper nodded at the pile of books on the table. "Got enough to get you started?'

I had a book about whales, a book about elephants,

a book about coral reefs, a book about what the future could be like if we didn't start taking care of the planet (and what it could be like if we did), and a story about a moose.

"Are you kidding? I probably have enough to get me through the year."

"Right." Cooper was drumming on the tabletop with his fingers. "Then how about we check these out and then go over to the café at the Meeting House for a drink?" He started drumming faster. "I'd like to hear some more about the devastating effects of global warming."

"Really?" It didn't seem possible. The only other person who didn't start groaning and stop me after the first five minutes when I launched into one of my monologues about the environment was my dad. "You don't consider yourself an expert yet?"

"Don't worry, there's a price to pay." He rubbed his hands together. Gleefully. "When it's my turn, you have to listen to me go on and on about the global economy. You won't believe how many fun-filled hours of gloom and doom there is in that."

I laughed. "You haven't met my father," I said, "or you wouldn't think that's a threat."

"I'd like to meet him," said Cooper. "He sounds like an interesting dude."

I said he was. I said my dad thought Cooper looked like a nice boy.

116

"Well, I am." Cooper laughed. "Didn't you know that?"

You might think it'd be kind of demoralizing talking to someone who was as worried about the future as I was, but, in a weird way, it was almost comforting. I guess it made me feel less alone.

But Cooper and I weren't talking about doom and gloom as we stepped out of the library. We were talking about the peanut-butter cookies at the Meeting House café.

"Wait till you taste them," Cooper was saying. "I always thought the best thing about the Quakers was the pacifism, but this is definitely a close second."

I didn't laugh. I was distracted. Savanna Zindle was maybe five yards away from us, waving so hard it looked like some giant, invisible hand was shaking her. Something awful had happened. I caught my breath. I'd been a total, self-centered creep. There I'd been having a good time without her, while Savanna really needed me. Maybe she was locked out of the house again, or her mother had finally followed through on all her threats and thrown all of her stuff out of her bedroom window. I could feel guilt start seeping up from my toes.

"Gracie!" screamed Savanna. She zoomed toward us. "What perfect timing. I was just coming to look for you."

"What happened?" At least it couldn't be that Morgan

had finally called to tell her he didn't want to see her again because she wasn't in tears. "What's wrong?"

"Nothing." She gave me a hug, hitting Cooper in the knees with her bag. "I just, like, suddenly remembered I still have to get Marilouise a birthday present. So I thought you could come with me and help me pick it out. I don't have, like, a single idea. . . ." She slipped her arm through mine, leaning her head close to my ear. "I mean, omigod, Gray, what do you get for the girl who is nothing?"

I didn't laugh at that, either.

I was relieved that she was all right and everything, but at the same time I really wished that she could've waited till tomorrow to get Marilouise's present. You know, when I didn't have something else to do.

"Oh, Savanna . . . I'm . . ." I looked over at Cooper. His eyes were on Savanna. He was smiling his private-joke smile. "We were just going for a coffee." I nodded across the street to the Meeting House. It wasn't the kind of place Savanna would go to unless you paid her. A lot. "They've got this really cute café. And these peanut—"

"But you don't *have* to go there, do you?" Savanna was beaming back at Cooper like a high-powered flashlight. "I'm, like, just going to get her something in the gift shop. It's on the same block as Java. You can have your coffee there." The flashlight swept from him to me and back. "We can all go."

OK, I know how bad this sounds—you know, like I

was a really rotten friend—but I didn't want us all to go. To tell you the truth, now that I knew Savanna wasn't in some kind of trouble, the only place I wanted her to go was away.

"I don't know. . . ." I looked over at Cooper again.

"Don't worry about me." Cooper was still looking at Savanna, but he wasn't smiling anymore. "You two go do your shopping. I've got a lot of homework tonight. I should get moving anyway."

And what about the doom and gloom and peanut-butter cookies?

"But—"

"Well, that's perfect." Savanna squeezed my arm. "Thank God I caught you before you, like, totally left the library and I didn't know where to find you."

"Yeah," I said. "Thank God for that."

Savanna's big smile disappeared at about the same time that Cooper did, replaced by the anguished look of a heart in torment.

"I don't know what to do, Gracie!" Her hair shivered with suffering. Her face contorted in pain. "I mean, I really don't know how much more I can take. I, like, literally found myself staring into the medicine chest this afternoon, wondering if Zelda's got enough sleeping pills to put me out of this torture and misery."

"Oh, Savanna." Fresh guilt kicked me in the stomach. Hard. I gave her a hug with the arm that wasn't involved with holding my bike up. "I thought you said nothing happened."

She gave a hedgehog-in-distress kind of cry. "Nothing has happened, Gracie! That's the trouble. Nothing. Nada. Zero. Absolute zilch. I might as well be on top of some mountain with no phone and a couple of goats for company."

I made a wild guess that we were talking about Morgan Scheck again. That would be why she'd come after me. He still hadn't called.

"I can't believe it! I really can't believe it. I mean, can you believe it? It's, like, Wednesday, Gracie. Wednesday. Which is, like, three days after Sunday. Seventy-two hours. People have been born and died in that time. They've gotten married and gotten divorced. But I haven't heard a word from Morgan. Not one infinitesimally tiny word. I was really positive I'd hear from him this afternoon."

And I'd been pretty positive I wasn't going to be hearing about him this afternoon. I ignored the feeling of annoyance this change of my plans had caused and tried to be comforting. As a best friend should.

"Well, you did say he's really busy." She had said this more than once. Morgan had classes. Morgan had to study. Morgan had a part-time job. Morgan had a lot of extracurricular activities. Morgan had a ton of friends. If Morgan got any busier he'd have to have himself cloned.

"Busy was yesterday, Gracie." We turned onto the

main road. Savanna wasn't walking; she was stomping. "And Monday. Monday could be busy, too. Two days is understandable. I mean, it's not like I'm one of those clingy girls. And I do have other things to do myself. But this isn't busy anymore. Three days is not understandable. Three days is way past busy." She stopped so suddenly I rolled my bike over my foot. "Why hasn't he called, Gracie?"

Why was she asking me? I wasn't the expert on men.

"I mean, I do know he's got a really crazy schedule," Savanna went on. "I got that part. But he could just, like, text me and say that he's got a trillion things to do and he'll call when he gets the chance, couldn't he?"

That seemed pretty reasonable to me. You know, unless he'd broken both his arms and all his fingers and was in a coma. I said maybe she should call him.

Savanna made one of her um-duh faces. "I did that Monday, Gracie, remember? I left a message that I thought I'd lost an earring in his car."

"You lost an earring?"

"No, of course not. But I don't want him to think I'm after him, do I? Men like to do the pursuing."

Yet more wisdom from the pages of the glossy magazines.

"Well, maybe you should call him *again*."

She waved one hand in the air. Dismissively. Been there . . . done that . . . "I left another message yesterday—you know, in case he didn't get the first one. But I can't call again. It's like three strikes and you're out. I mean, I don't want him to think I'm all desperate and needy."

God forbid.

"So what do your magazines say you should do if he doesn't call?"

"You're not funny, Gracie." She stuck her tongue out at me. "And, anyway, he will call. I know he will. I mean, he said he would. That was the last thing he said on Sunday. *I'll call you.* . . . I can still hear him saying it."

"Well, then, he will call."

"You don't think something's happened to him, do you?" asked Savanna.

I decided against mentioning broken arms and digits and comas. She was upset enough.

"Of course not."

"But you can't be sure about that, Gracie." She was looking at me, but she was pretty much talking to herself. "I mean, this is a really dangerous world. There are mass murderers all over the place. And terrorists. And kidnappers. And *birds* . . ."

Birds?

"You know, that flu thing they were warning us about. He could've eaten, like, contaminated chicken."

Or spinach. A lot of people had gotten E. coli poisoning from spinach. It was pretty hazardous, too.

Savanna scowled. "This isn't exactly a laughing matter, Gracie. I'm serious. He could've had an accident. You know how many accidents happen every day? Like millions. And I don't mean just cars. People slip in the shower and get hit by things falling out of windows."

"I'm sure nothing's happened to him." My dad taught at the state college. If one of the pre-law students had been poisoned by poultry or knocked out by a suicidal TV, he would have heard about it. "He probably just, you know . . . forgot."

"Forgot?" She let go of me as if I was hot. "You mean, like, I'm so boring he forgot about me? Is that what you think? What am I, Marilouise Lapinskye?"

"Oh, Savanna, please . . . Of course you're not boring. You're the least boring person I know." Leaves scudded past us and Savanna's hair blew around us. "All I meant was that he doesn't seem able to plan ahead, does he?" Or even get to a phone.

But that wasn't the right thing to say, either. She was standing with her arms folded in front of her, staring at me. It was the Zindle scrutinous mode. She really reminded me of her mother.

"Now what are you saying?"

What was I saying?

"I'm not saying anything. It's just that . . . Well, it's not like he's in the Sahara without a cell phone, is it? You know, unless he has been abducted, it does seem a little weird that the one time he did make a date with you was at the last minute." To be honest, it hadn't seemed weird to me before, but now that I was actually thinking about it, it did. I know I'd never had a date myself, but I did have the impression that you usually got more than an hour's notice. "So, you know, maybe he intends to call you, but then . . . I don't know . . ." I couldn't stand her looking at me like that. I started walking again. "Something else comes up."

"You think he's seeing another girl?"

Did I say that?

"He's not seeing someone else, Gracie. Morgan would never do a thing like that."

Why not? She was doing it.

"Savanna, please. I've never even met this guy. Why would I think he has another girlfriend? All I'm saying is that you're obviously right—he's really busy. He probably just loses track of time. He'll call you. You should try and chill out until he does."

"But I can't chill out!" cried Savanna. "That's why I had to come and get you. I mean, I just couldn't sit in my room all afternoon waiting for my phone to ring. I'd have gone totally nuts." She threw back her head. "Oh, why doesn't he call?"

Good God. We were starting all over again. It was the conversational equivalent of the wheel in a hamster's cage. You know, going in circles. Around and around. I was the one who was going to go nuts. I had to change the subject.

We'd come to the bridge over the river that borders Crow's Point at one end. It's a narrow bridge, so we were walking single file. "Speaking of calling," I said to her back, "why didn't you call *me*?"

She stopped and turned around. "What?"

"Why didn't you call me while I was in the library to tell me you wanted to meet me?"

"Because you were in the library, Gray." Savanna was speaking very slowly. And distinctly. "Your phone was turned off."

"You could've left a message."

"Which you would've gotten when? After you got home?"

"Not necessarily."

Savanna tilted her head to one side, studying me like I was a dress in a store window. "Am I missing something here?"

"I just wondered why you didn't tell me you wanted to meet me. You know, since you knew I was busy." I nudged her with my front wheel. "Go on, Savanna, we're blocking the sidewalk."

She didn't go on.

"Are you mad that I turned up, Gracie? Is that why you're being so unsympathetic to my emotional needs?"

"Of course not." I gave her another nudge. "And I'm not being unsympathe—"

"Omigod!" shrieked Savanna. "Omigod! That's it, isn't it? You wanted to be alone with Mr. Misfit!" She steadied herself against the bridge. So she didn't fall over laughing. "Oh, I don't believe this. It can't be true. That's why you told me you weren't going to join that dumb do-gooders club and then you did. You like the King of the Cretins!"

"Don't be ridiculous." If she didn't get moving, I was going to run her over.

Savanna wasn't listening. "Oh, Gracie . . . I mean, I don't want to, like, sound mean or anything—and I am totally not saying that you're not attractive or anything like that because you know that isn't true—but you can't possibly think Cooper's interested in *you,* can you?"

I hadn't actually given it any thought. Could I think he was interested in me? How would I know? I didn't think he was uninterested. Or disinterested. Or physically repulsed. I was pretty sure he liked me as a friend. He laughed at my jokes. He let me drone on about stuff that I cared about. You know, a person doesn't offer to share peanut-butter cookies with someone who isn't a pal.

"Of course I don't."

"I mean, just because he's started coming to school before the second bell doesn't, like, signify anything. You know that, don't you?"

"Of course I do."

Savanna's mouth puckered as if worry was making it shrink. "I just don't want to see you get hurt, Gracie. I mean, you haven't had much experience with guys. . . ."

That was like telling a fish that it didn't do much flying.

"I'm not going to get hurt. Cooper and I are just friends, Savanna. You know, like we were last week and the week before that?"

"I hope so. I mean, you do realize that he's *never* had a girlfriend."

"But neither has Pete or Leroy."

"That's different. I mean, they, like, talk about girls all the time, don't they? But Cooper never does. Not even to Archie."

"And?"

"And you do understand that Cooper's not really interested in girls, right?" Her voice sounded like it was wringing its hands. "Like, not at all."

I thought she was talking about the time in the summer that she and Archie dropped by Cooper's place and found him in the backyard wearing a "skirt." She'd thought he must be gay.

"It wasn't a skirt, Savanna. It was a sarong. Lots of men wear sarongs when it's hot."

"Not in Crow's Point," said Savanna. "And, anyway, that wasn't what I meant. I meant that he's not like the other boys. They're always staring at breasts and stuff like that. They're *into* girls. The only things Cooper's into are causes." She looked like she wanted to pat my shoulder. "And I'm worried that you're just another one of his causes. He thinks he can convert you to his wacky ideas because you cry when sea turtles die in fishing nets and want to save everything."

Boycott Coca-Cola. Don't buy stuff made in China. Save Gracie Mooney.

I saw you in the window as I was walking past. In a trance of terminal boredom . . . Was that really why Cooper came into Java? Because he thought I looked like I needed his help?

"I know what he's like, Savanna. And I'm not into him." I wasn't.

"Are you sure, Gracie?"

"Of course I'm sure." But maybe I was a little, you know, flattered by the attention.

Savanna laughed. "Well, that's a relief. I mean, Mr. Holier-than-thou, he's like such a major pain in the butt — always moaning about starving children and telling you not to wear labels and stuff."

You'd think he could worry about drunken movie stars and TV shows like everyone else.

She started walking again. "Come on, let's find something for Marilouise and go to Java. I could really use a coffee."

Make mine a double espresso.

CHAPTER TEN

Savanna Changes Her Plans (and Everybody Else's)

It may sound weird, since I wasn't one for social gatherings, but I was really looking forward to Marilouise's birthday outing. It was going to be fun. Savanna said the only way it would be fun was if Marilouise stayed home. "Marilouise could make a Hollywood party seem like waiting in line at the airport," said Savanna. I laughed. But I wasn't going to let her bring down my enthusiasm. It was the girls-going-out-together part that really appealed to me—away from school and any mention of Morgan Scheck and stuff like that. It seemed pretty grown-up, almost like the girls' nights out Savanna and I were going to have when we had our own apartment.

The birthday dinner was on Saturday night. Which meant I had to leave Neighbors' right after the class ended so I'd have enough time to get home, shower, get dressed, and then walk over to Savanna's. It would have made more sense for her to come to my house, but I was worried that if I wasn't there to hurry her up she'd never be ready in time.

Cooper walked me home, anyway. "I still remember Marilouise's sixth birthday party when her dog ate the cake," said Cooper. "It was a truly memorable event."

Savanna was still in the bath when I got to the Zindles' house. "For God's sake, Savanna, you've been in there for hours," Zelda screamed from downstairs. "Anyone would think you must've drowned by now." She smiled sourly. Smiling sourly was Zelda's speciality. "Go on up, Gracie. Maybe you can get her to move her butt. She never listens to me."

Half an hour later, I was sitting in Savanna's armchair, wearing my special-occasions black skirt and my favorite top (gauzy and stretchy and patterned to look like lizard skin) and with my hair spiked up, idly flicking through one of her magazines (the educational kind that tell you how to figure out what your most flattering color is and how you know if a boy really likes you), still waiting for Savanna.

At least she was out of the bathroom. She was in the doorway, bellowing to her mother downstairs. "No, it's a *dress*—it's gray and red and blue and white. . . . Yeah, it's short, Mom, but it's a *dress*—not a top, not a skirt, not a kilt, a dress! You, like, wear it with leggings or tight jeans or whatever. . . ." She leaned back into the room, sighing and rolling her eyes. "God help me. . . ." she muttered.

"How can I be related to a woman who flunked Fashion 101?" Her head went back out of the door. "But I, like, put it in the hamper *weeks* ago. How is it possible that you haven't even washed it yet?"

I stared down at a picture of a girl who didn't look like she ever had bed-head or got zits. She was wearing this flowery, flowy kind of dress. Really feminine in a romantic, meet-me-on-the-clifftop-in-a-thunderstorm kind of way. I was trying to picture the dress on me. It didn't look feminine or romantic. It looked like a little kid dressing up in her mother's clothes. Ready to trip over the hem and fall right over the cliff if she so much as took one step.

"But I wanted to wear it tonight. . . ." wailed Savanna. "Well, excuse me for breathing, but I don't want to wear something else. I had it all planned. I was going to wear it with my gray silk pants. Nothing else really goes with them." Savanna slammed the door shut. "I swear, sometimes I think she does it on purpose!"

I looked up.

"What about all the stuff you've got on the bed?" Which would be the dozens of things she'd pulled out of her closet and drawers when she was looking for the short gray, red, blue, and white dress. Which explains why I was sitting in the chair.

Savanna sighed. "But it's all so dull and *regular*. . . . I wanted something, like, really kapowy."

"I thought you didn't care about tonight. I thought

131

you said it was like going out with your parents." Only without any major fights.

"Omigod!" Savanna put her hand to her mouth, her eyes peering over her fingers like two full moons. "I was sure I told you. Oh, I am such a flake. Didn't I tell you? How could I forget to tell you?"

I believe in being positive, but sometimes it takes a really gigantic effort. I dropped the magazine back on top of the pile on the floor. I had the same sort of bad feeling I got when I heard about another melting glacier. "Tell me what?"

She started rummaging through the clothes on her bed. "I can't go to Anzalone's with you guys after all. Something came up at the last minute."

"What do you mean, *something came up*?" I unlooped my legs from the arm of the chair and sat up straighter. This *was* the last minute. "We're meeting Marilouise in less than an hour."

"I'm not." Savanna was shaking her head. Disappointedly. I couldn't tell if the disappointment was because of Marilouise or because her mother was a better Realtor than she was a laundry lady. "I mean, I'm really sorry, Gracie, you know I am. I mean, I'm, like, really devastated, but I just can't go to Marilouise's dinner thing tonight after all. I was sure I told you."

And when would that have been? I'd been at Neighbors' all afternoon.

"I don't know. . . . I thought I told you when you got here."

"You were in the bath when I got here."

Savanna sighed. "I'm reallyreally sorry, Gracie." She gave me an apologetic smile. "I guess it just slipped my mind."

"It *slipped* your mind?" What had she been doing all day, patching up the hole in the ozone layer?

Savanna twisted a stray strand of hair. "Well, if you'd hung out with me instead of doing good deeds, Gracie, you would've been with me when all this came up, wouldn't you, and then I wouldn't've forgotten to mention it."

"When what came up?" As if I couldn't guess.

"Morgan finally called! Isn't that great?" Savanna wasn't looking disappointed now. "And guess what? He's taking me out for dinner!" If she smiled any more, her teeth would fall out.

"But you're already going out for dinner."

"Yeah, I know, but"—Savanna sighed—"only now I'm not, am I? Now I'm going out with Morgan."

You'd have thought that one of her magazines might have had something to say about dumping your friends because some boy asked you out at the last minute.

"Savanna, you can't just change your plans because Morgan suddenly decided he can see you. That's not right."

"It's not like that, Gracie." She tossed a couple of tops

aside. "It wasn't sudden. He always wanted to see me tonight; he just didn't know if he could."

"Why, because the UN special meeting might go on longer than he'd thought?"

"You're not funny. You know how busy he is."

"Oh, Savanna . . . It's Marilouise's birthday, remember? She's been planning it for weeks."

Savanna groaned. "As if I didn't know. It's practically all she ever talks about."

"I don't know why you ever said you'd go. All you've done is complain about it right from the start."

Savanna pouted. "You think I'm a lousy person."

"No, I don't. I just think—"

"You're disappointed in me. You think I'm a crappy friend."

"I didn't say that, Sav. You're a great friend." She was always trying to boost my morale. Telling me I was cute and funny and not as short as I thought. Last year, when I'd been teased a lot for being small or a vegetarian or a brain-box, she'd always stood up for me. And I knew that if I was in trouble she would help me out. When I was home with the flu for two weeks in the spring, she'd come over every afternoon to bring me my homework. "I just think that if you tell someone you're going to their birthday dinner, then you should go. You know, unless something really major happens." Like your house is hit by an asteroid.

"But something major *has* happened." She looked like a little kid who can't understand why her pet gerbil is lying on the floor of its cage with its feet in the air. I was starting to feel as if I was the one who was being unreasonable. "Morgan can see me tonight. I mean, you know what his schedule's like. Who knows how long it'll be before I see him again if I don't go tonight?"

"It'll be a year before Marilouise has another birthday."

"Gee, really?" Savanna widened her eyes. "I didn't know that."

"Oh, come on, Savanna. You know what I mean. You'll have a date with Morgan a lot sooner than Marilouise gets to put another candle on her cake. This is an important night for her."

Her whole body shrugged. "But it's an important night for me, too. I've been waiting, like, days for this." She stuck out her lower lip. "I don't know why you're being so hard on me, Gracie. I mean, what would you do if you had to choose between a date with this totally awesome guy at some sophisticated restaurant and a bowl of spaghetti with Marilouise Lapinskye at a place where they sell pizzas in the foyer?"

"You already bought her a present."

Savanna smiled. "Well, you can give it to her, can't you? That way, she'll know I really was going to come, and she won't feel so bad."

Part of me felt like saying, *Give it to her yourself,* but

it wasn't the dominant part of me. The dominant part of me knew that arguing with Savanna when her mind was made up was like thinking you could stop climate change by only using your car six days a week instead of seven. Pretty pointless. So I said, "What excuse did you give Marilouise for not going?"

Savanna held up a long black skirt and a metallic-pink top. "What do you think?" She shook the top so it shimmered. "Or maybe *this* with the silk trousers and my red miniskirt?"

Maybe I wasn't the only one who knew how to avoid answering a question. I was sitting up so straight by now that I was practically rigid. "Savanna, what did you tell Marilouise?"

"I haven't told her anything." Savanna was still studying the top, her head on one side.

"What do you mean, *you haven't told her anything*?"

Now she was looking at me, but not what you'd call right in the eyes. More like right near the side of my head. "I kind of thought that maybe you could tell her."

"Excuse me?"

"Oh, Gracie . . . You're, like, so much more diplomatic and kind than I am. You know you are." She gave me one of her three-year-old smiles. "And she doesn't know you as well as she knows me. She won't get mad at *you*."

"Oh, no, you don't. . . ." I was shaking my head. Very firmly. "This isn't my problem. There is no way I'm

136

breaking this news to her. You're the one who's . . ." I hesitated, searching for the right words. Letting Marilouise down? Lying to her? Jacking her dinner for something better? "Not coming. You should be the one who tells her." And the one who apologizes. Abjectly.

Savanna moaned. "But you know I hate to be criticized, Gray."

"That's ridiculous. The most judgmental thing I've ever heard Marilouise say was that she doesn't like peanuts."

"That's exactly what I mean. Marilouise is the worst. I mean, she doesn't shout and tell you what a jerk you are like a regular person. She just makes you feel like you stepped on the last butterfly or something."

"Well, that's too bad, isn't it?" Maybe next time she'd look where she was going.

"But I can't tell her, Gray." Savanna dropped the skirt and the top back on the bed. "I mean, how can I tell her when I'm so sick I can't even pick up the phone?"

"Oh, Savanna . . . That is really feeble." You'd think that, with all the lying she did, she'd be better at it. "Marilouise isn't stupid. She'll see right through that."

"Not if you're convincing."

"Savanna—"

She sighed. "Well, can you think of a better excuse? I mean, like, be reasonable, Gracie. There isn't time for anything more complicated. Sudden, paralytic illness is the only possible reason I could come up with at such short notice." She put her hands together. Pleading. "Please, Gracie. Don't let me down. I'm counting on you."

"Savanna, you can't count on me. I mean, you can count on me, obviously you can count on me — you're my best friend — but not for this. I really don't like lying."

She shrugged. Philosophically. "And who does?"

I could think of one person who didn't seem to have a lot of trouble with it.

"I mean it, Savanna. I tried to tell you the other day. I was really uncomfortable with that whole thing about telling Archie we went to see my dad in a play."

"You were? Why?"

Why did she think? Because my bra was too tight?

"Because I had to lie."

"And I told you I was sorry about that, Gracie. I mean, Archie surprised me just as much as he surprised you. I don't see how that gets to be *my* fault. I mean, I can't control what comes out of his mouth, can I?"

"That's not what I mean, Savanna. All I'm saying is that I didn't like lying to him. But this is even worse."

She looked at me. Curiously. Inquisitively. A naturalist discovering a new species of iguana. "How come?"

"Because it's Marilouise's birthday, that's how come. And she's been looking forward to it." I did some more head shaking. "I really don't think I can lie to her like that. I'll feel like a total creep."

"But you're not being a creep. You're being a loyal friend. You're the loyalest friend anyone could ever have. That's why I love you."

"Savanna—"

"I don't mean a loyal friend just to me, Gracie. I mean to Marilouise, too." Now she was looking me right in the eyes. "I mean, what are you planning to do? Tell her what's really going on? Be honest with yourself here, Gracie. How do you think poor Marilouise'll feel if she finds out I skipped her birthday because I'd rather go out with Morgan? You think that's going to boost her self-esteem? You think that's going to cheer her up a whole lot?"

Probably not. Probably it would make her feel like a small piece of dog poo on the bottom of someone's shoe.

"See? That's, like, exactly what I mean," said Savanna. "So you wouldn't be doing her any favors, would you? You'd be making things way worse."

I wasn't sure about way worse, but I could see that I wouldn't be making things way better.

"Well . . ."

"I knew you'd help me!" She ran over and threw her arms around me. "Thankyouthankyouthankyou, Gracie." She squeezed me so hard I gasped. "I'll call you the minute I get home."

Oh, good. At least I still had something to look forward to.

CHAPTER ELEVEN

Eggplant and Angst

Mrs. Zindle gave us a ride as far as the bridge. I'm sure Zelda and Savanna were bickering most of the way because bickering was pretty much their default mode, but I don't really remember the drive. I was pretty preoccupied with swamping myself with guilt about Marilouise. Marilouise had never been anything but really nice to me. Even when Savanna started being best friends with me instead of her, Marilouise never got snappy or snarly the way a lot of people would have. I didn't know how I was going to be able to explain to Marilouise how Savanna was practically on death's front lawn. How could I possibly face her? The way I felt, if I looked her in those clear blue eyes, I was liable to blurt out the truth and beg for mercy.

Savanna was almost out of the car before it stopped, but I climbed out slowly. I felt like I was about to shoot the last silverback gorilla.

"Wish Marilouise a happy birthday for me!" ordered Mrs. Zindle.

Savanna said we would. Mrs. Zindle waved as she drove off. Savanna waved back. The Zindles' gas-guzzler passed the lawn decorated with dozens of smiling garden gnomes and disappeared around a bend. Oh, how I wished I was in it.

"Right, I have to go." Savanna turned and gave me a hug. "Kisskiss, byebye. Don't forget to tell Marilouise how really sorry I am." She thrust her present into my hands. "Tell her I'll call her as soon as I'm feeling better."

Horns honked as Savanna dashed across the street.

My excitement about the evening was as gone as the Mohicans. I'd rather have been digging potatoes. I'd rather potatoes had been digging me. So instead of going right into the restaurant, I hung around in the parking lot for a while. Postponing the inevitable. Psyching myself up. *Marilouise, you'll never guess what happened. . . . Marilouise, it's just totally awful. . . . Marilouise, Savanna is sooo sorry. . . . Well, what's good here besides the eggplant parmigiana?* Eventually, some guy stuck his head out the kitchen door and asked me what I was doing. I went inside.

Anzalone's was always busy on a Saturday night, but that night it was packed tighter than a cattle pen. The first thing I saw after I pushed past the mob of people by the register waiting to pick up their pizzas was a cloud of silver star balloons, swaying over a table at the back.

Everyone at the table was wearing a sparkly paper hat. *Balloons . . . paper hats . . . Happy Birthday, Marilouise!* The icy hand that had been squeezing my stomach relaxed its grip a little. This wasn't what I was expecting. This was a real party, after all. Which was good news. Marilouise wasn't going to be all torn up by one less guest the way she would have been when there were only two altogether. Savanna wasn't really going to be missed. Marilouise might not even notice that she wasn't there. I hovered on the edge of the dining room for a couple of minutes. Maybe I could sneak back out, go home, and leave Marilouise a message on her phone that Savanna and I were both sick. Victims of a small localized epidemic. And then a couple of subzero fingers started squeezing me again. Who *were* all those people? Did any of them look even vaguely familiar? Why hadn't Marilouise told me she'd invited them, too?

Which would be when I finally spotted Marilouise. She wasn't anywhere near the balloons and the sparkly hats. She was sitting by herself at a table set for three in the middle of the room. She was all dressed up as if she was going to a wedding—or, possibly, a party. She was wearing a blue-green dress and a corsage of tiny white flowers pinned to one shoulder, and she'd done something to her hair. Or someone had done something to her hair. Usually it was straight and pulled back in a ponytail, but tonight it was piled on her head in a shiny, solid clutch of curls. For a minute, I was really glad that Savanna wasn't with me. *Omigod,* she would have hissed in my ear. *Do you think they're glued together?* And I would've laughed—because that's exactly how they looked. That was the kind of diplomatic, kind person I was. Marilouise's cell phone was in front of her on the table. She kept glancing down at it.

There was no escape. You could possibly disappoint someone celebrating her birthday with twenty other people, but there was no way you could disappoint someone whose only companion was her phone.

"I'm really sorry I'm late, Marilouise." I sat down and gave her my biggest smile. "Wow," I said, "you look really nice."

"You think so?" Marilouise touched the curls. "My mom treated me for my birthday." She looked behind me. "Where's Savanna? I thought you guys were coming together."

Despite my misgivings, I made myself look right into her eyes. If you're going to lie to someone, you might as well try to make it look like that's not what you're doing.

I explained that Savanna was sick.

"She was fine until about half an hour before I got to her house, and then it all started. It was pretty gross." Vomiting, fever, aches and pains. I made it sound like the return engagement of the Great Plague. "She wants you to know how gutted she is that she couldn't make it, but Zelda wouldn't let her out of the house. I mean, not that she could actually walk as far as the front door. But if she could've, Zelda would've been blocking her way."

"Gee . . ." murmured Marilouise. "Poor Savanna. That sounds awful. I hope it's nothing serious. Did she call the doctor? There's always stuff going around at this time of year. What a drag being sick on a Saturday night."

"Yeah," I agreed. "It's a real bummer. Especially since she was really looking forward to tonight." I crossed my fingers so hard it hurt. "She hasn't talked about anything else all week."

Marilouise's eyes darted to her phone. "Do you think we should call her and see how she is? I hate to think of her lying there all by herself while we're here having a good time. Maybe it would cheer her up."

"She'll be sleeping by now." I wouldn't say that I was proud of how fast I seemed to be getting the hang of lying, but I was definitely relieved that I had more talent for it than I'd thought. "And I'm pretty sure Zelda took her phone away. So she can't be disturbed? Anyway, I'm sure she'll be fine. You know, eventually." I smiled. Positively. "It's probably just one of those twenty-four-hour things. Like you said, there's always a lot of stuff going around at this time of year."

"Yeah." Marilouise nodded. "Even my dog's been sneezing."

I laughed, looking on the bright side. "Well, at least we have each other."

144

Marilouise smiled. Ruefully. "I'm really sorry, Gracie. I mean, it does seem kind of minimal, doesn't it? Just the two of us." She looked at the empty place between us. "It's too bad I didn't invite Jem after all."

Maybe it wasn't too late.

"But, I couldn't ask her now." The curls moved back and forth on her head like a helmet. "She'd think I only invited her because Savanna couldn't make it. That would be really mean."

If there was one thing Marilouise Lapinskye wasn't (you know, besides sexy and gorgeous and scintillating), it was mean. I bet she never lied, either.

"Here." I pulled the presents from my bag. "This one's from me." The one wrapped in newspaper — the ecologist's choice. "The one with the bow is from Savanna."

Marilouise made a big deal of opening her gifts. She carefully peeled back the tape. She patiently untied the ribbon. She slowly unfolded the paper. She could have opened them blindfolded with a hatchet as far as I was concerned. At least watching her was something to do besides feeling like a creep and wishing the evening was over before it had really started.

She made a major fuss over the earrings. "Look!" She held them up on either side of her head. "They totally match my eyes." Her eyes were actually much bluer. She made a major fuss over Savanna's friendship bracelet, too. "If you talk to her before I do, make sure you tell her how much I love it. I don't think I've ever seen anything like it." She obviously hadn't been in the gift shop lately.

Then we pored over the menu for a while.

"Gosh," murmured Marilouise. "There's not much for vegetarians, is there?"

Not if you didn't eat chicken or fish.

"There's plenty," I lied. "I think I'll start with the bruschetta."

"Are you sure that's OK?" asked Marilouise. "They have that salad with the avocado and the mozzarella. . . ."

I gave her a reassuring smile. "I love bruschetta. Really."

"Great." She gave me one of her nervous smiles. "Is it OK if I get the shrimp cocktail for my appetizer? It won't gross you out, will it?"

"Of course not." She could eat raw meat if it made her happy. I wouldn't care if the blood dripped down her chin. "Have whatever you want."

"Then I'll have the shrimp." Marilouise closed her menu. "And the eggplant. It's really, really good." She gave me another nervous smile. "What about you?"

I felt so bad about everything that I went for the eggplant, too — you know, because she was so crazy about it — even though eggplant made me think of slugs.

The meal went slowly. We sat smiling at each other and making polite conversation, surrounded by the noise and hilarity of the other diners like a couple of gulls stranded on a piece of driftwood on an enormous, churning sea.

Every time I opened my mouth, my voice sounded anxious and insincere, so I let Marilouise do most of the talking. She got us through our appetizers talking about school and her dog and stuff like that. Normally, I would have held up my end of the conversation by telling some funny stories or going on about the life and habits of lizards till she begged for mercy, but tonight I didn't have the heart for funny stories or even lizards. I was feeling really down. Which is what being a heel does to me. All I wanted was to go home and put on an old movie to cheer me up and forget that this night had ever happened. *Relax,* I told myself. *It can't get any worse.*

Which would be an example of famous last words.

Our entrées arrived.

Marilouise smiled down at the casserole the waiter put in front of her. "I know it sounds silly, but I've practically been dreaming of this. It is so terrific."

I stared down at my own casserole. "Yeah, it looks really good." It looked like lasagna, all bubbling cheese and tomato sauce. I liked lasagna. Maybe it was going to be all right after all.

Marilouise held up a forkful and blew on it a few times. "It's delicious!" she proclaimed. "It's even better than I remembered."

"Um . . ." *Lasagna*, I told myself. *It's just like lasagna.* I dug in. It was nothing like lasagna underneath. Underneath, it was layers of very large slugs. Sliced and covered in sauce. I cut a tiny piece. I figured that if I kept the pieces really small I'd be able to swallow them whole without having to bite or chew or anything revolting like that. "It's great."

"Savanna would be totally grossed out if she was here. One time she came over for supper and my mom made moussaka and Savanna wouldn't touch it. All she'd eat was the salad." Marilouise broke a bread stick in half. "She said cooked eggplant reminded her of slugs."

I smiled. "She's got a really vivid imagination."

"Tell me about it!" Marilouise laughed the way I would if someone told me that carbon emissions are killing the planet as if it was major news. "She is such a character, isn't she?" She bit into her bread stick. "I mean, she's nothing like me. I'm so quiet and shy and everything, but she's larger-than-life, isn't she?"

I said Savanna was pretty much one of a kind.

Marilouise sighed. "To tell you the truth, I was kind of surprised she said she'd come tonight. I mean, this isn't really her usual scene, is it? Plus she has so many other things to do. And Archie . . ." Her mouth shrugged. "Sometimes I have the feeling she must think I'm pretty boring."

"That's not true. She thinks you're great." I stuffed a forkful of eggplant into my mouth so I didn't have to say anything else—at least not until I'd figured out how to eat it without chewing.

"Well, Savanna isn't boring, that's for sure," said Marilouise. "I guess that's why I've always liked hanging out with her. Because she's so exciting." Crumbs lined her smile. "Did I ever tell you about the time we got locked in her attic?"

"No." I swallowed hard. "I don't think you did."

She rolled her eyes. "I don't even remember *why* we went into the attic in the first place. It was a pretty dumb thing to do, really." I bet I could guess whose idea it had been. "But it was even funnier than the time we were stranded on the lake because Savanna knocked the oars overboard. I mean, we were really lucky there were these boys nearby who rescued us."

What fresh hell was this? I wondered. Was she going to talk about Savanna for the rest of the meal, reliving every fun-filled adventure and hilarious disaster? You know, so it wouldn't be so obvious that we were two dull girls eating slugs together? At the rate I was swallowing, we were going to be at Anzalone's till it closed.

I'd caught the Lapinskye nervous laugh. "Never a dull nanosecond."

Marilouise told me all about the time she and Savanna got locked in the attic. Then she told me all about the time they were stranded on the lake. They were funny stories. And Marilouise told them the way I would have told a funny story about Jackson's chameleons. With warmth and affection. Which meant that I kept picturing Savanna, sitting with Morgan Scheck at a table that, unlike our table, didn't feature a candle stuck in an old wine bottle. I wondered if there was any chance that she was thinking of Marilouise and me.

I'm going to die here, I thought. *Either I'm going to choke to death on a piece of eggplant or the guilt's going to kill me. . . .*

And then I heard someone call my name. "Gracie! Oy, Gracie!"

I didn't care if it was Death himself come to get me. I looked up.

Zebediah Cooper, wearing his old fedora and what looked like a WWII aviator's jacket, was jostling his way between the tables. Archie Snell (dressed like a regular boy) was trotting behind him.

It might have occurred to me that this wasn't necessarily good news—because now I had two more people to lie to. But I'd never been so happy to see anybody in my whole life. I waved like someone drowning. *Thank God!* I thought. *A distraction!*

Cooper came to a stop next to Marilouise. "Happy birthday, Marilouise." He took off his hat with a flourish and bowed. "Many glorious returns of the day."

"Yeah," echoed Archie. "Happy birthday, Marilouise."

"Thanks." Marilouise giggled and blushed. "How did you know?"

Cooper nodded toward me. "Because Gracie Mooney has a big mouth."

"Don't tell me that's why you're here!" Marilouise's cheeks were now the color of a Grand Canyon dawn. "To wish me a happy birthday?"

"One of the reasons," said Cooper. "The other's that Archie suddenly realized he'd never see another day if he didn't get some pizza tonight." He put his hands on the empty chair in front of him. "You guys still eating? You mind if we sit down?"

"No, please . . . sit down." Marilouise pushed her empty plate away. "I'm all done."

"Me, too." My plate wasn't empty, but it was significantly mauled. "I can't eat another bite. It's really filling."

"I'll finish that, if you want," volunteered Archie. "I'm starving."

Cooper grinned at Marilouise. "I must say, you're looking suitably celebratory and fetching tonight. I really dig the corsage."

Marilouise did some more blushing. "Thanks."

Cooper looked over at me. "You look nice, too, Gracie. Kind of post-punk with an ecological theme."

I wasn't used to getting compliments from boys, either. I knocked my fork off the table.

"Hey!" Archie was looking around as if he'd only just noticed that it was just Marilouise and me. "Where's Savanna? I thought she was coming, too."

151

In an ideal world, Marilouise would have explained where Savanna was—on the grounds that it's not a lie if you don't know it is—but Cooper had gone off on one of his tangents, explaining the history of nosegays and tussie-mussies to her, so I was the one who had to explain to Archie about the twenty-four-hour bug and poor Savanna being back at home, feverish and all alone. Missing out on the fun.

"Gee," said Archie, "that's too bad. She said I should . . . I thought she was going to be here." He looked disappointed.

"Yeah," I mumbled. "So did she."

"You think I should call her?" He was reaching for his phone. "Tell her I'm sorry she's sick?"

No, I definitely didn't think he should do that.

"She's not well enough to talk," I said quickly. "Her mom's fielding all calls."

Archie was afraid of Mrs. Zindle. You know, because she was always yelling at Savanna.

"Oh, right." He let his phone drop back into his pocket. "I don't want to bother her if she's that sick."

"So," said Cooper, "now that Archie doesn't need any pizza, since he's eaten half of Gracie's dinner, what say we join you two for dessert?" He leaned back in his chair. "Our treat, of course."

"That's really nice of you. . . . But we're going back to my house for dessert. My mom's made a cake." Marilouise was blushing again. "I guess you're probably busy, but you guys could come, too, if you want."

"I don't know. . . ." Cooper looked at Archie.

"We don't want to intrude," said Archie.

"You wouldn't be," promised Marilouise. "We were just going to eat our cake and maybe play a game of pool."

"Pool?" repeated Cooper. "You've got your own table?" He winked at me. "She's not a hustler, is she?"

I laughed. "Paul Newman and Jackie Gleason."

"What kind of cake did your mom make?" asked Archie.

CHAPTER TWELVE

My Dad Starts Getting Curious, and Savanna Decides She's in Love

So, after all my anxiety and worry and guilt, it turned out to be a really ace night. We hung out at Marilouise's till midnight, playing pool and talking. We laughed a lot. Normally when a few of us got together, Savanna was pretty much the center of the group, but I don't think any of us actually felt there was anything missing. I definitely didn't. I felt kind of guilty about that, too, of course, but I know I wasn't missing Savanna. It wasn't something I'd have said out loud or anything, but I had the sneaky feeling that I'd had a better time than I would have if Savanna hadn't abandoned ship. And I had a hunch that Marilouise did, too. Like me, she was a ten-watt bulb next to Savanna's spotlight—it gave her a chance to shine. Who could have guessed that beneath her quiet, dull surface, Marilouise was really a pool shark with a killer sense of humor?

But I was still pretty glad to get home. Triumphant. I couldn't wait to talk to Savanna. I figured she was going to be as over the moon as I was. Mission accomplished and everybody happy—even me. And something else. After spending the night with Archie, I was feeling really bad for him. I wanted to talk to Savanna about that, too.

The person I didn't want to talk to right then was Robert Mooney. Since I'd done more lying that night than the spokesman for a lumber company in the Amazon does in a week, I was hoping to get to my room without having to do any more.

I should have known my luck couldn't last.

My dad was in the living room, reading homework papers. Which means he was waiting up for me in his old-fashioned caveman way. He raised his head as I shut the door behind me. "Have a good time, honey?"

At least I could start out with the truth.

"Yeah, I did. I had a really good time." I headed for the stairs. "But I'm beat. I didn't realize how late it was."

"What about the birthday girl?" asked my dad. "She have a good time, too?"

I grabbed hold of the banister. "Yeah, she had a really good time, too." I yawned.

But my dad is nothing if not thorough.

"And Savanna?"

I was willing to bet that she'd also enjoyed tonight. Which meant that, technically, I was still telling the truth. "Yeah, she had a really good time, too."

"So where is she?" He cocked his head like he was

listening for something. "I thought she was staying over."

She was—when we were spending the night together with Marilouise. But I'd been so relieved that things had gone well that I'd forgotten that part. Which meant that I had no excuse ready. Unfortunately. Because I couldn't tell my father that Savanna hadn't been with me because he'd want to know why, and (the truth being completely out of the question) there was no way I could say that it was because she was sick. Every Sunday morning, my dad rode his bicycle into town for the Sunday paper. And every Sunday morning Mrs. Zindle drove her gas-guzzler into town for the paper. What if they ran into each other?

I could hear my dad saying, *Hi there, Zelda . . . Savanna feeling better?* And Mrs. Zindle asking, *Better than what?*

"She changed her mind." Strictly speaking, this was true, too.

"Really? Why was that?" My dad's stare seemed to be pinning me to the foot of the stairs. "Don't tell me something came up again."

You had to wonder if he'd become a historian because he had a suspicious nature, or if he had a suspicious nature because he was a historian.

"No . . . You know . . . She just decided not to come back with me."

He tapped his pen against the arm of the couch. "This seems to be happening a lot lately."

"No. You know, not really." I managed to move onto the bottom step. "She always changes her mind a lot."

He nodded. "She's just a woman of whims."

"Yeah." I slipped onto the next step. "She's a woman of whims."

My dad smiled. "So who was that on the porch with you, if it wasn't Savanna?"

Suspicious and with the hearing of a bat.

"Nobody." I shrugged. "You know, just Cooper."

"Cooper," repeated my dad.

"Yeah, you know . . . The guy you saw the other day? The one who got me interested in Neighbors'?" When I'd finally told him about Neighbors', my father had thought it was great that I'd joined. He's a big believer in community spirit. "He walked me home."

Robert Mooney's eyebrow twitched. "Again?"

I started edging farther up the stairs. Casually. "Yeah. You know . . . He likes to walk."

But Robert Mooney wasn't done with me yet.

"I didn't know you were seeing Cooper tonight. I thought it was just you girls."

"It was. You know, just us girls." Even though I was now back in a truth zone, I was still edging ever upward, casual as a leaf in the wind. "He and Archie just happened to show up at Anzalone's. For pizza. And, well, you know . . . they went back to Marilouise's with us—you know, for ice cream and cake—and then Cooper said he'd walk me home so Mrs. Lapinskye didn't have to drive me."

"I see . . ." My dad nodded. "He sounds like a very considerate boy."

Boycott Coca-Cola. . . . Don't buy stuff made in China. . . . Do good deeds. . . .

"Yeah," I muttered. "I guess he is."

"Next time you should invite him in," said my dad. "I'd like to meet him."

"Sure," I answered. "Next time."

As if.

Savanna said she'd call me as soon as she got home, so I went to my room to wait. I was getting into my pajamas when my phone rang. I had to hop over to my dresser on one foot, but I got it on the second ring.

"Omigod, omigod, omigod!" shrieked Savanna. "I'm in love. I mean, really. Reallyreally in love. You wouldn't believe it; I've never, ever felt like this before. I mean, seriously. Not ever. I feel like I've been in a coma for sixteen years and I've finally woken up!"

"Who is this?" I got the other leg of my pajama bottoms on and pulled them up. "What number did you want?"

"Don't tease me, Gracie." Savanna laughed. "I am, like, so totally, ecstatically happy. I mean, like, really. I mean, like, any other time I thought I was happy, I wasn't even in the same room as happy. If I was any happier, I'd probably pass out from joy. I mean it, Gray. This was like the most incredible night of my life. Really. Like, totally incredible."

I wriggled my LOVE IT OR LOSE IT T-shirt with a satellite picture of Earth on it over my head. "So you had a good time?"

"Do birds fly in the sky? Do fish swim in the sea?"

So far they did.

"But it wasn't just good," Savanna rolled on. "To describe it as good is like describing Mount Everest as a big hill. I mean, like, really, Gray, you just wouldn't believe how different going out with a college man is from dating high-school boys. It's like moving into a mansion after you've been living in an apartment over a garage. I mean, talk about sophisticated! He opened doors for me. He pulled out my chair. . . ."

I assumed she didn't mean the way Pete or Leroy would, just as you were about to sit down.

Savanna did her deliriously happy goose impression. "Do you want to hear every supremely wonderful detail?"

"Of course I do. I'm all ears."

"He took me to this really classy restaurant over by Lebanon Springs—"

"Lebanon Springs? But that's miles away."

"He had the car, Gracie, remember? He's old enough to drive at night."

Unlike boys who were still in high school.

"Anyway, you wouldn't have believed this place,

Gracie. It was sooo cosmically cosmopolitan. There's nothing like it in Crow's Point or even Lawson except in the Sunday *New York Times Magazine*. It was all, like, understated and miniature—"

"*Minimalist.*"

"Right. Really elegant and linen napkins. And each place had all this cutlery, like we were going to be eating for the next ten hours or something. It was awesome."

"I'd have been terrified." The two forks at Anzalone's were enough to confuse me. "How did you know which to use when?"

"I just did whatever Morgan did." Just saying his name made her sigh. "Anyway, it was, like, so cool. I felt like I was in my twenties."

Unless I had a sudden growth spurt, I'd be lucky to feel like I was in my twenties when I was thirty-five.

I sat down on my bed. "So what did you eat? How did you know what to order?"

"I said I couldn't make up my mind. You know, because everything sounded so good? So I let him do the ordering."

You had to hand it to her, she was a natural. Either that or she'd learned more from her magazines than I'd thought.

"Well, that must've made him feel needed."

"Gracie, please!"

First they had this amazing salad with noodles and

shrimp and mango and avocado. Then they had this awe-some fish with a squiggle of green sauce next to it on the plate. Then they had this thing that looked like a cup-cake, but when you cut into it, it was filled with melted chocolate.

So much for Mrs. Lapinskye's carrot cake and choco-late ice cream.

"Not that I could eat much," said Savanna. "I mean, I was like sooo charged up and nervous and everything. You know, in case I did use the wrong fork or spoon or something. I really wished you were there, you know, to calm me down like you do."

Aside from the fact that it's really hard to be in two places at once, where would I have been? Under the table with a book on etiquette?

"You know what I mean?" Savanna giggled. "Even if you were just across the room, I wouldn't have felt so nervous."

"You couldn't have felt more nervous than I—" I began.

"No, really," cut in Savanna. "I was, like, totally terrified of saying something that would tell him my real age or what the 'rents really do or something like that. You can't imagine how stressful that is."

I tried again. "I bet that I can."

She wasn't listening.

"So, after we ate we took this, like, awesomely

romantic walk in the moonlight. You know, just like on television."

"You mean life doesn't imitate art; it imitates bad TV?"

"Oh, Gracie, don't. It was really fantastic."

They held hands. They talked about life and stuff like that. They saw a shooting star.

"You know what that means, don't you?" demanded Savanna. "A shooting star?"

Normally, I would have said that it meant some interplanetary dust had burnt out in the upper atmosphere, but I was still thinking about walking in the moonlight. Technically, I'd been walking in the moonlight, too, but it had only been romantic if you consider discussing pool shots a prelude to falling in love.

"No, what?"

"It's a sign, that's what! You know, that my meeting Morgan and everything was, like, really destined. It's the real deal."

This, of course, would be ignoring all the people who saw the same star fall while they were putting gas in their cars or taking out the garbage. But I didn't point that out, either. I would've felt like a grump.

"And then he kissed me!" Savanna crowed. "That was like nothing else I've ever experienced, either. I mean, you remember what Archie was like when we first started going out?" I did. She'd said then that kissing Archie was like biting into something that bit back. "This was more spiritual than physical. It was, like, electric. It was like kissing clouds. . . . Oh, I can't describe it, Gray. It makes me go all weak and swoony just to think about it."

It wasn't making me feel weak and swoony. The more she gushed about Morgan, the more I thought of Archie, spending the night with Cooper, Marilouise, and me—while the person he wanted to spend it with was exchanging saliva with Morgan Scheck.

I gave her a couple of seconds to recover, and then I said, "So now that you're officially in love, does that mean you're going to tell Archie about Morgan?"

"Omigod," said Savanna. "Will you listen to me go on and on about myself. I never asked you how it went with Marilouise. Did she like my present?"

"She loved it. She was really sorry you're so sick."

"You see?" Savanna laughed. "Didn't I tell you she'd buy it?"

"And guess who came into Anzalone's while we were there?" I went on. "Archie and Cooper. They said they wanted a pizza, but I think, really, they dropped by because Archie thought he was going to see you. You know, I got the impression you told him he should drop by."

"I don't remember saying that," said Savanna.

"Anyway, they wound up going back to Marilouise's with us and—"

"Hang on a second," interrupted Savanna. "I have

another call." She was back in a minute. "It's *Morgan*! Can you believe it? He didn't even wait till the morning. I have to go. I'm probably seeing him tomorrow, but I have to babysit Sofia tomorrow night. Mother Zindle's going out at six. Come over at six thirty and spend the night. Then we can really talk."

"Right. Six thirty it is," I said.

But I said it to myself.

Savanna was already gone.

CHAPTER THIRTEEN

*I Talk to Archie,
and Savanna Talks to Me*

I'm not sure why (since we did have a date for that night), but I kind of thought Savanna might call me on Sunday morning. You know, because she'd had to hang up so abruptly. Only she didn't. It was Cooper who called.

Cooper said he and Archie had had such a good time last night, they wondered if Marilouise and I wanted to go bowling with them and Leroy and Pete that afternoon. I wasn't what you'd call a great bowler. I was more what you'd call a really bad one. Balls rolled behind me instead of in front, or bounced into the gutter. I figured it was because I was so short. Everyone else strode gracefully, while I scurried. Practically the only thing I'd ever knocked over was a giant-size soda Leroy put down on the bench. The only reason I ever went bowling with the others was because Savanna wouldn't go without me. She wasn't as humiliatingly awful as I was, but she wasn't nearly as good as the boys.

I was surprised Archie wanted to go without Savanna.

"Why not?" laughed Cooper. "He was bowling a long time before they started dating, you know."

"And you? *You're* going bowling?" Cooper never came with us.

"I'm usually busy on Sundays," said Cooper. "But I'm not busy today."

I wasn't busy, either. I said yes. Marilouise said yes, too.

Usually, our games were more like a dramatic event than a sport. It always took us a long while to settle down because Savanna had to get the right pair of shoes and the right ball and exactly the right position before she could throw, which meant the boys had eaten all their snacks before we began and had to get more. There were always arguments over who was keeping score and whose turn it was. But somehow the presence of Marilouise and Cooper changed all that. Marilouise didn't mess around. She took charge of the scoring, put on her shoes, found a ball she liked, and got a strike on her first go. In fact, she turned out to be almost as good at bowling as she was at pool. And Cooper turned out to be even better than Archie, who actually owned his own ball. We still had fun and laughed a lot, but it was more like we were goofing around while we played, not playing while we goofed around.

After my first ball bounced into the gutter, Cooper decided to show me what I was doing wrong.

"Loosen up. You're not rolling it; you're dropping it."

I said that I knew that.

He stood behind me, his arm over mine. "Don't let go, Gracie. Just go through the motions with me."

Up . . . back . . . forward . . . forward . . . swing . . .

"Watch out!" warned Pete. "You know what a player he is!"

The others all laughed. I dropped the ball.

"Yo, Cooper!" called Archie. "Maybe you should become a professional coach."

But by the second game, I was knocking down pins every time. Not a lot, maybe—but more than I would have if I'd sat out my turn.

"You see?" Cooper winked. "You just needed the right teacher."

I started having a really good time.

And then, just before our last game, I decided to get myself a drink. Which would be about when my good time ended.

"I'll come with you," offered Archie. "I'm still hungry." He looked at the others. "Anybody else want anything?"

After Archie had taken the orders and we were walking across the lanes, he glanced over at me and said, "So . . . did you talk to Savanna?"

I hesitated for a few seconds. Was she off the critical list yet? Should I say yes? If I said yes, what should I say that she'd said?

"No." I went straight for the lie. "I called her this morning, but her mom said she's still, you know, not well enough to talk. She's still pretty much sleeping all the time."

"Right." Archie opened the door to the snack bar, but instead of walking through it he came to a stop. "Gracie?" He was practically whispering. "Gracie, can I ask you something?"

I must have known that he wasn't going to ask me about the probable effects of unchecked global warming, but my guard was down. I walked into his question like a dolphin swimming into a tuna net.

"Sure," I said. "What is it?"

"It's just that . . . you know . . ." He took hold of my arm and guided me into the snack bar, steering me into a corner. Gently but firmly. "Since you're Savanna's best friend and everything . . ."

I nodded. Slowly. I was getting one of my bad feelings. Polar bears were pitching into icy seas. "Uh-huh . . ."

"Well . . . it's just . . . I mean . . ." He was shifting his weight from one foot to the other. I could hear him swallow. "OK . . . Look, it's just that—" He took a really deep breath. "Is Savanna mad at me or something, Gracie?" He looked really worried. "Is that what's going on? She's mad at me?"

"Mad at you?" I laughed the way you do when someone tells a joke that isn't funny. "Savanna's not mad at you, Arch. I don't know what you're talking about. There's nothing going on."

"Well, she's acting like she's mad at me." He stopped shifting and stood dead still. "Like I did something . . . or said something . . ." His foot tapped against the linoleum floor. "You know Savanna . . ." *Tap, tap, tap.* "Sometimes it's hard to tell."

"Well, she hasn't said anything to me." I smiled in a bright, end-of-conversation way. "You must be having another one of your hallucinations."

"I'm not so sure." He didn't smile back. "And I'm not sure you're being straight with me. Maybe you're just trying to spare my feelings."

If I was, I wasn't doing a very good job.

"Archie, I'm telling you the truth." I crossed my heart. "Smokey Bear Junior Forest Ranger's honor. Savanna isn't mad at you."

He finally managed half a smile, but it wasn't what you'd call happy.

"Really, Archie. I'd know if she was."

Somehow it was more horrible seeing someone as confident and happy as Archie undermined by doubt and worry than it would have been to see someone more like me bottoming out. I might have hugged him if it hadn't meant burying my head in his stomach.

"Then why is she acting so weird?"

I said that I thought he was asking the wrong person.

"But I did ask Savanna." Archie's shoulders moved slowly up and down like the flippers of a dying seal. "She said that she didn't know what I was talking about. She said there's nothing wrong."

I gave him an affectionate shove. "Well? What more do you want?"

"Yeah, but she didn't hang out with me all last week, Gracie. She always had some lame-o excuse—either she had too much homework, or she was tired, or her mother needed her for something. And when I do see her at school . . . Well, you know how she is at lunch. She hardly talks at all anymore. She acts like she's had an iPod implanted in her brain and she's listening to that."

I smiled. Cheerily. "Well, maybe she's just going through a quiet phase," I suggested. "People do. Even really talkative people." Even people who never shut up.

"Is that how she is with you?" asked Archie. "Quiet bordering on comatose?"

No, when we're alone she talks about her other boyfriend so much that I don't know when she has time to breathe.

"Well, you know, Archie . . . We talk about girl things. It's different." If my smile got any cheerier, I was going to start singing and dancing. "Except for not having much to say sometimes, Savanna seems the same to me."

"Well, not to me," said Archie. "It's like every time I go to touch her, she moves out of my way. It's gotten so bad I'm afraid to put my arm around her anymore. I can't even remember the last time she kissed me."

Necessity isn't the only mother invention has—it has desperation, too.

"Well, maybe she knew, you know, subconsciously, that she was coming down with something and she didn't want you to catch it."

"That's another thing." Archie did his dying-seal impersonation again. "Last night—"

"Last night she got sick, Archie. Unless you're Typhoid Mary, that had nothing to do with you."

"But she wasn't sick yesterday morning," said Archie. "Yesterday morning, she said she was going to be at Anzalone's. Definitely."

"I told you. It was sudden." I had to resist the temptation to pat his arm. "Really, Arch, Savanna isn't mad at you. It's just one of her moods. She's probably just a little stressed out. You know, with school and her family and everything."

I thought I sounded pretty convincing—but not to everyone.

"Look, I won't say anything to Savanna," promised Archie. "I just want to know if she's not into me anymore or what. It's kind of driving me nuts. And there's nobody else I can talk to about it."

What about Cooper? Wasn't that what friends were for?

The only extrasensory perception I'd ever noticed in Archie was the ability to know if I had a brownie in my lunch box before I opened the lid, but now he seemed to be able to read my mind.

"Not Cooper," said Archie. "He thinks Sa— Well, you know what Cooper's like. He'd say I should tell her to get a life and stop messing with my head."

And I should have said, *Dump her! Dump her now, before she causes you even more pain, humiliation, and heartbreak.* Only I didn't.

I said, "I think that would be overreacting."

"Well, I don't want to." Archie sighed. "I don't want to break up with her. I just want her to be nice to me again."

"Oh, Arch . . ." It was like hearing baby orangutans say that they wished the men would stop bulldozing their habitat and shooting their mothers. Enough to break your heart.

"Please, Gracie. If Savanna's through with me, I really need to know." Archie patted my arm. "You can tell me the truth."

No, I couldn't.

"I told you." I wondered if, besides being able to read my mind, he could tell that my palms were sweating. "I *am* telling you the truth, Arch. As far as I know, there's nothing wrong."

His frown softened. "You're sure?"

I felt as if I was waving good-bye to someone who was walking backward and straight off a cliff.

"I'm absolutely, totally positive."

"Really?"

"Yeah, really."

He looked as if he might cry with relief. "Thanks, Gracie. You're a pal." He grabbed my hand and started shaking it. "I feel much better."

That made one of us.

"We'd better go and get the supplies." I laughed. "Pete and Leroy will be eating the bench by now." I was ready to run to the bright lights of the snack bar.

"Gracie." Archie grabbed my arm. "Gracie, this is just between you and me, right? You won't say anything to Savanna, will you?"

"Of course not," I said. "My lips are sealed."

"I am sooo sorry, Gracie." Savanna pulled a box of pasta and a jar of tomato sauce out of the cabinet and handed them to me. "I mean, like, really, I wouldn't even want that troglodyte Jemima Satz to get stuck by herself with my psycho sister, never mind you."

"Sofia was fine." She was in the family room, wearing her tutu and watching TV with the sound turned down when I'd arrived, and she was still there. She hadn't said a word to me. "It was your mom who kind of gave me a hard time."

I'd showed up at six thirty, as we'd arranged, but as soon as I rang the bell, Mrs. Zindle started shouting. *Don't tell me you forgot your key again. . . . Where the hell have you been? Why can't I ever depend on you?* I knew she wasn't talking to me. I got on all right with Mrs. Zindle. I'd seen her yell at her family pretty much the way you see clouds (you know, in the background and on a regular basis), but we weren't related so she never yelled at me. My wild guess was that Savanna wasn't back yet.

"Poor Gracie . . . It's all me, me, me with Zelda," sympathized Savanna. "I mean, it's not like she was going to the Oscars or something. It's just some dinner with people she works with. She *has* eaten with them before." She bent down to the cabinet where the pots were kept. "Was she totally mad-eyed berserk?"

That was one way of putting it. If Mrs. Zindle had been an air force, she would have been in über-carpet-bombing mode.

"I am, like, really sorry, Gray." She handed me the spaghetti pot. "I mean, I planned to be home on time, but what was I supposed to do? I couldn't turn into a pumpkin at exactly five o'clock, could I? Love doesn't own a watch."

Or even glance at the clock on its cell phone, apparently. Savanna rolled up after seven.

"Zelda was really curious about where you were." I

went over to the sink and started filling the pot with water. "You know, because she thought you were with me."

"Omigod . . ." Savanna covered her mouth with her hand. "I guess I should've warned you." She smiled. Warily. "What did you tell her?"

I carried the pot of water to the stove. "I said we'd all gone bowling, and then you and Archie went off together and I went home to get my stuff."

"Gracie Mooney, you're a genius!" She took out a saucepan and handed it to me. "That was, like, totally inspired."

"Not really." I opened the jar of sauce and emptied it into the pan. "It was pretty much the truth. You know, except that you weren't with us, of course."

"What?" Savanna straightened up. She was smiling as if she thought I was pulling her leg. "You really went bowling? With the boys?"

I nodded. "Yeah."

"You all went bowling without *me*?"

I looked around to see what else there was to do. "You want me to set the table?"

"You can't be serious. I mean, like, *really*? You all went bowling without *me*?" The way Savanna was smiling made it look like she didn't have any teeth. "Nobody even asked me if I wanted to go?"

"You were doing something else, Savanna, remember?

And, besides, you were sick. How could they ask you to come when you were sick?"

"But you don't even like bowling, Gracie. You always complain when I want you to go."

"Well, this time I didn't."

"Oh, and why was that, Gracie?" She was going to have frown lines just like her mother if she didn't stop making that face. "Because Archie called you up and asked you to go bowling with him and Leroy and Pete? Without *me.*"

"Don't be ridiculous. Besides, it was Cooper who invited me."

This laugh was nothing like a honk—or like falling beads. It was like someone coughing out a nut that had gone down the wrong way. "Cooper? But Cooper doesn't go bowling. He's never gone with us even once."

I checked to see if the water was boiling yet. "Well, this time he did."

Savanna made an exaggerated, jokey face. "That must have been a lot of fun. You and four boys. I mean, most of the time you hardly talk to them. You usually grouch if I leave you alone with them for, like, half a second."

"I wasn't alone." I lowered the lid again. "Marilouise came, too."

"Marilouise?" Savanna's eyebrows practically hit her hairline. "*Marilouise* went with you?"

"Oh, for Pete's sake, Sav." I was starting to see

certain advantages in sticking to Morgan as a topic of conversation. Boring but safe. "I don't know why you're getting all bent out of shape about it. We went bowling. You know, like millions of American teenagers do every day. What's the big deal?"

"That's not the point, Gray." Her lower lip was down. "The point is that it's a little hurtful to see how nobody was even a tiny bit concerned about me. I mean, I was supposed to be really sick. For all Archie knew, I was on my deathbed. What would you have done if I'd died? Thrown a party?"

"You're being completely ludicrous." I thrust the box of pasta into her hands. To give her something to do besides fester and fume. "And, anyway, Archie was very concerned about you."

She stopped sulking aggressively. "Really?"

"Yeah, really." When I told Archie that I wouldn't say anything to Savanna about our conversation, I'd meant it. But I could tell that I was on the brink of breaking my promise. I turned away from her and got involved with the pasta water again.

"What did he say?"

"You know . . ." I shrugged. "That he hoped it wasn't anything serious. I had to stop him from coming over to see how you were."

"There's something you're not telling me," said Savanna.

"No, there isn't." I reached for the box. "The water's ready."

"Are you sure there's nothing else, Gracie?" She narrowed her eyes. Thoughtfully. "What are you holding back? Your ears are going red."

I really had to think about growing my hair.

"*Me?*" I choked. "You're the one who's holding back, Sav. You haven't said a word about your date with Morgan since you walked through the door." I frowned. "Don't tell me you didn't have a good time."

"Don't try to change the subject, Gray," ordered Savanna. "I know you too well. What did Archie say?"

"I can't tell you. I promised."

"Gracie . . ." She had that take-no-prisoners look in her eyes. "What did Archie say? You're my best friend. You can't keep something like that from me."

"You swear that you won't tell him I told you?"

"On a bear." She handed me the pasta.

"He thinks you're mad at him. You know, because you haven't been hanging out and hardly talk to him."

"Oh, for Pete's sake . . . He never listens to what I say anyway."

"He thinks you've been acting weird. You know, avoiding him." I sighed as I watched the fusilli fall into the water. "He seemed really upset."

Just call me Little Big Mouth.

"And what did you say?"

"What do you mean, *What did I say?* I said there was nothing wrong. I said you definitely weren't mad at him."

"Thankyouthankyou, Gracie!" Savanna threw her arms around me. "I knew I could count on you."

"You know what?" I said as we disengaged. "Maybe now would be a good time to tell Archie the truth."

"I know you think I'm being awful, Gray, but actually I'm trying to be kind. Really. I mean, the point is that I can't say anything till I'm really sure about Morgan. You don't want me to hurt Archie for no reason, do you?" She smiled. Shyly. "Anyway, you know what they say: a bird in the hand is worth two in the bushes."

"Bush," I said.

CHAPTER FOURTEEN

Back with a Vengeance

Savanna and I were running a little late on Monday morning because she had to have an argument with her mother and find her cell phone (in the box of remotes by the TV) before we could leave the house.

"I've been, like, thinking about what you were saying last night," said Savanna as we hurried to school. "About Archie being so upset at the way I've been acting? I mean, I do think it's pretty self-centered of him to assume it, like, has anything to do with *him,* but I guess I have been a little self-absorbed lately. And I'm not mad at him, you know I'm not. I really like him a lot. I don't want him to get all bitter and twisted or anything."

"So what are you going to do?" I figured there wasn't much point in saying "Tell the truth" again.

"Watch this space," said Savanna. "This week is going to be different."

The boys were already in the lounge by the time we got there. Archie, Pete, and Leroy were talking among themselves—in the way boys do when there are no girls there to get bored by a verbal replay of Saturday's game. Cooper was sitting next to Pete, his eyes on the door. He waved when he saw us.

We both waved back.

Savanna sailed across the lounge as if a strong wind was pushing her. "Hi, everybody!" she called. "I have returned!"

And, just like that, zombie girl was gone.

Leroy, Pete, and Archie all looked up. Archie's smile was wary.

Cooper scooted over so I could sit between him and Pete. "I didn't know you'd been away," he said to Savanna.

Savanna made a face that was guaranteed to get her massive wrinkles in thirty years. "I wouldn't expect *you* to notice." She plonked herself down so close to Archie she was practically in his lap. She leaned her smile next to his face. "Kisskiss." She rubbed her nose against his cheek. "But *you* were worried about me, weren't you, Arch? *You* missed me."

"You know I did." Archie was kind of blinking as if he thought he might be dreaming. He touched his cheek.

"What are you looking like that for?" Savanna hooked a foot around his ankle. "Aren't you glad to see me?"

"Yeah, of course I'm glad to see you." Though maybe he wasn't expecting her to be speaking to him again so suddenly. He slipped an arm around her shoulder.

Gingerly. She didn't squirm or pull away. "I just didn't think you'd be in today. From what Gracie said. I thought you were really sick. She said you couldn't even talk on the phone yesterday."

And here we had living proof of the miracle that is modern medicine.

"I *was* really sick. I don't think I've ever been sicker in my whole life." Savanna shook her hair and sighed. "And I'm still not, like, a hundred percent. I mean, my muscles ache like I've been working out for the last two days. But I couldn't stay in bed another second without dying of boredom. I mean, I, like, missed you so much. . . . Anyway, I vowed that if I didn't have a fever this morning, I'd come in no matter how bad I felt." She snuggled against him. "So what did you do while I was all by myself on my bed of pain?" She looked up at him, smiling almost shyly. "I hope you didn't have too much fun."

Archie started to tell her what he'd done while she had the twenty-four-hour plague, trying to make it sound like a lot less fun than having a near-death experience.

Meanwhile, Leroy leaned across Pete and tapped my knee. "Gracie," he said. "I need your help. Remember you were talking yesterday about that book you read a—"

"Hey, wait your turn." Pete shoved him back. "I need Gracie to check my math for me. It's my first class, so it has priority."

"You can both get to the back of the line," said

Cooper. "I have something really important I have to discuss with Gracie." He pulled a notebook from his mailbag. "Remember we were talking about how boring the language manuals are at the project?" He opened the notebook across our knees. "Well, I had this earth-shaking moment of inspiration last night, and I had this really great idea—"

Out of the corner of my eye, I saw Savanna pull out of the snuggle and sit up so quickly Archie practically fell over.

"Omigod!" shrieked Savanna. "That reminds me. I have this really great idea, too!"

That got everybody's attention. The boys all stopped talking and looked at her.

"It is, like, so awesomely fantabulous!" Her hands flapped in the air as if she was about to take off. "I mean, I can't believe I forgot about it for even a second!" She straightened up.

It was Cooper who said, "So what's this great idea?"

"That we all go to the Christmas dance together." If Savanna had been the sun, it would have been high noon. "I mean, haven't you seen the posters? They're all over the place. It's like the social event of the winter."

Just in case you forgot, the Christmas dance had been mentioned—briefly and fairly unfavorably—the week before. That would be when Archie asked Savanna if she wanted to go. And she pretty much said no.

"Forget it," said Leroy. "There's nobody I want to ask who isn't already going with someone else."

"And there's nobody I want to ask, period," said Pete.

"Yeah, but that's why my idea is so abnormally fantastic. I mean, nobody has to have a date." Savanna looked so pleased you'd think she'd come up with an alternative and sustainable fuel to oil. "Instead of going as couples, we all go with each other. That way, it'll be more like a party. Think what a blast it'll be!"

Archie had been looking at Savanna as if he didn't know the dog could speak English, but now he said, "What are you talking about, Savanna? When I asked you, you said you didn't want to go to the dance."

"I said I'd think about it, Archie. Remember?" Savanna laughed and leaned against him. "And now I've thought about it. And I've decided we should all go."

"Does that mean you're paying for the tickets?" asked Pete.

Savanna pretended to laugh.

"Well, you can count me out," said Cooper. "I'm not a dancing man. And even if I was, it's the same night as the Neighbors' Christmas bash. There's no way I can pass up a potluck supper and accordion music." He glanced over at me. "So I'll be otherwise engaged."

I nodded. "Me, too." It isn't true that anyone with a heartbeat can dance. This is a myth I'd disproved when I was five and was asked to leave Miss LeBlanc's ballet class. "I'm not a dancing man, either." The potential for public humiliation was virtually limitless.

"But the beauty of my idea is that it doesn't matter if you can't dance," insisted Savanna. "We'll all be together. Hanging out. You don't even have to tap your toes in time to the music if you don't want to."

What I didn't want to do was go to the dance.

"And what sense does that make?" I argued. "It's like going to a buffet and not eating."

"You what?" Savanna's smile set like cement. "What are you saying, Gracie? Are you saying you'd rather go to some *church supper* than the Christmas dance?"

I'd rather go to Florida in August than the Christmas dance.

"You know I don't like stuff like that, Savanna. Dances really aren't my scene." Nor were parties, of course. I hadn't even thought about the Neighbors' bash. "And, anyway, I didn't say I was go—"

"I mean, that's not, like, the point, Gracie," said Savanna. "The point is that it's, like, really hurtful to me that you'd rather . . . that you don't want to come. Pete and Leroy are coming." She turned to Pete and Leroy, the selling-ice-in-Alaska look on her face. "Aren't you?"

Pete shrugged. "I guess so. Since it's Christmas."

"Yeah, why not?" said Leroy. "I suppose it could be fun."

I said, "Oh, Savanna . . ."

Cooper leaned toward me. "I guess that means you're dreaming of a white Christmas," he whispered.

"Bing Crosby and Fred Astaire, *Holiday Inn*," I whispered back.

"Ow!" screamed Savanna. "You don't have to yank the hair out of my head, Gray. When I said I wanted to look different, I didn't mean bald."

"But I have to get the hair through the little holes in the cap, don't I? And I can't do that without pulling."

It was almost Thanksgiving and Savanna wanted a new look for the holidays, so I was giving her lowlights. When she'd wanted to revamp her image for the summer, we'd dyed her hair black, but she'd had an allergic reaction and her face had swollen as if she'd been stung by a swarm of bees, so this time we were going for a less radical change. You know, one that wasn't life-threatening.

"Just be, like, gentle, OK?"

I said that I'd be as gentle as someone pulling hair through tiny holes in a plastic cap with a crochet hook could be.

"So what were you and Archie being all conspiratorial about this morning?" asked Savanna as I started applying the colorant.

"We were plotting the overthrow of civilization."

Savanna laughed. "Yeah, right. What's Archie's role? Is he in charge of bringing the snacks?"

I said that if he saw her the way she looked now—like a refugee from *Star Trek* with her hair all sticking out and an old beach towel wrapped around her—he'd probably bring a camera.

When Savanna stopped honking, she said, "So what was it? You were thick like thieves."

"*As* thieves." My voice was a little muffled because I was wearing a bandanna across my face so I didn't inhale any death-ray fumes. "Anyway, we weren't conspiring; we were just talking." The plastic gloves protecting my hands crackled. "He was just telling me how happy he is. You know, now that everything's normal again."

This was practically the first time Savanna and I had been alone since Monday morning. While I was "watching this space" as Savanna had told me to, she had spent the week putting the "in" back into "inseparable." Whenever they weren't in a class, she and Archie were together. Holding hands. Rubbing shoulders. Kissing good-bye as if they were going off to war and not history and gym. She'd spent a couple of afternoons with him, playing footsie under the table while they did their homework together in the library. She even went to the basketball game on Thursday night. It was as if the week before— when she'd been distant and distracted and checking her phone every three minutes—had never happened.

"Me, too." Savanna smiled at me in the mirror. "Not that I, like, had any doubts. I knew it would work."

"Excuse me?" I dropped the strand of hair I'd been dabbing with dye. "Are you saying it's all an act?"

"Not an act, Gracie," Savanna corrected. "It's called being philosophical. I mean, I couldn't take another week like that last one, all warped out because of Morgan. It was way too stressful. Look, my nails even started breaking." She held her hands in the air so I could look. "Anyway, it isn't like I haven't figured out Morgan's MO by now."

Self-centered. Pretty self-absorbed. Inconsiderate. So hard to get on the phone you'd think he was a spy.

"He's very disorganized, Gray. And that's, like, really not helpful when you're so busy all the time. I mean, I know I'm going to see him before he goes home for Thanksgiving next week—he absolutely promised I'll see him this weekend—but I just have to accept that there's no way he'll call till the last minute."

This was Friday. There couldn't be too many minutes left.

"Exactly. Like, what's the point of me being all miserable when I could be having a good time? I mean, not to mention poor Archie. You have to think of him, too, you know."

I thought I had.

"Yes, you did," agreed Savanna. "And I'm really grateful to you for making me see that. I mean, why should he suffer? It's not like I don't still like him." The towel shrugged and the tentacles shook. "I just like Morgan a little more."

I started dabbing again. "So you're not really back with Archie."

"Never mind about me." Savanna was watching me in the mirror. "What about you?"

"Me?"

This was what happened when I spent a few days without Savanna: my thought processes slowed down. I had no idea what she was talking about.

"Yeah, you—"

"Savanna!" I tugged on her hair. "Stop moving your head. I'm getting this junk all over me."

"Don't change the subject," said Savanna. "When I asked you what was going on with you and Cooper, you told me nothing was going on."

Which would be because it was true.

"Really?" Arching your eyebrows doesn't really work when you've got tentacles sticking out of your head and a Bart Simpson beach towel wrapped around you. "Well, that's not what Archie says. Archie says that he definitely thinks there's, like, something going on." She twitched her shoulders and Bart kind of winked. "At least with you . . ."

I stopped dabbing again. "What do you mean, *at least with me*?"

She shuffled in her seat. "Well, it wouldn't be Cooper, would it? I mean, like I tried to tell you, Gracie, Cooper's never shown any teensy-weensy interest in girls. I'm not saying he takes the other road or anything, Gray, but Archie says he's never even said he thought someone was hot or anything like that. And he's never said anything about you. As a person, maybe, but not as a girl." She raised her eyebrows. Pointedly. "You have to think what that means."

It was amazing how she could look totally ridiculous and smug at the same time.

"I think it means that he's not a testosterone-drugged jerk, that's what I think it means."

The tentacles shook. "Oooh, somebody's touchy."

"I'm not touchy. I just don't know why you're all of a sudden on my case about Cooper." Again.

"I'm not on your case. I'm just concerned." She looked concerned. A concerned visitor from another planet. "You're my best friend, remember? I don't want you to get your hopes up or anything."

"Oh, for Pete's sake, Savanna." She wasn't looking in the mirror, so she couldn't see the scornful expression on my face. "I'm sorry, but didn't we have this conversation already?"

"That was *then*," said Savanna. "*Now*, Archie says you stuck as close to Cooper as a stamp to an envelope when you all went bowling without me. He told me all about it." She stopped looking at her lap. "Which is, like, more than you did."

"Because there was nothing to tell. And I didn't—"

"Archie was full of all kinds of information, Gracie." Maybe it was because of the plastic cap on her head, but she reminded me of one of those old movies where the women all sit under the dryers at the hairdressers', gossiping about their neighbors and friends. "He said you even got Cooper to put his arms around you."

If I hadn't had gloves covered with gloop on my hands I would have slapped my forehead. "I didn't *get him to*, Savanna. He was showing me how to bowl. That's why I finally managed to knock something down."

Just to prove that her repertoire of animal sounds wasn't limited to honking like a goose, Savanna snorted like a horse. "In the snack bar?" She smiled. Thinly. "Don't the balls trip people up? That must get kind of messy."

"No, not in the snack bar. In the lanes."

"Archie said that you were practically on Cooper's lap in the snack bar."

This was so ridiculous that I burst out laughing.

"Have you and I met, or what?"

Savanna's lips were twitching, but she wasn't going to give up yet. She single-handedly redefined the limits of stubbornness.

"You *have* been hanging out with Cooper a lot," she said.

"No, I haven't."

"You went to the library with him."

"One time. To get some books. And it was *his* idea."

Even though Savanna didn't wear glasses, the way she was looking at me made it seem as if she did. "But you did tell him you'd be at Anzalone's. *And* you invited him back to Marilouise's for cake."

"No, I didn't. Marilouise—"

"You go to that quacking thing with him."

"They're *Quakers*. Some of them. And I don't go *with* him. I—"

"Well, he's there, Gracie. And you didn't used to go, did you? You only went in the first place because of him."

"Oh, you really are too much." I was ready to throw the disposable sponge applicator at her. "I don't even like Cooper. I only got to be friends with him because of you."

I don't know why I said that. You know, about not liking him. It sounded like I disliked him. It just came flying out of my mouth like a bat from a cave at dusk. It was like the time when I was little and I told my dad that I wished he was dead. I didn't want him to be dead. I never want him to be dead.

"Really?"

"I told you before, Savanna. I could never like him like you're saying."

"Phew!" Savanna pretended to wipe sweat from her forehead. "Archie really had me worried. He seemed so sure. And I really didn't want to see you make a fool of yourself."

I gazed at the two of us in the mirror. Octopus Woman and a short bandit.

Me, neither.

She rolled her eyes. "I should've known Archie was up the wrong tree."

"Exactly. Way the wrong tree."

CHAPTER FIFTEEN

Savanna and I Finally Go to the Mall

Even though he'd absolutely promised, Morgan couldn't see Savanna that weekend after all.

"He's just, like, really busy, Gracie," Savanna explained. She meant that he was *still* really busy. "I mean, Thursday *is* Thanksgiving, so, obviously, he's got a lot going on. He said that he'll see what he can do."

He was either a spy or a turkey farmer.

"You should've heard him on the phone, Gray. He was, like, so sweet and sorry I thought he was going to cry."

I thought I was going to cry, too. One of the things I'd always loved about Savanna was her optimistic nature. You know, because I was such a worrier. But now I was starting to worry about her optimism.

"At least this gives us a chance to go to the mall on Sunday," Savanna said. Besides needing something for the Christmas dance, she didn't feel that her wardrobe was really worthy of Morgan Scheck. (Just in case she ever saw him again.) "And we can't go next weekend when everybody else starts their Christmas shopping—because the Professor's doing that thing he does, so we're busy."

I didn't really want to go to the mall. I wanted to help my dad start getting ready for that thing he does. Which is Remember the Wampanoag Day. My father never makes a big deal out of Thanksgiving. He has issues with the Pilgrims. The day he makes a big deal of is Remember the Wampanoag Day. The Wampanoag were the people who helped the colonizers. My dad says we should never forget the arrogance of the invaders or how the Wampanoags' trust and kindness was repaid with genocide and theft. So every year, on the Saturday after Thanksgiving, my father invites all his friends and his whole department and their families over for a major meal. Everybody brings something to drink and a dessert, and he cooks succotash and stuffed squash, talks about the Iroquois Confederacy until you feel like you'd been there, and, after dinner, he and his band play and everybody sings along to "The Ballad of Ira Hayes" and "Pocahontas." It's a big deal for me, too. It's the kind of day that makes you think you've always been happy. That's why we were busy the next weekend. Savanna was coming to remember the Wampanoags.

So on the Sunday before Thanksgiving, we took the one o'clock bus to the mall.

* * *

Savanna twisted to the left, then twisted to the right. "What do you think, Gray? Does it make me look older?"

"Older than what?"

She sighed. "Gracie . . . I'm dating a college man, remember? I don't want to look, like, juvenile. I want to look mature and sophisticated."

"It's yellow." I was getting really bored. It was at least the twelfth outfit she'd tried on. "Yellow doesn't make anyone look older, unless it's the color of her skin."

Savanna screwed up her mouth, still staring at the mirror. "You're right. It makes me look like something you'd get in your Easter basket." She heaved another sigh.

"Well, what about that red skirt and jacket we saw? There was nothing juvenile about that. I'll go and get it if you want. It'd look great on you."

"Oh, nonononono." She shook her head. "Not red. Red's, like, totally not in the equator."

"*Equation*. And I don't see why. I mean, half of your clothes are red. You love red. Red's your color."

Not anymore it wasn't.

"Yeah, I know that. I mean, I did really used to like it a lot. But that was when I was a lot younger."

"You mean two weeks ago?"

She stuck her tongue out at me. In a mature and sophisticated way. "Anyway, *now* it just seems loud and, you know, really childish."

"I thought red was supposed to be sexy."

"If it's a Dior cocktail dress or something like that, Gray, you can, like, maybe get away with it. But not if it's just for casual. And, anyway, the point is that Morgan's a muted-colors man. Didn't I tell you he was wearing this awesome desert-pink shirt the last time I saw him?"

"Yeah," I said. "You did mention it. But he wouldn't be wearing the suit, Savanna. You would."

There was another woe-is-me sigh. "Maybe I'll check out the green again." She reached over and took a dress from one of the hooks on the wall. "Here," said Savanna. "Why don't you try this on while I'm changing?"

I stared at the dress she was holding. It was short and thin and bandage-like and looked like it was probably the reason they invented thongs.

"Me? I thought that was for *you*."

"It was." She gave it a shake. "But I'm not sure about black. Black is more your color, isn't it?"

"It's not black," I argued. "It's covered in glittery stuff."

"Don't quibble." Savanna sighed. "Anyway, I got the wrong size by mistake. It's way too short for me."

"But I'm not here to buy anything."

"You don't have to buy it, Gray, just try it on." She shimmied it toward me. "So we can see what you look like when you're being feminine."

I knew what I'd look like—an unconvincing female impersonator.

"I think I should go and get that red outfit for—"

"Oh, please, Gracie. It's not going to kill you just to try it on." She edged it closer. "It'll be fun."

"Funny is not the same as fun."

"Pleasepleaseplease . . ." She pretty much shoved the dress into my arms. "Your inner girl will thank you."

My inner girl must have been more eager to get out than I'd thought, because (and against my better judgment) instead of arguing, I put on the dress. With difficulty.

"There," I said, when I'd finally managed to struggle into it. "Are you happy now?"

Savanna stepped back so she was against the door of the changing room. I could see her in the mirror with her chin in her hand and her eyes narrowed, studying me in a critical will-this-boat-float? kind of way. "Yes, Gracie. Yes, I am happy now. I really like that dress." She nodded. Slowly. "It's simple but classic. It's definitely you."

Simple, maybe. I wasn't so sure about classic.

"It is?" It looked like someone else to me. Someone taller. And with breasts. Someone who risked hemorrhaging to death by shaving her legs more than once every couple of months.

She nodded faster this time. "Yes, it is. It's exactly what I've been telling you about the real, feminine you lurking under your grab-that-lizard facade, Gray. You look, like, totally great in that dress."

198

I could see that I didn't look horrifically hideous or anything—I just didn't look like me.

"You really think so?" I turned around to see myself from the back. At least I was never going to have to go into massive debt to have fat sucked from my butt. "I think it looks weird." Aside from the problems with breathing and walking, I couldn't see how you could possibly sit down in this dress unless you had a blanket to throw over your thighs.

Savanna hummed like our old refrigerator. "That's because you're wearing basketball boots, Gracie. Try to picture it with heels and stockings."

I could picture the dress with heels and stockings all right. But I wasn't in them. I was still wearing my basketball boots and my giraffe socks.

"You're wrong, Sav. The real me likes jeans and shoes you can walk through the woods in. I wouldn't wear this in a zillion years. "

"Yes, you would," said Savanna. "It's absolutely perfect for the Christmas dance. The glitteriness makes it look like you've been dusted with snow."

Or like I had terminal dandruff.

"Savanna, I am not buying something new for a dance I don't actually want to go to. And if I was, you know I wouldn't buy it here."

She rolled her eyes. "Please! Spare me the high moral principles, Gray. This is going to be a really special night.

You're going to need something festive . . . and dressy. . . ." She leered. "And sexy. Which means that you, like, totally can't buy a dress for the Christmas dance in a thrift store. It's out of the question."

"Excuse me, Ms. Zindle. But I never said I'd go to the dance, remember? I'm still thinking it over."

She pretended to yawn. "OK, so you're *still* thinking it over. But just in case you *do* decide to go, you're going to need something to wear, aren't you?"

"Well, it won't be this." Not only was it steeped in toxic chemicals and human misery, it was mega-expensive. Considering how little material there was in it, it was more expensive than gold. I tugged the dress over my head. "I can't afford it."

"Of course you can. What about all your babysitting money?"

Most of what I made went straight into the bank— into my Send-Gracie-Mooney-to-College Fund—or paid for my cell phone.

"Well, you could use a little tiny bit of it," argued Savanna. "Just this once."

"You know I don't like impulse buying. I have to sleep on it." I reached for the hanger. "And I don't have the money to buy it now, anyway."

"That's not a problem. I'll get it for you." Savanna's smile got brighter. "I'll put it on my mother's card. You can pay it back whenever."

"No, I don't wa—"

"You don't have to thank me." Savanna snatched the dress from my hand. "I mean, like, really, what are friends for?"

We were on our way to the cashier when Savanna was distracted by a display she hadn't seen on our first trawl through.

"Wait a minute, Gray. These are kind of cool." She handed me the dress and held a pale blue sweater up in front of her. "What do you think?"

"It's nice." It was a plain pullover. There wasn't that much to say about it. Unless it was to point out that it was probably made in China.

She dropped the blue sweater and picked up a beige one. "How about this?"

"That's nice, too." Except for the color, it was exactly the same.

Savanna smooshed her lips together. "Gracie, that is not being helpful. Which one do you like better?"

"I don't know . . ." I looked from one to the other. You wouldn't be able to tell them apart in candlelight. "I guess the blue."

"Really? What's wrong with the beige?"

"Nothing's wrong with the beige. But you asked me my opinion and—"

"Omigod!" Savanna's eyes were focused behind me and transfixed with horror. If we weren't standing under the fluorescent lights in the leisure-wear section of The Clothes Horse, I'd have thought she'd seen a ghost. She clutched my arm. "There's Archie!" I was pretty sure her nails were making holes in my flesh. "I can't let him see me." That would be because she'd told him she was grounded so she could keep the weekend free for the Scheck. Just in case. (I did say she was an optimist.) Savanna dropped to the floor.

For about half a nanosecond, I kept looking at the space where she'd been, and then I slowly turned around. Archie wasn't alone. He and Cooper were riding down the escalator together.

I felt as if I'd fallen through a hole in the ice. You know, frozen. Now that I knew that everyone thought I was after Cooper, running into Archie and Cooper was embarrassing enough—but running into them with Savanna crouched under a clothes carousel beside me put it into a whole other league of humiliation.

"For God's sake, Gracie!" hissed Savanna. "Get down before they see you!"

But it was too late.

"Hey, Gracie!" Cooper waved. Like normal. Maybe nobody had told him I was after him.

I waved back.

"Don't just stand there like you're made of salt," hissed Savanna. "Stop them from coming over here!"

I took a deep breath and headed for the escalator.

"Hi!" I put on a big boy-am-I-glad-to-see-you smile. "What are you guys doing here?" I was looking at Archie. So he wouldn't get the wrong idea and think I was only interested in talking to Cooper.

"Shopping." Archie held up the large paper bag he was carrying. "It's my dad's birthday next week. So I figured . . . since I couldn't see Savanna, I might as well get the shopping ordeal over with. You know she's grounded, right?"

I said I'd heard. I said that the only way Savanna would get out of the house today would be to set it on fire.

"I'm only here because Archie doesn't like shopping by himself and he bribed me with lunch," said Cooper. "What about you? I thought you were mallophobic."

"I am . . ." Now I was focusing on a sign that said WINTER FUN behind him. But I couldn't look at him. In case it looked like I was after him. "I just . . . you know . . . I had some time on my hands. . . ."

"What's that?" Archie nodded to my hands—which, unfortunately, were not holding a lot of time. What they were holding was the black dress. "That can't be *yours.*" He laughed, but he got that little thought ravine between his eyebrows. Had aliens taken over my body? Did I secretly wear dresses in the privacy of my own home the way Cooper wore sarongs? Or maybe he was thinking: Is she holding it for someone else? Who could that someone be? "Are you with somebody, Gracie?" His eyes flicked back and forth behind me. Looking for someone who was seriously in touch with her inner girl.

"It's mine." I jammed it under my arm so it looked more like a T-shirt than a slinky where-are-those-six-inch-heels-and-the-bodysuit? kind of dress. "And of course I'm not with anybody." Who would I be with? There was only one person I hung out with who would wear something that sparkled, and she was under house arrest. "I'm, you know . . . by myself." My voice was squeaking like a cornered mouse.

Cooper was staring at the lump of material under my armpit. "So what's the dress for?" Now he was frowning. Thoughtfully. "Don't tell me it's for the Christmas dance."

"Well, yeah . . ." I nodded. "You know. Probably. Unless I decide to wear it when I go climbing in the spring."

Cooper was still looking pensive. "I thought you said you didn't want to go to the dance."

"I didn't. But, you know, maybe I will. After all, I didn't say I wouldn't." Hahaha. "Savanna can be pretty persuasive."

Archie joined in my laughter. But nervously. You know, the way you laugh at someone on TV who does something really dumb or gross because you do it, too.

"So was the snake in the Garden of Eden persuasive,"

said Cooper. He half smiled. "I guess it's lucky Savanna's never tried to persuade you to rob a bank."

He sounded like my father. I could hear my dad when I was little saying, *If Candy Russo tells you to jump off the roof, are you going to jump?* so clearly he could have been standing behind me. Or behind Cooper. I felt like the kind of person who'd swim the Amazon if someone told her to. Someone persuasive.

I tried to laugh, but it came out more like I was gagging.

"I'm only teasing you, Gracie." He switched to a full smile. "I'm just surprised, that's all. You know . . ."

I didn't know. Know what?

He shrugged. "I guess I thought you'd be coming to the Neighbors' bash. Everybody's going to be really disappointed."

"So what are you doing now?" asked Archie. "I've got to buy Dr. Doom here lunch. Why don't you come, too? We'll give you a ride home."

"Oh . . . thanks . . . I mean, no. I'm not done . . . you know . . . I have to pay for this . . . and I wanted—" What? Wanted to run away? Wanted to drop through the floor? "I wanted to look at some other stuff."

"Well, meet us when you are done," said Cooper. "We'll be over at the taqueria."

"Yeah," Archie agreed. "We'll be there awhile."

"Oh, no . . . no . . . that's all right." I started shuffling away from them—as if I was being dragged away by The Call of the Shoes. "I mean, I don't know how long it'll take me. I'd really like to . . . I mean, really . . . But you know, it could take me a couple of hours." I backed into a carousel of skirts.

"Well, come if you can," said Archie.

"Yeah." Cooper untangled a hanger from my bag. "You don't want me to be stuck talking to Archie all afternoon, do you?"

"I'll try," I lied. "But I don't think you should count on me." I put a hand to my forehead. "I think I'm getting one of my headaches." This was true.

"We'll get a table for three," said Cooper. "See how it goes."

Edging back to the counter of sweaters, I watched them walk away—past the checkouts, past the security guard, and out into the plaza.

"The coast's clear," I announced.

A head rose over the sweaters. "What does he mean: *So was the snake in the Garden of Eden persuasive?*" asked Savanna.

CHAPTER SIXTEEN

Savanna Has Another Change of Plans

On the day of the Remember the Wampanoag dinner, I was in the basement getting the folding chairs out and cleaning them off when the doorbell rang. It was way too early for guests.

"I'll get it!" I could hear my father's footsteps over my head and the front door opening. "Gadzooks!" he cried. "It looks like Savanna Zindle. But it can't be! The Savanna Zindle I know never arrives *ahead* of time. Don't tell me the prophecies of Tavibo are finally coming true and the world's about to end."

"Hahaha, Professor Mooney." Savanna always laughed at my dad's jokes, even when she didn't understand them. "My mom was, like, driving this way, so I thought I'd come over and give you and Gracie a hand getting everything ready. I figured you could use the help."

For once, my dad was too surprised to make a joke. "You did?"

"Yeah," said Savanna. "I've been totally looking forward to today. It sounds really cool. My family's traditions are, like, pretty traditional, you know? I mean, if Hallmark doesn't make a card for it, then it doesn't exist. I never even heard of the Wampums before Gracie invited me."

"Wampanoags," said my dad.

"I, like, can't wait to hear your band, too," Savanna went on. "Gracie says it's really good. What's its name? The Woollies?"

Even though he knew she wasn't kidding around, he laughed. *"The Wobblies."* But he didn't bother trying to explain who they were.

"Is it OK if I put my stuff upstairs?" asked Savanna. "So it's not in your way?"

"Sure," said my dad. "Gracie's in the basement. You can give her a hand with the extra chairs when you're done."

So after she'd dumped her bag in my room, Savanna came down to the cellar to give me a hand.

"How come you came over so early?" Not to be rude, but volunteering for work wasn't something she was known for. I picked up two clean chairs and started up the steps. "Is your family driving you really nuts?" The Thanksgiving holiday was a long one for Savanna because all her grandparents moved in for the entire weekend. Which meant there were four more people to

208

argue with. She'd called me every hour, on the hour, to give me frontline bulletins on how insane they all were.

"You know, for someone who can find something to love in a boa constrictor, you can be very cynical, Gracie Mooney." Savanna picked up two chairs and followed me. "It just so happens that I couldn't bear the thought of you slaving away by yourself all afternoon. I mean, you want to have a good time tonight, not pass out from exhaustion."

I was touched. I looked over my shoulder at her. "I didn't know you cared."

"Yes, you did." She winked. "Anyway, it's not, like, totally selfless of me, is it? I mean, you're my best friend. I don't want to see you die young because you overtaxed yourself. Then I'd be all alone in a hostile world."

I laughed. You had to love her. Really. There was no choice.

Savanna was at her best that afternoon. Her best was really good. She whistled while she worked. She asked my father questions about the Wampanoags, actually listened to his answers, and complimented him on everything from the shirt he was wearing to the smell of the pies he was baking.

After we swept the front porch and decorated it with baskets of squash and colored corn and garlands of the festive leaves of autumn, she stepped back to see how it looked. "It's totally cool," she decided. "Zelda would put lights all around the baskets." Savanna's mother put lights up for every holiday going. At Christmas, she covered the house in so many lights it could probably be seen from space. "But this is, like, real, isn't it? You know, gifts from the earth."

Gifts from the earth? When I said stuff like that, Savanna always said that the only gift from the earth that she wanted was gold.

"My God," I joked. "Don't tell me you're finally going green?"

Savanna laughed. "You must be wearing me down."

She didn't even complain about having to wash the cutlery and dishes by hand. And while we worked she entertained me with true horror stories of Thanksgiving with the Zindles. The arguments over how to roast a turkey, mash potatoes, and make cranberry sauce. The battle over which set of dishes and silverware they were going to use (the ones Gus's parents gave them or the ones given to them by Zelda's), which ended with them using the paper plates left over from Sofia's birthday and plastic knives and forks. How Mrs. Zindle Sr. threw her apple juice at Mr. Zindle Sr. because he said that Zelda's stuffing was better than hers. How Zelda lobbed a bread roll at Gus because he said there was too much paprika in the gravy. "She's getting worse," said Savanna. "It won't be long before she totally loses all rational processes and just howls all the time. Her moods swing more than every five-year-old in this country put together." I said that maybe it was the menopause. Everybody said it could make you act weird. "Omigod!" wailed Savanna. "Just when you think things can't get any better!" We laughed so much that my dad finally came into the kitchen to see what was so funny.

Then we went upstairs to get ready.

As soon as we got into my room, Savanna collapsed on my bed with a sigh of relief. "Thank God!" she cried. "Alone at last! I can't keep it in any longer. I thought I was going to explode."

"Explode?" I thought she meant that she had to use the bathroom.

"Don't be so literal!" She propped herself up on her elbows. "Gracie," she said, "I have something I've been dying to tell you all afternoon. Something of truly awesome importance and juvenation."

"You mean *jubilation*?"

She snapped her fingers. "Yes! Jubilation. To be jubilant! To jubilate!" She hugged herself. "Oh, Gracie! Wait till you hear what happened!"

It hadn't occurred to me to wonder why she was in such a good mood. I just assumed that it was because she was happy to be with me—and because she was excited about remembering the Wampanoags. Maybe it wasn't Savanna who was the optimist after all.

I leaned against the door. "What?"

"Guess!" She rocked back and forth, hugging herself. "Think of, like, the most fantabulous thing that could ever happen to me."

I didn't really want to. I was getting another of my bad feelings. Baby orangutans were scrabbling through the ruined forest, looking for their mothers and crying.

"Your parents won an around-the-world cruise, but there are only three tickets so they're leaving you home alone."

"Better than that."

"They'll be gone forever?"

The honking of deliriously happy geese filled my room. Savanna leaped to her feet. "I have a date with Morgan, Gracie! Can you believe it? I have a date with Morgan! He got back from his folks sooner than he was supposed to. Isn't that awesome? So he can see me after all!" She spun around like the heroine in one of those old musicals—you know, the ones where the girls all wear ponytails and full skirts and can't stop singing. "Oh, I am sooo happy!"

"So when are you seeing him?" My stomach had more knots in it than a macramé bracelet. Which meant that I already knew the answer. Coming early . . . helping out . . . admiring squash . . . Everything was adding up. But I was really hoping that I was wrong. "You're not going to have to leave too early tomorrow, are you?"

"Oh, I'm not seeing him tomorrow, Gray." She reached

for her backpack and plopped it down on the bed. "Tomorrow he has to get ready for classes on Monday. I mean, he has, like, a gazillion things to do." She didn't look at me as she unzipped her pack. "I'm seeing him tonight."

I laughed. It was a hollow so-that's-what-rain-forests-used-to-look-like kind of laugh. "What do you mean, *you're seeing him tonight*?"

"What do *you* mean, *What do you mean*?" She started taking things from her bag. "I mean that I'm seeing him tonight, Gracie." She flashed me a smile. "You know, like, after the sun goes down?"

"This night?"

"I know it's, like, really short notice—and I probably should play harder to get—but the point is that he only got back this morning. I only just found out myself."

That wasn't the point I was concerned about.

"But you're spending tonight with me."

"Of course I am. I mean, I'm here, right? I'm just not going to spend like the whole night with you. I'm going to spend some of it with Morgan."

Had she cloned herself? Had she discovered how to defy the laws of science by being in two places at once?

"What are you, a necromancer?"

"I'm a romancer!" She threw her arms around me as best she could, since I still had my back against the door. "Oh, Gracie, I knew you'd understand. And it's not like

I'm going to be gone *all night*. It'll just be for a couple of hours. But I have to see Morgan. I mean, if I don't see Morgan I think my heart will break into, like, millions of pieces. And it has been nearly two weeks, Gracie. That's a really long time when you're in love."

Disappointment tended to make me petty. "I thought love didn't have a watch."

Savanna cackled happily. "But it does have a calendar."

You should never have invited her, whined a disloyal voice in my head. *You should have invited Cooper. At least you know he'd dig the music. And not leave in the middle to do something better.*

"But it's Remember the Wampanoag Day," I bleated.

Savanna went back to her unpacking. "I haven't forgotten them, have I, Gray? I've been here helping you all afternoon. Remember? And I know the party's going to be, like, mega-great and everything, and I'm reallyreally sorry I have to miss even the teensiest bit of it. But I'm going to be here for most of it. And, anyway, what can I do? I'm like a prawn of Fate."

"Pawn." I couldn't tell any more where the door ended and my back began.

"Right." Savanna took her makeup bag from the backpack and laid it on the bed. "He's picking me up at seven."

"Here?" That wasn't possible. The house would be

filled with tons of people. And my father. It would be especially filled with my father.

She shook out a pale green shirt with a scoop neck and wide sleeves. "Of course not here. I'm not stupid, Gracie. I'm meeting him in town. It only takes, like, five minutes to get there from your house."

I couldn't see how this eliminated the basic problem. You know, that she was supposed to be in our living room eating succotash and corn bread, not sitting in a car exchanging saliva with Morgan Scheck. "But what about my dad?"

Savanna sighed. "Well, that's why I'm meeting Morgan in town, isn't it?" She laid a short black skirt on the bed. "I mean, Morgan can't exactly knock on the door and ask for me, can he? The Professor would want to know who he is."

"But he's going to notice that you're missing."

"No, he won't." She took out her toilet bag. "That's why I came early, Gray. So he knows I'm here. I mean, later he's going to be, like, über-busy with his guests and hooting the nanny and everything, isn't he?"

"*Hootenanny*. And it's not really a—"

"Whatever. He's going to be occupied. That's the important thing. He'll never notice that I'm not around. If he doesn't see me in one place, he'll just think I'm somewhere else."

Maybe she really was crazy. Not just flamboyant and

confident and daring—all of which can be attractive and positive qualities—but certifiably insane.

"Are you totally nuts? It's not going to work, Savanna. My dad teaches classes with dozens of kids in them. He always knows when someone's absent."

"But not if he *knows* they're there, Gray. If he knows they're there, he doesn't think about them again unless one of them starts snoring. Don't you get it? Your dad *knows* I'm in the house! And I'll be mingling downstairs with everybody when they first get here—and then I'll just slip out of the back door for a little while. So if, like, later your dad thinks, *Gloriosky, where's Savanna Zindle?* he'll figure I'm in the bathroom or something and forget about me again."

"And what if he doesn't?" It was bad enough lying to my dad without him finding out that I was lying. The guilt would kill me. "What if he decides to look for you?"

"Oh, please . . ." Savanna waved this aside as if it was a gnat. "He's not going to look for me. He'll be playing the banjo."

"Guitar." There was a stain I hadn't noticed before on my bedspread. It looked like a heart. Slightly torn. "And he's not going to be playing it all the time, Sav. He's going to be hanging out with his friends. Circulating . . . Making sure everybody's having a good time . . . Being the host . . ."

"Which will keep him really busy, won't it?"

"Savanna . . ." I'd passed disappointment and gone straight to world-class worry. There was the little matter of us being caught. "Savanna—"

"Oh, please, Gracie, you have to help me. I promisepromisepromise, I'll be back by ten thirty. He'll never even know I was gone."

It was like looking into the pleading eyes of an orphaned baby chameleon. A really beautiful baby chameleon with intricate markings and its skin flashing shades of metallic blue. The chameleon was lost and frightened and shivering from cold. All it wanted was to find someplace safe where it would be fed and loved. *It's only for a couple of hours. . . .* I heard myself thinking. *It means a lot to her. . . . It's not like you're really doing anything wrong. . . .*

"Nine thirty, Savanna." I might be the girl who wanted to take six cats, ten dogs, an iguana, two rabbits, and a chicken home from the rescue center when I was ten, but I did have some limits. "I mean it. You have to be back in this house by nine thirty."

"Thank you, thank you, thank you, Gracie! I knew I could count on you. You are the truest, bestest friend there ever was." She threw her arms around me. "I'll be back by nine thirty. Swear on a bear. I don't want you turned into a pepper."

"Pumpkin." I hugged her back.

CHAPTER SEVENTEEN

Remembering the Wampanoags

If they gave out awards for mingling with people you never met before, Savanna would have won every one. No contest. She was never the kind of person to wait for people to talk to her, but today she was in über-gregarious mode. She was right behind my dad when the first guests arrived so he had to introduce her. She took coats and got drinks. She passed around the nuts and chips. She chatted away about the weather and the holidays and what she saw as the failings of the Crow's Point educational system. As more people started arriving, she answered the door herself. "Hi, I'm Gracie's best friend, Savanna. Who are you?" Every time one of the band members arrived, she made a big fuss. "I can't wait to hear you play. I mean, Gracie says you're, like, totally great." When it was time to put the food out, she was standing by as the oven door opened. "Oh, wow, Professor Mooney, that looks sooo good. My dad thinks cooking is opening a can." She helped carry out the dishes to the buffet table in the dining room. She went back to the kitchen for more serving spoons. She went back to the kitchen for more napkins. She went back to the kitchen for another jug of cider. And then, as everyone started piling food on their plates, she slipped into the kitchen and didn't come back.

The kids who had come with their parents were all younger than I was and had gone down to the basement, where there was a Ping-Pong table and board games and no adults asking them about school and stuff like that, so I went into the living room and started to do some mingling of my own. *How're things going . . . ? Still obsessed with iguanas . . . ? I hear you're doing some teaching, Gracie. . . . Are you still planning to go to Costa Rica in the summer . . . ?* Since I'd been answering adults' questions for sixteen years, I managed that part OK—*Fine. . . . Yes. . . . Right. . . . You bet. . . .*—I even managed to ask some questions of my own, but I was way too stressed out to actually eat. All I could see was the space where Savanna should have been. It was enormous. It was like looking into the open mouth of a whale. And now that I wasn't staring into Savanna's big brown imploring eyes, worry had stalked back into my mind. *What was my problem? Why was I so easily persuaded? Was it actually a miracle I was alive?* (You know, because no one I cared about ever told me to jump off a cliff.) It was all I could do to push food from one side of my plate to the other. When I did manage to get some into my mouth, it tasted like ashes. The ashes of someone who's gone down in flames. Ms. Salter, who taught yoga and played the fiddle, was worried that I was coming down with something. Only guilt. I said that I was just too excited to eat. I got rid of my plate and got myself some cider. I spilled it on my 500 YEARS OF GENOCIDE T-shirt and Mr. McKlintock's shoes. I laughed too loudly whenever someone made a joke. I called Fergal, the banjo player, Fergus, even though I'd known him since I was ten. "You'll be forgetting your own name next," he joked. I said that seemed pretty likely. And all the time I was mingling and wreaking havoc, I kept watching my dad. I was waiting for him to look over at me and shout, "Where's Savanna disappeared to, Gracie?" But he didn't. It began to look as if Savanna was right. He was too busy talking to his friends and giving out his corn bread recipe to pay much attention to the exact location of Savanna Zindle. When he did walk by me, to fill up his plate again, he whispered in my ear, "I think it's going well, don't you, Gracie? Even better than last year."

I said that I thought it was going super-well. "Everybody's having a really good time."

I wouldn't say it was the kind of evening that made me think I was always happy, but as it wore on, hope finally put in an appearance. My breathing started to return to something close to normal and my palms stopped sweating. I promised every god in the universe and the ghosts of the Wampanoags that if they got me through this in one piece, I would never ever lie to my father again. Not even if it was for his own good.

At nine o'clock, the band started playing. As far as I was concerned, it was like the all clear after an air raid. You can come out now. You're not going to get a bomb through your living room tonight. I began to relax and enjoy myself. My foot tapped. My head bobbed. *"Call him drunken Ira Hayes,"* I sang with the others. *"He won't answer anymore. . . ."* We were home free. My dad gets really absorbed when he's playing; he wouldn't notice if half his guests went home until he stopped. And by the time he did stop, Savanna would be back in the house and standing right beside me, shaking her hair and swinging her earrings and clapping along with everybody else.

At nine forty-five, I stopped tapping my foot and bobbing my head and slipped into my dad's study, to see if the clock there had the same time as my watch.

A little after ten, the band took a break. I stared at the kitchen door. It was opening. Slowly. My heart threw itself against my rib cage. Professor Reich, the head of the history department, stepped into the dining room with several bottles of beer in his hands. He gave me a wink.

At ten fifteen, I went to the kitchen for some more cider. I looked out the side window. I went into the little glassed-in porch off the kitchen and squinted into the darkness that was the backyard. I stuck my head through the door. "Savanna?" I whispered. "Savanna, are you there?" A bat flew past. I turned off the light by the door and went back inside. I stayed close to the dining room. You know, so I'd be right there when Savanna finally slipped in from the kitchen.

At ten twenty-five, the phone rang. I was too far away to get it without shoving Mr. Shiloh, the Wobblies' other guitarist, out of the way and jumping over the back of the couch. I caught my breath instead.

My father was only a foot or two from the phone. "Now, who could that be?" he laughed. "I thought everybody was here!" He put down his beer and went over and picked up the receiver.

I told myself not to panic. It *is* a big country. Vast. There were a lot of people who could have been calling our house right then—my grandmother in Florida, my aunt in San Francisco, someone offering my dad a time-share in the South of France, a wrong number. The options were pretty endless. It was Mrs. Zindle.

I knew it was Mrs. Zindle because my dad shouted, "Who? Oh, Zelda. How are you? No, of course you're not disturbing us. Yeah . . . yeah . . . we're having a great time."

I moved a little farther away from the living room, studying the desserts on the table as if I was having a hard time deciding what to have.

"Savanna? Yeah, sure she's here. Just a sec. I'll get her

for you." From where I was, I couldn't see him looking around for me, but I could feel it. "Gracie!"

I acted like I hadn't heard him. *Should I have a pecan brownie? Should I have a slice of pie? Oh boy, that cranberry cake sure looks good. . . .*

"Gracie!"

Several people who were hanging out in the dining room joined in. "Gracie, your dad wants you." Sara Nickerman, specialist field medieval history, leaned over and gave me a poke.

I turned around. At about the speed of a slow loris.

Robert Mooney, PhD in American history and single parent, was standing right behind me. He was looking really tall.

"Gracie, where's Savanna? It's her mother. She's been calling her, but her cell phone's switched off."

"Savanna?" I shrugged. "Isn't she in the living room?"

My dad laughed. "Do you hear her?" And then he frowned. I could tell he was thinking. And I knew what about. He was thinking about how he hadn't heard Savanna shrieking or honking for a long time. He was thinking about how he hadn't seen her talking or eating. How he hadn't seen her leaning against me or heard her singing the wrong words while we listened to the music. He moved his head down toward me. "Gracie, Savanna *is* here, isn't she?"

"Yeah, of course she's here." I laughed as if you couldn't

get more ridiculous than thinking that Savanna wasn't in the house. "I was just talking to her."

"Really?" He was doing that thing where he pushes his tongue against his cheek as if it helps him think.

"Yeah. Just a little while ago." I smiled. Like someone who's telling the truth. "I don't know where she's gone—you know Savanna—but she's around here somewhere." I made myself look right in his eyes. Where else would she be?

"Well . . . I don't remember seeing her for a while now. Not with you, and not with anyone else." Unlike me, Robert Mooney still wasn't smiling. He was watching me with the same serious expression he had when he read the newspaper. He never trusted anything he read in the papers; he was always looking for the parts of the story that had been left out. "You know, I wouldn't want to find myself inadvertently lying to Mrs. Zindle, Gracie. If Savanna isn't here, I think you should tell me. If anything happens to her, I'm the one who's responsible, you know."

My stomach pretty much cemented itself into a ball. This was something I hadn't thought of—that my dad would end up lying for Savanna, too. It wasn't bad enough that I was lying to *him*, now I'd made him an accessory to my deceit. That was the thanks he got for all the sacrifices he'd made raising me by himself.

"You're not lying," I lied. "She's around here somewhere, Dad. You know what she's like. She gets bored staying in one place too long." I gave another shrug. "Maybe she went out on the porch. Or upstairs."

"Ummm . . ." My dad nodded. "Go and get her." He didn't believe me. He was calling my bluff.

"I didn't say that she's definitely upstairs or on the porch. She could've gone downstairs. You know, to see if the little kids are OK."

"Get her, Gracie." My dad almost never yelled. The way you knew that he was upset or angry was that he spoke so quietly you practically had to stand on tiptoe to catch what he was saying. "Tell Savanna her mother's on the phone."

"She could be in the bathroom," I babbled on. "You know how long that can take. Remember that time she was in there for over an hour and you had to go next door? Maybe you should just tell Mrs. Zindle that Savanna will call her back."

"Gracie . . ."

"Or maybe I should talk to her. I can take a message."

My dad put his hand on my shoulder. He leaned down, close to my ear, so no one else could hear what he was saying. "I know Savanna is—has her own way of doing things, Gracie. But I've never known you not to tell me the truth. So if she really is here, I want you to get her. Now."

I figured that I had two choices. One: I could go through the motions of looking for Savanna—really thoroughly and so slowly that a snail could have walked from our front porch to town before I was done — hoping that by the time I was finished she'd be back in the house. Two: I could tell him the truth and get it over with. Which would probably mean that I'd spend the rest of high school in Florida with my grandmother because my father wouldn't speak to me anymore and had sent me to live with her in her trailer with the vultures circling overhead.

"Gracie?" He squeezed my shoulder. "Gracie, what's going on?"

I'd make a really lousy politician. When politicians get caught lying, they just lie some more. But I couldn't do that. It had to be option two.

"It's just that Savanna —"

My father suddenly straightened up. "Well, speak of the Devil." He sounded really surprised. "There she is." He was looking behind me.

I turned around.

Savanna was coming out of the kitchen with a glass of soda in her hand.

"Savanna!" I thought I was going to faint with joy.

She clocked the looks on our faces — relief mixed with the remnants of horror (mine) and deep suspicion and bewilderment (my father's). She gave us her what-a-wonderful-world smile. "What's up?"

My dad didn't smile back. It was possible that he was never going to smile again. "Where have you been, Savanna?"

I would have hemmed and hawed and looked shifty and evasive. My ears would have turned the color of a cardinal. Savanna's eyes didn't blink and her smile didn't flinch. She wasn't even flushed the way you'd expect someone who'd just come into a warm house from the cold would be. "I was out in the backyard." She made it sound like a normal thing to do.

Though not to everyone.

"The backyard?" My dad's eyebrows rose. "Is something happening out there that I don't know about?"

Savanna laughed. "Oh, Professor Mooney . . . I mean, I think this party's really affected me. Spiritually. All of a sudden, all I could think of were these long-ago people, living nobly and in harmony with nature, and I just had to go outside to try to communicate with them. And it's such a beautiful night with, like, a gazillion stars. I mean, it's like they know we're honoring them and are telling us thank you. And it's so timeless—you can imagine that there aren't any cars or planes or electric plants or anything like that. . . ."

"Really?"

"Uh-huh. I just stood there looking and thinking that, like, hundreds of years ago, a girl like me probably stood where your backyard is now and looked up at those exact same stars. I mean, that's really something, isn't it?"

"Yeah," said my father. He was looking at me. "It's really something."

I said, "Savanna, your mother's on the phone. It could be important."

CHAPTER EIGHTEEN

Savanna and I Have Our First Fight

The phone call wasn't really important. Zelda couldn't find her favorite bath gel. Figuring out that Savanna had used it and not put it back where it belonged was pretty much a no-brainer. "She is, like, sooo anal," said Savanna after she hung up. "I mean, what's the big deal? It's not like she's got some major date. She's taking a bath and going to bed." I said that I didn't understand why Zelda didn't keep everything she valued locked up.

Savanna and I went up to my room before the band called it a night and the last guests left. Two guitars, a banjo, and a fiddle didn't really make the kind of music Savanna could listen to for more than half an hour without falling asleep, and, now that I knew my dad wasn't going to disown me and send me to live in a trailer in Florida, I felt as if I'd spent the night rescuing animals from a flood. I was wiped out.

Savanna put the plate of desserts she'd brought up

with her on my night table and threw herself on my bed. "I can't believe you were worried for even one tiny second. Didn't I tell you everything would be OK?" she crowed. "You just get so nervous about everything, Gray. It can't be good for you. I'm really scared it's going to do you some permanent damage. I mean, look at how you twitched and fretted about my plan, and it totally worked like a dream!"

I locked the door behind us. "Not a good dream."

Savanna groaned. "That's exactly what I mean, Gray. You have to stop being so negative all the time. . . . It's a real turnoff—especially for guys." She kicked off her shoes. "I went, I came back, and no one's the wiser." She raised her arms. Victorious. "You did all that worrying for nothing."

I hadn't planned on saying anything about how guilty I was feeling and what a lousy time I'd had and everything. Savanna and I never fought. Partly because I wasn't confrontational. And partly because she had her family to fight with; she didn't need to fight with me, too. Besides, I was so relieved that we'd actually got away with it that all I really wanted was to forget about it.

But, instead of keeping my mouth shut, I said, "That close." I held my thumb and index finger so you'd just be able to slip a hair between them. Maybe. "If you had been two seconds later, it would all have been over except for the tears. That's how close we came to being busted by my dad."

"But we weren't, were we?" Savanna smiled. Brightly. "*If*s don't count, Gracie. It's only the *did*s that matter. Did I get back too late? Did your dad find out the truth? Did we get in trouble?"

"You forgot one." I was still standing. "Did I lie?"

Savanna bit into a brownie. "You didn't lie, Gray. You just edited the truth a little. Really a little. Because the point is that I *was* in the house most of the night. But not, like, all of it."

Words are funny. They are important, but not as important as what they describe. You know, like in a war when civilians are being bombed into oblivion and the army calls it "collateral damage." You could call it chicken soup, but it would still be killing innocent people. Editing the truth . . . fictionalizing . . . omitting a couple of tiny facts . . . It didn't matter what you called it. It was still lying.

"I don't like lying to my dad, Savanna." I moved away from the door, pulled the chair out from my desk, and sat down. So she'd know that I was being serious. "It makes me feel really lousy."

"Oh, Gracie, don't say that." She brushed some crumbs off her top. "I mean, it's not like he'll ever know."

"But *I* know."

She took a cranberry-and-orange cookie from the plate. "I'll tell you what. If it makes you feel better, you won't have to lie to him again. Ever. I mean, this was, like, an emergency. Swear on a bear, any future excuses will not involve the Professor." She gave me a smile. "Just Archie and the 'rents."

In movies and books, people who survive a near-death experience—like some terrible accident or a heart attack—often have a moment of truth afterward. Suddenly they understand what's really important in life. They find God. Or they give up drinking. Or they don't lie anymore.

I shook my head. This was my moment of truth. "No, not them, either."

Savanna stopped in mid-bite. "Excuse me?"

"I'm really sorry, but I can't cover for you anymore. Not with Archie, not with your folks—not with anyone."

She smiled as if I was teasing. "But you have to."

"No, I don't." I didn't.

"What do you mean, *No I don't*?" She dropped the cookie back on the plate. "You can't abandon me now, Gray. Not when everything's, like, going so well. I need you to support me. I depend on you. Without you, I might have to stop seeing Morgan. I mean, how can I keep it all together by myself? And if I have to stop seeing Morgan, it'll be just like you took a gun and shot me through the heart."

And if I kept lying for her, it would be like I took a gun and shot myself through the heart.

"I'm sorry, Sav. I really am." I leaned forward. I

was earnest, but I was calm. So calm you'd think we were having a regular conversation about how she was going to survive till the next time she saw Morgan or what color she should do her nails next. "But I can't go on with this. I just can't. I feel like an impersonator." Impersonating myself—the honest Gracie Mooney. The girl who always told the truth.

"Oh, Gracie . . ." Savanna's whole body sighed. "How many times do I have to tell you to lighten up? You're taking this way too seriously." She smiled again. "I mean, it's not like you're killing white rhinos for their horns or anything like that. This is, like, totally harmless. All you're doing is backing me up." She winked. "By not quite telling the truth."

Downstairs, my father started belting out "There Once Was a Union Maid."

I took a deep breath. "No, I'm not. From now on, I'm quite telling the truth."

"Which means what exactly?" She tilted her head to one side. "That you won't lie for me, or that you won't back me up?"

"She never was afraid . . ." sang my father.

"Both." The relief of not getting caught was nothing to the relief I felt at finally taking a stand. Of knowing that things really would be different from now on. I felt like I'd been walking across a minefield, and now I'd made it back on safe ground. "If you tell Archie you were with me when you weren't and he asks me how I liked the flying seals or the kazoo orchestra, I'll tell him the truth." I made myself look her right in the eye. "That I was home by myself."

I didn't get long to enjoy my relief. Savanna's face lost its smile. It looked like it should be up there on Mount Rushmore, squeezed in between Teddy Roosevelt and Lincoln. "You couldn't do that to me, Gracie. You wouldn't dare."

"I could." I focused on her hair. "I would."

"But that would be, like, the biggest, most major treachery ever. I mean, I would never do something like that to you. Not even if I was being tortured." She wasn't sprawling against the pillows anymore; she was sitting up straight. Exactly as if she was carved out of sacred stone. "You're supposed to be my best friend. Best friends stick by each other. They help each other out. Like I always help you out."

"I *am* your best friend. That's why I'm telling you how I really feel." You can tell your best friend *anything,* right? Even about them. "Who else is going to tell you when you're—you know, making a big mistake."

"Who else?" Her curls snapped. "Well, that's a laugh. Because you know just as well as I do, Gracie Mooney, that practically everybody in the world is always telling me I'm wrong. I get nothing but criticism. From Gus and Zelda . . . from teachers . . . from kids at school . . . and

234

now from you!" Her voice was getting louder. I couldn't hear what was happening to the union maid anymore. "How come I'm always the one who's in the wrong, huh? How come everybody's always down on *me*? How come everything's always *my* fault?"

"Everything isn't always your fault, Savanna. All I'm saying is—"

"I thought you— I thought you really understood me, Gray." She was kneeling on the bed now, so that her body was wobbling as much as her voice. "I thought you were on *my* side."

"I *am* on your side." I looked her straight in the eyes. "But I don't think what you're doing is right. And not just all the lying. Cheating's bad, Savanna. Somebody could get really hurt."

"Oh, for God's sake, Gracie. You are sooo melodramatic." Savanna had gotten up off the bed. She'd folded her arms across her chest and was tapping her foot on the floor. "I told you, it's not cheating unless—"

"Then tell them," I said. "Tell Morgan and Archie. Tell them both that you're seeing someone else, but it's OK because you aren't married."

Tap, tap, tap. Her eyes narrowed. "Why are you doing this to me, Gracie?"

"I'm not doing anything *to you*, Savanna. Just count me out, that's all I'm saying. I don't want to be a part of it anymore."

"But you *are* doing something to me." She sounded like the digital voice on an answer machine. *Tap, tap, tap.* "You're ruining my life, that's what you're doing. I'm supposed to be able to depend on you. But I can't, can I? You're just not *there* for me!"

"What are you talking about? I'm *always* there for you." Even when *there* was someplace like the mall or the beach or the gym, where I really didn't want to be. Even when she never showed up. "You're the one who never thinks of me or what I feel or what I want to do." I couldn't seem to stop. Now things I hadn't even thought had bothered me at the time were racing out of my mouth. "You never once came to see my butterfly garden in the summer. You never once went camping with me."

"You know I don't like The Great Outbores, Gracie. I totally can't sleep in dirt and bugs. I have, like, a phobia. And I was going to check out your butterflies, but it just so happens that I was busy, too. In case you forgot. I mean, I'm the one who got stuck babysitting Sofia all the time. *By myself.* And I'm the one who had to deal with Archie and his demands last summer. *By myself.*" Savanna's hair moved like storm clouds in a heavy wind. "And, anyway, that's not the point. The point is that, instead of supporting me, you're going against me. I mean, this isn't just you having other things you have to deal with. This is you deliberately sabotaging me."

It was? This had to be the fastest transformation since

Clark Kent stepped into the phone booth and came out as Superman. From best friend to enemy agent in under a minute.

"But that's ridiculous!" Now I was standing, too. "I'm not sabotaging you. I want to help you."

"Oh, right . . . So long as *you're* not inconvenienced."

"Oh, Savanna. You know that's not true. I—"

"And don't kid yourself about why you're doing this to me, either. It's not because you're so perfect and principled and don't like to do anything wrong." Her arms weren't folded in front of her anymore. "That is, like, so incredibly far from the truth it's practically in another galaxy."

Never mind another galaxy, I was starting to feel like I'd stumbled into a parallel world.

"I didn't say I was per—"

"I know exactly why you're doing this to me, Gracie Mooney. Don't think I don't. You're doing it because you're jealous."

Now there wasn't a doubt in my mind. I'd definitely stumbled into a parallel world. Gracie through the looking glass—and straight into a ravine.

"I what?"

"You heard me." She was so angry that I wouldn't have recognized her if I hadn't seen her get dressed before the party. "You're jealous." Savanna waved her arms and shook her head so that her hair blew around as if a hawk wind was moving through my room. "I can't believe I've been so blind! Now I see it all, Gracie Mooney! *You're* the worst best friend I've ever had. You're way worse than Lena Skopec. I mean, all she took was my boots. But you! Right from the start you've been trying to turn me against Morgan. Making me doubt him. You're like that dude in that play we did in English last year—you know, where he makes her husband jealous and she dies in the end? What's his name? Eon—"

"*Iago.*"

"Whatever. Trying to poison my mind. Always saying that Morgan's making up excuses for not seeing me. That he has another girlfriend."

I felt like a one-girl climate-change disaster: my stomach was a block of ice, my palms were damp, and my heart was pretty much crumbling into the sea. "But I've never said any of those things. I've never even met Morgan, Savanna. Why would I want to turn you against him?"

"Oh, I don't think this really has anything to do with Morgan." All of a sudden, she was dead calm in this really creepy, unnatural way. The way psychos are in the movies when they call up the police to tell them where the next body is. I'd have liked it better if she was still screaming. "I think you've always been jealous of me. Probably before I even knew you. Probably when I was just someone you saw around school, you were already plotting how you could ruin my life! I bet that's why you wormed yourself between me and Marilouise like you did."

"What are you talking about? Marilouise was in my English class. I was friends with her first. I—"

"Exactly! And then she introduced you to me, and you shoved her out and made yourself my best friend."

That wasn't the way I remembered it. Savanna saw me and Marilouise talking outside of class one afternoon, and she came over and introduced herself. "Hi," she said, "I'm Savanna Zindle. Who are you?" And then, after a while, she kind of lost interest in Marilouise, and Marilouise just seemed to drift away.

"It was your plan right from the start, wasn't it? You were jealous of me because I'm all the things you'll never be—"

"You mean like tall?"

"You wanted to pretend to be my best friend so you could really hurt me."

What was I, some kind of criminal mastermind? Could she hear herself? Had we ever met? But the biggest question was: did she believe what she was saying—was that what she really thought of me?

"Savanna, you're being completely ridiculous."

"Oh, am I?" she sneered. "Well, I disagree. I don't think I'm being ridiculous at all. I think I'm finally seeing the *real* you, Gracie Mooney. And the *real* you just can't stand to see me happy. You want me to be a pathetic loser, so you can feel better about yourself."

"That's not true!"

"Isn't it?"

"No, it isn't! I've been helping you."

"Have you?"

"What do you mean, *have I*? Of course I have, I—"

"Well, if you ask me, the person you've been helping is yourself. I heard you, Gracie. I *heard* you dissing me to Archie and Cooper."

"When? I never—"

"Oh, yes, you did. At the mall. You said I was a snake."

I opened my mouth to correct her, but she rolled on like a tsunami. "And don't you just love all the attention the boys give you now? They're all over you!" Her voice went grating and tinny. *"Oh, here's Gracie. . . . Oh, Gracie, help me tie my shoelace. . . . Oh, Gracie, wasn't the bowling a blast?"*

"Savanna—"

"And don't think you fool me, sucking up to Cooper the way you've been doing, pretending to be interested in him. I mean, you don't even *like* him. You made that totally clear. No, I know what you're up to. You're trying to get close to Archie."

"Archie?" Even though we were in the middle of an argument, it was an effort not to laugh. "Do you mean Archie Snell?"

"Yes, poor little Miss Innocent Gracie Mooney, Archie Snell. Maybe you can fool him and Cooper, but not *me*.

You think that if he cries on your shoulder and you're, like, sooo sympathetic and understanding, you'll get him on the rebound."

Why would I think a thing like that?

"But I don't want Archie. I—"

"Well, you don't want Cooper. So why else are you burrowing in with them like a tick on a dog?"

"But I'm only even friends with them because of you."

"That's *your* story. But you're a liar, aren't you, Gracie? You said so yourself. So why should I believe anything you tell me? I mean, like, if you told me it was raining, I'd probably throw out my umbrella. All I know for sure is that you and Archie are all palsy-walsy now. You're always whispering together."

"No, we aren't. The only time we talk alone is when we're talking about you."

"And I wonder what you tell him, Gracie, huh? What do you tell him? Because Archie's being, like, very suspicious lately. He always wants to know why I can't see him and what I'm doing. I'm surprised he hasn't started stalking me."

"But that's not my fault. You're the one who—"

"Oh, please. . . . Spare me the pathetic excuses."

"Savanna—"

"I can't take anymore!" She grabbed her bag from the foot of the bed. "I'm going home."

"You can't go home." I was amazed at how reasonable I sounded. "It's after midnight. And you don't have your shoes on."

She raised her chin. "Then I'll sleep downstairs."

Now that she wasn't screaming anymore, you could hear the Wobblies, still going strong.

"Won't the music keep you awake?"

Savanna's face was all crushed together as if it was a tin can someone had stomped on. And then she collapsed back onto my bed, tears streaming down her face. "I can't believe you're doing this to me. I really can't."

"But I'm not, Savanna! I'm not—"

"I told you . . . all my secrets . . . and everything . . . and you're, like . . . the only person who, like . . . who really knows me . . . who loves me . . . and you turn on me. . . ." Her words got swallowed in sobs.

"But I haven't turned on you!" It was a chain reaction. I was crying now, too. "I do love you. I'm sorry. I'm really, really sorry. I didn't mean to upset you. I just— Oh, please, Savanna . . . Please say you forgive me."

Her bottom lip quivered. "I don't know. I feel, like, sooo betrayed."

I sat down next to her—near but not touching. "I'm sorry. Savanna, I'm really sorry. Please. Say you're not mad at me. I just . . . you know . . . It's been, like, really stressful for me. Especially tonight . . ."

"I'm not mad. . . . I mean, not that mad. . . . Anyway, I don't think I can stay mad at you, Gray." She snuffled back a few million tears. "And I don't know . . . maybe you're right. Maybe what you said to Archie and Cooper is true. I'm like too—" She wiped her sleeve across her eyes. "Too persuasive or something."

"You're not! I was just saying that because I was embarrassed. You're just you. Please. Say we're still friends."

"Oh, Gracie . . ."

I threw my arms around her.

We both started crying again.

CHAPTER NINETEEN

The Difference Between Truce and Peace

I didn't sleep very well that night. I didn't toss and turn—because I didn't want to disturb Savanna—but I lay there staring into the dark, going over and over everything Savanna had said and everything I'd said, trying to make them go back in the box so I could forget about them forever. I could tell from her breathing and the fact that she didn't have her knee in my back that Savanna wasn't sleeping, either. I whispered, "Savanna?" But she didn't say anything.

When I woke up the next morning, she was already dressed. She was standing in front of the mirror, putting on her makeup, humming under her breath. I didn't recognize the song.

I rubbed my eyes. "What time is it?"

She pulled the top off her mascara. "It's after nine thirty."

"But your mom's coming at ten." I pretty much jumped

out of bed. "We won't have time to make pancakes." Pancakes were our favorite sleepover breakfast.

"I know." She held her mascara wand in the air and looked at me in the mirror. "But I didn't know whether I should, like, wake you up or not. I mean, I figured you needed to sleep." She started stroking her lashes. "Yesterday was pretty mega."

I pulled on my jeans. "My dad's probably got some coffee made." I yanked my genocide T-shirt over my head. It smelled like sour apples. "I'll fix you some toast."

"That's OK." She slid the wand over her lashes. "I'm not really hungry."

"Well, what about juice? Don't you at least want some juice?"

She batted her eyes at her reflection. "Really, Gracie. I'm fine."

I watched her put the brush back into the mascara tube. I watched her unscrew the top on a little bottle of cologne and dab some behind each ear. I watched her fluff out her hair with her fingers, tilting her head to the left and the right and giving it a shake. I had this weird feeling that I wasn't really there. I said, "Savanna, about last night . . ."

"Forget it, Gracie. I have." She dumped her makeup back in its case. "You know, it's all just water over the bridge."

"Under."

She snapped the lock. "Whatever."

A horn honked in the driveway.

"Omigod! Mother Zindle's early!" Savanna stuffed her things into her backpack.

I put on the flip-flops that I used as slippers and followed her out of my room.

"I don't think you should come outside with me," said Savanna when we reached the bottom of the stairs. "You know, in case Zelda asks you something about last night. I don't want to put you on the spot."

"It's OK, I—"

"No, really." Savanna grabbed her jacket from the hooks by the front door. "I thought about what you said after you fell asleep last night. I mean, I know I can be, like, pretty self—pretty self-involved. But that's going to stop. From now on, I'm going to pay more attention to how you feel and what you want."

I didn't really like the sound of that. "I think I went a little over the top," I said. "I was really stressed. I don't want you to—"

"Kisskiss, byebye." She gave me a hug. "I'll talk to you later."

I waved to Mrs. Zindle from behind the storm door as Savanna ran to the car. When she got inside, Savanna rolled down her window. "Tell your dad thanks again!"

she called as her mother backed out of the driveway. "I had a really great time."

I spent the rest of the morning helping my dad clear up and put the good dishes back in the cabinet and the chairs back in the basement.

"You guys went to bed kind of early last night," he said, as we moved the furniture back to where the band had set up. "I was afraid we might keep you awake. We played pretty late."

I said that it was OK. "We didn't fall asleep right away. You know, we had things to talk about."

"Oh, right." He picked up a broken guitar string from the rug. "I thought I heard you." He looked from the string to me as though he was waiting for me to say something. And then he said, "I had the feeling something was going on with you and Savanna."

"Oh, Dad . . ." I laughed—at what a father he was being. "Something's always going on with me and Savanna. We're best friends."

He nodded. "Best friends or not, if there is anything bothering you, Gra—"

"No." I straightened out the fireplace screen. "Nothing's bothering me."

"Right." My father slipped the broken string into his pocket. "But you know where to find me if you do want to talk."

"Yeah." I didn't want to talk. Not ever. As far as I was concerned, the sooner everybody forgot about last night, the better. "Thanks."

"You know what?" He gave me a big smile. "You're not going to believe this, but I'm already looking forward to the leftovers."

In the afternoon I finished my homework, and after supper I watched an old movie by myself. I finally went to bed around midnight — after I realized that when Savanna said "later," she didn't necessarily mean *later today*.

The next morning at school, we all hung out in the lounge as usual. Cooper wanted to know how the Remember the Wampanoag party went, and Savanna said it was cool. "Wasn't it, Gracie?" asked Savanna. That was the only thing she said directly to me.

She didn't come to lunch that day.

"You know Savanna," said Archie. "She left all her homework till last night, so she had to go to the library to do her history now."

That afternoon, when I met up with Savanna after school, Marilouise was with her. "We've got this psycho-killer history test on Friday," Savanna explained, "so Marilouise's coming over to study. She is sooo good at history. I mean, you'd think she'd lived before or something." This was the first I'd heard of Marilouise's past lives. And, from the look on Marilouise's face, I guessed it was the first she'd heard of it, too. Savanna talked about Manifest Destiny all the way to the Old Road.

Savanna called me after supper. "I'm sorry about that," she said. "It was, like, not my idea, believe me. I mean, I *can* study by myself. But you know Marilouise. She's pretty needy really."

"That's OK." I laughed. It wasn't what you'd call echoing with joy. "Only, I was, you know, a little worried that you were avoiding me or something. Since you didn't come to lunch today."

"Avoiding you?" she repeated. "Why would I be avoiding you? I just had stuff to do."

And that was pretty much the way it was for the rest of the week. She stopped meeting me in the morning because her dad was leaving earlier and could give her a ride to school. We still hung out with the others before the bell, but mainly she sat with Archie's arm around her, talking to him. We ate lunch together with the others, but there was never an empty seat next to Savanna anymore. We met in front of the main building at the end of the day—but on Tuesday her mother picked her up to go somewhere after school, on Wednesday she went to Marilouise's to study some more for the history test, and on Thursday she had somewhere to go with Archie. We'd still talk on the phone most nights, but our conversations lasted minutes, not the hours my dad always joked about—and were usually cut off in the middle of a sentence by some crisis in the Zindle household or another call.

I started feeling really lonely. It was as if Savanna and I were in some kind of suspended animation. We weren't exactly fighting, but we weren't exactly not fighting. We weren't exactly *not* speaking, but, unless you count *hello, yeah, see you,* and *bye* as a conversation, we weren't really speaking, either. It was pretty weird to think that not so long ago I could have told you what color bra Savanna was wearing and what she'd had for supper, and now I didn't know anything about her that everybody else didn't know. A dozen times a day, I'd hear something or see something and I'd think: *I have to tell Savanna that.* . . . And then I'd remember that I probably wouldn't get the chance. I'd be smiling and telling jokes at school, but as I pedaled home I'd feel like the last Wampanoag, wondering how everything had managed to go so wrong.

I tried not to let anyone see that I was upset. I didn't want to take Savanna's behavior personally. I wanted to believe that she just happened to be really busy that week. But it was hard not to. I felt as if I'd driven her away by criticizing her and refusing to help her. I wasn't the friend she'd thought I was. I was less. I figured that if I were Savanna, I'd feel completely misunderstood. And let down. It was as if I'd said to her, "Jump and I'll catch you," but, when she jumped, I stepped out of the way. Then I told myself that I was overreacting as usual. Maybe Savanna was acting weird, but, if you looked at it objectively, that was pretty understandable. We'd never had a fight like that before. She was shaken. In shock. It would just take a little while for things to get totally back to normal.

"Did you lose your phone?" my dad asked me on Wednesday, while we were doing the dishes. "Or did Savanna lose hers?" He half smiled. "It's been pretty quiet in here the last few nights."

I said that Savanna had been really busy. "You know, coming up to Christmas and everything."

"I see." He nodded as if that made perfect sense. "It's just that you seem a little mopey." His eyes were on the plate he was rinsing. "Are you certain everything's OK?"

I said that I was positive.

He slipped the plate into the drainer. "You know, Savanna isn't always right, Gracie. No matter how confident she seems."

I said that of course I knew that. "She's not exactly the pope, is she?"

He didn't so much as crack a smile. "No," he said. "Not exactly."

"So what's going on with you and Princess Zindle?" asked Cooper as we were leaving the cafeteria together on Thursday.

"Nothing." I put on a puzzled face. As if he'd asked me how many pairs of socks I owned. "Why?"

"*Why?*" Cooper cocked an eyebrow. "Because I thought I detected an atmospheric shift. A little darkening of the usually cloudless blue skies over the peaceful village. An unseasonable drop in the temperature. The subtle distancing of twin stars."

I laughed. Hahaha. "What is this? Meteorology for beginners?"

"Let me put it more succinctly, Ms. Mooney." Cooper came to a stop and leaned against the wall. "The eggs and bacon are both out, but they don't seem to be together anymore. The egg is on one plate, and the bacon on another."

I'd stopped, too, but I was shuffling from foot to foot. "What's that supposed to mean?"

"You and Savanna seem to be on the outs."

"We're not on the outs." Not officially. "We . . . you know . . . we did have a little argument about something really stupid, that's all. But we made up. It's not a problem."

"Right, it's not a problem," said Cooper. "Only the white water of Savanna's conversation doesn't seem to be flowing toward you anymore."

I said that I hadn't noticed.

"Really?" Cooper was holding on to my book bag as if he thought I might run away. "So you're telling me that any parting of the ways I've detected is just a figment of my warped imagination? You're telling me that nothing's wrong?"

I said that that was what I was telling him.

Savanna said she wasn't still mad at me when I spoke to her on the phone that night.

"I don't know what you're talking about." She was on the landline. I could hear the TV blaring behind her. It was something that involved a lot of shrieking and laughter. "We made up, remember? It's, like, way in the past."

"Yeah," I said, "but you've been acting strange all week. Kind of distant."

"No, I haven't, Gracie." Savanna's laugh was sharper than the laughter on the television. "I think you've been working too hard—as usual. You're imagining things."

Was I imagining that I hadn't been sitting next to her at lunch?

"*And?* I sit right across from you, don't I? I am allowed to sit with other people, you know. It's not like we're going steady, Gracie. Or Siamese cats."

"*Twins.*"

"Anyway, it's just how it's been working out," said Savanna. "It isn't part of some fiendish plan."

The fact that she'd been busy every afternoon wasn't part of some fiendish plan, either.

"Of course not. I've had stuff to do. Don't you ever have stuff to do?"

"But we don't talk on the phone anymore."

"Um, duh . . ." She choked. "I don't want to shock you or anything, but it just so happens that we're talking now."

"Yeah, but you don't really tell me anything."

"I'm trying to think of you and how you feel, Gracie. I'm trying to give you some space. Isn't that what we said?"

"Well, yeah, it is, only—"

"My cell phone's ringing, Gray. I'll talk to you later. Kisskiss, byebye."

At lunch on Friday, Archie asked Savanna if she wanted to go to the lake the next day. "It's still warm enough to take the boat out."

Savanna made a disappointed pout. "I can't. We're going shopping." She leaned her head against his. "I still have to get something totally special to wear to the Christmas dance, don't I? I can't go in something *old*."

I stopped in mid-chew. This was the first I'd heard of another shopping expedition.

"What about when you get back?" asked Archie.

Cooper turned to me. "You mean you're not going to Neighbors' this week?"

I looked from him to Savanna.

"Oh, I'm not going to the mall with Gracie!" Savanna laughed. "You know how much Gracie hates the mall." She was looking at the gap between Cooper and me. "And, anyway, Gracie's not going to the dance. Because she doesn't want to do that, either. She hates dances, too." She smiled as if she was in a toothpaste ad. "And I'm, like, not going to make Gracie do something she doesn't want to do."

"Oh. Right." Cooper nodded at me. "So you decided not to go after all."

Well, someone had.

"Yeah . . . You know, it's not really my thing."

"I'm going shopping with Marilouise." Savanna stabbed at her salad. "She needs something for the dance, too."

"Marilouise?" I put down my sandwich. "Marilouise is going to the Christmas dance with you?"

Savanna made a what-can-I-say? kind of face. "I know, it's, like, blue snow or something, isn't it?" She was wearing tiny Christmas-tree earrings that shook when she laughed. "I mean, I figured I'd see Marilouise skateboarding on the moon before I'd see her at another dance after what happened in middle school, but she thought all of us going together like it's a party was a *great* idea." The teeth flashed. *Unlike some people.* "She's really excited about it."

"So what about tomorrow night?" Archie was saying

to Savanna. "Maybe we could all go to a movie or something."

Savanna glanced at me. "I'm not sure. I may have something to do with the Zindles."

I once asked my dad to explain what the difference between a truce and peace was. It must have had something to do with what I was doing in school. "I don't get it," I said. "Aren't they pretty much the same thing?"

My dad said no. He said peace means things are settled, but a truce is temporary. A truce might be called to give the armies a chance to regroup. Or because they wanted a break from mutual annihilation. Or because it was Christmas. The war wasn't over. The problem hadn't been solved. There was no forgiveness—and no forgetting, either.

So now I knew.

CHAPTER TWENTY

Yet Another Change of Plans

I was always happy to go to Neighbors', but that Saturday I was really happy to go. Everywhere else, I missed Savanna—even sitting at home on the couch, where we always scrunched up together watching movies, made me feel lonely. But she'd never been to Neighbors'. It was all mine—a Savanna-free zone. As soon as I walked through the doors, I felt better. I wasn't some kind of outcast; I was a regular person that other people liked and chatted to. The kids all came running as soon as they saw me. "Miss Mooney! Miss Mooney!" *Look what I wrote . . . look what I made . . . listen to this . . .* It was the only place where I didn't feel alone.

The book I was using that week was called *And Then The Moose Got into the Pool.* It was about this really baking summer and a baby moose who is so hot he wanders into someone's backyard and gets into the wading pool to cool off. Everybody loved it.

By the time the class was over, I was in a pretty good mood. But Cooper wasn't. He was waiting for me in the hallway as usual, but instead of smiling and humming under his breath as usual, he had a pained, stricken look on his face—you know, as if he had heartburn or his shoes were too tight.

"You mind if we skip the café today?" The all-purpose mailbag swung back and forth between us. "I thought mayhaps we could do something different. Change our habit. Break the mold."

What did he want to do, go rappelling instead?

"I thought we could go to Java."

Java?

"You don't have to come if you don't want to." He was shuffling in place so much that his mailbag banged against the wall behind him. "It was only a suggestion."

I liked going for coffee with everyone, but I liked my walks home with Cooper even more. I really looked forward to them. Hanging out with Cooper always cheered me up. I said that I'd rather go with him.

"You're sure?" His bag hit the wall again. "I don't want to pressure you."

I said that I was sure.

Cooper made a sweeping gesture with one arm. "In that case, shall we sally forth?"

But I was the one who did most of the sallying. Cooper

schlumped along beside me with his hands in his pockets and his eyes on the ground. Instead of the steady stream of anecdotes and thoughts I was used to, he let me do all of the talking, just grunting and *umm*ing and occasionally saying "Wow" or "Right" or "That's terrific" when I paused for his response.

"And not only that," I was blathering as we reached Java, "but they all totally got the idea that it was so hot because of global warming. Maria, you know the one with the braids and the bows? Maria even wanted to know if the moose was so close to the houses because there weren't many woods left! Can you believe it? Isn't that great?"

"Yeah," said Cooper. He tugged on the strap of the mailbag. "So this is my treat, understood? I'll even throw in the cupcake of your choice." Cooper wasn't exactly looking at me — as far as I could tell he was half smiling at someone behind me. "You won't get a better deal than that."

We sat by the window.

"You know, I kind of think of this as our table," said Cooper, as he ripped open a bag of sugar so hard it shot all over.

I shook sugar from my cupcake. The woman next to us shook sugar off her skirt.

"You mean, because no one's going to want to sit here after we go?"

He smiled sourly, darting a wary look at our neighbor.

"At least it wasn't milk," I joked. "Or soy sauce. I did that once in a restaurant and it went everywhere. It looked like there'd been an oil spill or something."

"Umm," grunted Cooper. He was concentrating on opening the next bag very carefully. "Taken in that perspective, I can see that I'm terrifically lucky. Fortune's child."

After he successfully got the sugar into his cup, Cooper dedicated his attention to smoothing out the bag and studying it as if he was trying to decode it.

I usually found talking to Cooper easy and effortless, but today it was about as easy and effortless as walking the Inca Trail in stilettos with an armadillo on your back.

"I've only had tea in here before," I said, breaking the uncomfortable silence. "This coffee's really good."

"I've never had the coffee here, either." Cooper picked up his cup to take his first sip of a Java latte. He missed his mouth and poured it down his shirt.

"It doesn't look like you're going to have it now."

It was the woman at the next table who laughed at that joke.

"Damn and tarnation." Cooper jumped up, knocking the napkin holder to the floor.

After things settled down, he held his cup near his mouth, gazing into it like there was something really interesting going on in there. You know, like a solar eclipse or a migration of starlings.

I bit into my cupcake. "This is good, too."

He eyed his cupcake over the rim of his cup as if he thought it was going to explode. "Yeah. It looks good."

I had to wonder what we were doing there. Were we on some reality TV show that I didn't know about? Had he lost some kind of bet?

"Is there something the matter?" I finally asked.

"The matter?" Cooper repeated. "What makes you say that?"

"Because you're acting like you have seven minutes to save the world and you don't think you're going to make it."

"Nah." He didn't laugh, but he did smile. Barely. "I only have five."

"I didn't mean to—you know, if it's none of my business—"

"There's nothing the matter, Gracie. I'm just being a total klutz today." He put down his cup. Coffee sloshed into the saucer. "But, you know, I was thinking . . ." His fingers drummed on the table. "Now that you're officially not going to the dance . . ." He had his eyes on the sugar bowl. "Well, I was wondering if you might want to go to the party at Neighbors' instead."

"The party?" I'd pretty much forgotten about the party.

"Yeah . . ." He picked up his cup. "You've seemed a little diminished with the cares and concerns of human life lately." He smiled. Encouragingly. "And the party's going to be fun. An interlude of comradeship and light relief in a troubled world as it hurtles toward oblivion." He put his cup down again.

"I don't know . . ." I wasn't a party person at the best of times—which this definitely wasn't. "I don't really function well in large groups of strangers." Not if most of them are over nine. "And I don't really know anybody except Mrs. Darling and Mrs. Hendricks."

"That's not true. You know Harlan and Anita and Mrs. Greaves." Those were the volunteers we usually hung out with after our classes. Having given up on his cup, Cooper picked up his spoon. "And you know me." He put down his spoon. "That's why I thought . . . Well, you know . . . that we could go together." He knocked his spoon to the floor.

I watched him retrieve the spoon. Did he mean go together like on a date or go together like we went to the library?

"Together?"

Cooper wrapped his fingers around his cup as if he was afraid it was going to take off. "Yeah, you know . . . To give each other moral support."

I don't want to, like, sound mean or anything, Savanna

Zindle was saying in my head, *but you can't possibly think Cooper's interested in you, can you . . . ? And he's never said anything about you . . . not as a girl. . . .*

That's when it finally hit me. He felt sorry for me. That's what it was: pity. Because he knew Savanna wasn't speaking to me and that she was hanging out with Marilouise instead. He was trying to cheer me up.

I didn't know what to say. I didn't want to be his charity case. And it wasn't as if I was gutted about not going to the dance. I never wanted to go in the first place. But even though I didn't want anyone to feel sorry for me, the truth was that I could stay home by myself any other night of the week. Preferably one when I wouldn't have to imagine Savanna all sparkling and laughing with Marilouise.

"Well . . ."

"You shouldn't let that dress go to waste," said Cooper. "Since you already bought it." He put his hands on the table and leaned back in his chair. "I'll dress up, too. Wear my sharkskin suit."

"Well . . ."

I pictured Cooper in a shark costume. *Didn't I tell you he's weird?* whispered Savanna.

And then I heard Savanna laugh. For a second, I thought it was just in my head, but Cooper glanced out the window, so I knew he'd heard her, too. Savanna was standing in front of Java with her back to us, watching Marilouise maneuvering her way off the bus with her arms full of shopping bags. Marilouise saw me and flapped a hand. Savanna didn't turn around.

"I guess so," I told Cooper. "You know, I don't get that many invitations from sharks."

CHAPTER TWENTY-ONE

Come Back, Gracie Mooney — All Is Forgiven

The next week was different. Which was mainly because of Cooper.

Since I wasn't meeting up with Savanna anymore, I took my time getting dressed on Monday morning. I dawdled over breakfast. I couldn't decide what I wanted for lunch. I had no reason to hurry. No one was going to miss me if I wasn't in time to hang out in the lounge. Cooper was waiting for me by the bike rack when I got to school.

"I thought I'd make sure you were all right. I was afraid you fell off your trusty steed." He scuffed one foot along the ground. "Or something." He seemed to be holding his breath. "You're not known for your tardiness."

I said that today I was. "You know, I just didn't feel like rushing the way I usually do."

Cooper nodded. "I've been thinking of going back to my old routine myself."

I bent down to lock my bike.

"And another thing I was thinking . . ." said Cooper. "You know that great idea I had?" Cooper's great idea was to write his own exercises for his students. He wanted them to be imaginative, relevant, and entertaining. Instead of dull, dated, and as dry as dust, like the ones in the old language books that had been donated to the project. "Well, I was thinking that maybe you might want to help me with it." He was scuffing his foot again. "I figured that we could work on it during lunch." I was afraid that he was going to fall over. "Instead of listening to verbal replays of Savanna's latest fight with her mother."

I laughed. I said that it sounded good to me.

So I stopped having lunch in the cafeteria and went to the study room with Cooper instead. Savanna stopped meeting me in the afternoon, because she always had some reason to stay late at school. Wednesday night, I tried to call her five times but the line was always busy and she never called me back, so I didn't bother after that. I figured that she knew my number if she wanted to talk. And every morning I'd meet Cooper at the end of the Old Road and we'd walk the rest of the way to school together. I guess I was exhibiting a belated animal instinct for self-preservation. Why get too close when you're liable to be shot?

I got so involved with working with Cooper on his great idea that I was too busy to miss Savanna so much.

Cooper and I were basing the exercises on stuff that had really happened—either to us, to someone in his class, to someone we knew, or from a story we'd read in the paper. We laughed a lot—because most of the stories were pretty funny. Like the time Archie's father got locked out of the house in his underwear. And the squirrel who stole candy from a vending machine. And the trouble Mr. Magyar had trying to make the plumber understand him over the phone.

On Friday Cooper had another great idea. "I was thinking we should celebrate," he said. "Since we've been working so hard." He wanted to bring a couple of old movies over to my house and order a pizza on Saturday night. "Maybe *Notorious*," he suggested. "Or *The 39 Steps*. I'm in a Hitchcock kind of mood." Unless I thought my father would object.

I said that my father didn't have anything against Hitchcock.

We hung out in the café after our classes on Saturday as usual. Everybody was in a pretty festive mood. You know, talking about the party next week and what we were bringing for the potluck supper and stuff like that.

Anita was worried about what to wear. "Are we supposed to get really dressed up?" she fretted. "I don't think I have anything that's fancy enough."

Mrs. Greaves said that she was wearing the red

wool dress she bought four years ago. "I only wear it at Christmas, so it's always like it's new."

Harlan said he figured that he'd wear a jacket with his good slacks. "And maybe a tie," he decided. "If I can find someone to knot it for me."

Cooper said, "Wait till you see me and Gracie. Fred and Ginger, eat your hearts out. The Meeting House has never seen the likes of us before!"

That would be when my phone rang.

"Gracie! Gracie! Gracie, it's me!"

And "me" would be Savanna.

"Gracie, are you there?"

I could tell that something was wrong. Not because she was shrieking, but because she sounded so normal. Like she always did when she was upset about something and needed to talk to me. As if it was three weeks ago and not a drop of water had passed under our bridge—or over it, either.

I turned my body so I wasn't looking at the others—and could pretend that they weren't looking at me. "What's the matter?"

"Oh, Gracie . . . Thank God you answered. Gracie, where are you?"

Where did she think I was? About to get on a plane for Hong Kong?

"I'm at Neighbors'. You know, where I am every Saturday afternoon?"

"Oh, Gracie . . ."

I could hear tears way at the back of her voice, the way you can sometimes hear thunder in the distance long before it even looks like it's going to storm.

"What is it? Savanna, tell me what happened."

"I'll tell you when I see you. I have to see you, Gracie. Like, right away."

"But I—"

"Please . . ." begged Savanna. "I'm on the bus—I'll be in town in, like, fifteen minutes. I'll meet you at your house."

"But I'm not at my house. I—"

"Please, Gracie. It's, like, life-and-death."

"Savanna . . ." Experience suggested that "life-and-death" didn't necessarily mean anyone's life was in danger.

"OK, not life-and-death exactly, but it's reallyreally bad."

"Are you all right?"

"Pleasepleaseplease. I, like, absolutely have to talk to you."

A lot of people—people who don't stand for anyone messing them around—would have said no. They would have said that they were really sorry, but they were in the middle of something important. They were busy. They had plans. They were feeling very hurt at the way she'd been treating them. It was way too soon to just forgive and forget.

But I wasn't one of those people. The fact that she needed me made all the bad stuff practically disappear. I said, "I'm leaving right now."

It was to Cooper, Harlan, Anita, and Mrs. Greaves that I said, "I'm really sorry." I jammed my phone back in my bag and grabbed my things. "I have to go. It's an emergency." I looked at Mrs. Greaves and Anita. I figured that neither of them was one of those people, either. "It's my best friend. Something's happened."

"Of course," murmured Mrs. Greaves. "If your friend needs you . . ."

Anita nodded. "It sounded like she was pretty upset."

Cooper, however, *was* one of those people who would have said no.

"Oh, come on, Gracie," said Cooper. "You're not going to drop everything just like that, are you? Why can't she tell you what happened on the phone? Damn and tarnation, that's what they're for."

"I'm sorry." This time I said it just to him. "I really am. Maybe we can watch a Hitchcock another time."

"As long as you have no regrets," muttered Cooper.

Margaret Lockwood and Michael Redgrave, *The Lady Vanishes*.

I expected to find Savanna pacing up and down on the porch, crying, when I got home, but she wasn't there yet. I sat by the front window to wait for her.

My dad came out of the kitchen carrying a mug of tea.

"What's up? You look like you're on sentry duty. Don't tell me the British are coming again." He gave me a fatherly smile. "Or are you waiting for your friend?"

I said Cooper wasn't coming over after all. I was waiting for Savanna.

"Um . . ." said my dad. Now he was looking at me with fatherly concern. "I'll be in my study if you need me."

I had the door opened before Savanna reached the porch.

"Oh, Gracie . . . Thank God you're here. What would I do if you weren't here?" She threw herself into my arms.

"What happened?"

"Uhgratecheese," she sobbed into my shoulder. "Uhgratecheese . . ."

"What happened?" I brushed curls out of my face. "Calm down and tell me what happened."

"Uhgratecheese . . . uhgratecheese . . ."

"Come on inside." I pulled her into the hall and shut the door with my foot. "Now breathe slowly and tell me what happened."

Savanna straightened up, wiping tears from her eyes with the back of her hand. She looked like a really unhappy raccoon. She glanced from the living room to the dining room. "Where's the Professor?"

"It's OK." I fumbled in the pocket of her jacket for the package of Kleenex she always carried. "He's in his study. He'll have the radio on." I handed her a tissue.

271

"Oh, Gracie, you were right. . . . If only I'd listened to you. . . . You were, like, so totally right." She blew her nose. "Why didn't I listen to you? You always know best."

Right about the catastrophe of climate change? Right that she wasn't being fair to Archie? Right that she ignored my feelings? Right that she should have bought the red suit?

Savanna started crying again. "M-Morgan," she gasped. "He was l-lying to me all along. Just like you tried to tell me he was." She smeared some tears across her eyes. "Practically everything he told me was a big fat lie."

"Look," I said, pointing her toward the stairs, "you go to my room, and I'll make you a soothing cup of herbal tea. It'll help you calm down."

"Coffee," snuffled Savanna. "You know I don't do flowers."

"Right." I gave her a hug. "One cup of coffee coming right up."

"And hurry, Gracie." She blew her nose. "Just wait till you hear what he did."

Once Savanna got over the you-were-right and I-should-have-listened-to-you part and had calmed down and stopped sobbing, it turned out to be the most interesting story she'd ever told me about Morgan Scheck. It beat how he got that scar over his left eyebrow by miles.

272

That afternoon Savanna's parents were going to Lawson, the biggest town for at least a hundred miles, to do some Christmas shopping, and Savanna had decided to go with them.

"I mean, like, how bizarre is that? I never go shopping with them. I'd rather shop at the Salvation Army. But I just suddenly heard myself saying, 'Wait for me.' I mean, it was like I was being guided. Like I had some psychotic premonition that I had to go to Lawson today."

It was a typical day out with the Zindles—Mrs. Zindle criticized Mr. Zindle's driving, Mr. Zindle insisted on keeping his window open so they all froze, and Sofia hit her mother over the head with a hairbrush and then cried the rest of the way because her mother hit her back. Savanna was huddled in one corner of the backseat, staring out the window as they drove through Lawson, watching all the other people who might have been her family, but weren't, walk by.

That was the psychotic part.

The psychic part was that while she was looking out the window, who should she see but Morgan Scheck.

He was standing across the street, under the awning of a Mexican restaurant, texting on his cell phone.

Here's another example of how the Fates were in control: the Zindles' car stopped at the light at the corner.

"There's that store I want to check out!" announced

Savanna. "I'll take the bus home." And she jumped out of the car.

She made sure that her parents were a block away before she shouted, "Morgan! Morgan! Hey! I'm over here!"

Hearing his name, Morgan looked up. But his face didn't light up with happy surprise, as it should have. It went blank. He looked down again.

"Morgan!" screamed Savanna. A truck rumbled between them.

"It was kind of like in a movie," said Savanna. "Where the good guy's chasing the bad guy and then a train gets between them and, when it finally passes, the good guy isn't there anymore?"

"He disappeared?"

"Worse than that." She sipped her coffee. "He was with another girl."

"I don't suppose she was just a friend?"

"She was kissing him."

"His sister?"

"On the mouth."

A lot of people—people like me—would have slunk back into the shadows if they'd seen a boy they were dating kissing someone else, or at least into the nearest store. You know, because they were confused . . . baffled . . . sure there had to be some kind of mistake. But not Savanna. She didn't respond well to being slighted.

She marched right across the street without worrying that she was going to make a fool of herself or cause a lot of trouble.

"I nearly got hit by a car. You should've heard what *he* called me." She made a warrior-queen kind of face. "But I didn't care. I was just sooo mad. I mean, like, *really*. Who does Morgan Scheck think he is?"

I said that he definitely had a higher opinion of himself than was probably justified.

"At least I was there when his other ex-girlfriend threw his cell phone under a moving car. But I still cried all the way back on the bus. I've never felt so awful in my whole life. Like I was totally alone." Savanna put her hand on mine. "And then I thought of you." She pressed against me. "I had to talk to you. I mean, if I couldn't talk to you, I don't know what I would've done. All I kept thinking was that once I'd talked to you, it would seem a whole lot funnier than it did right then."

It was pretty funny. You know, except for the part about finding out that Morgan had another girlfriend and getting her heart stomped on and stuff like that. There was a lot of screaming, mainly at Morgan. The other girl wanted to know who Savanna was, and Savanna wanted to know who she was, and both of them were so mad at Morgan that if he'd been an egg, he would have been scrambled. And, all the time that they were shouting, Morgan kept saying that they didn't understand and that it wasn't what they thought. Savanna said that at one point it looked like he was going to make a run for it, but she and the other girl both grabbed an arm and wouldn't let him go.

"I'm really glad you did call me." I leaned my head to hers. "You know . . . I just wish I'd been there."

She squeezed my arm. "Me, too. On both counts."

I looked over at her. "So this time it really is all right, right, Savanna? You know, before, you said—"

"I know . . . I know . . ." Her free hand flapped like a bird. "I was like a total witch to you, Gray. I can admit that. But I was so crazed over Morgan. I mean, I can't tell you the stress and emotional upheaval he put me through. I feel like I've been through the long cycle in the washing machine."

That would be the washing machine of love.

"And I felt like you were against me. That was, like, the last straw in the box for me."

"But I—"

"I know . . . I know . . . It was all my fault." She squeezed me again. "Let's make a solemn promise that we'll never fight like that again, Gray, OK? Because I really couldn't stand it. I missed you so much. These last couple of weeks've been the most awesomely awful thing I've ever been through."

"It's a deal," I said. "I missed you, too." All the time.

"Because everything's really going to be different from

now on. Swear on a bear. I mean, I know I made some mistakes, but not anymore."

"Right," I said. "We'll start all over."

She sighed. Happily. "And now we can go to the dance like we planned and have this awesome time, and I can forget all about Moron Scheck and what a total jerk I've been."

"I can't go to the dance." I said this gently. But firmly. "I told Cooper I'd go to the party at Neighbors'."

"Really?" She sat up a little straighter. "When did you do that?"

"Last weekend. You remember, when you weren't exactly speaking to me?"

Savanna rolled her eyes. "Yeah, but that was when I was mad at you, Gray. You can't punish me for that."

"I'm not punishing you. But Cooper said that since I wasn't going to the dance after all, maybe I'd go to the Neighbors' Christmas party instead—you know, to give him some moral support—and I said I would."

"Well, that's OK." She picked up her cup from the bedside table. "Just tell him you changed your mind."

"I can't do that, Savanna. I told Cooper I'd go." We'd spent the week talking about the party, the way you do. We wondered if Mr. Jerez really would bring his accordion. We joked about Mr. Lundquist's threat to put mistletoe in every doorway. We went shopping together for the token present everybody had to get for the little kids. Cooper gave me his to wrap because he always got tangled in the tape. He wanted to know if I thought my dad, being a folk singer, might have a string tie he could borrow to go with his sharkskin suit.

"Oh, Gracie . . ." Savanna nudged me. Affectionately. "That is, like, sooo *you*. You never want to let anyone down."

Considering how much trouble letting down Savanna had caused me, I didn't really think that was being unreasonable.

"This is Zebediah Cooper we're talking about here, remember?" She gazed at me from beneath her lashes. Appraisingly. "Even if he suddenly realized that besides all the poor, oppressed workers and starving children there are actually girls on the planet, you're not interested in him like that. I mean, that's what you said, right?"

"Yeah, I did say that. . . . But he is my friend."

"Exactly," said Savanna. "That's why he'll understand."

I had this sudden image of Cooper, wearing a shark costume, dumping coffee all over himself.

"Yeah, I'm sure he will, but I still think I should go." I shrugged. "You know, since I already said that I would."

"Whatever you want," said Savanna. "You're the boss. I've learned the errand of my ways."

"*Error.*"

"Whatever." She gave me a hug.

CHAPTER TWENTY-TWO

In the Lane, Tears Are Glist'ning . . .

The last thing Cooper said to me on Friday afternoon was, "See you *mañana*, Gracie." He rubbed his hands together. "Three-bean salad and mariachi music. I can't wait." He waggled his eyebrows. "And, with a little luck, the next time you see me I'll be wearing a string tie." He was going over to Archie's with Archie and Savanna to see if Mr. Snell had one he could lend him. Mr. Snell had gone through a square-dance phase.

And then on Saturday morning, he called up to say that he wasn't going to the Neighbors' party after all.

"What? What happened? Are you sick?"

"Not so you'd notice," said Cooper. "No headache or fever or nausea." He cleared his throat. "I'm simply not in the mood anymore."

"But you were looking forward to it." And so was I.

"Well, now I'm not. Now I'd rather stick needles in my eyes."

I said that at least he was honest.

"Someone has to be," said Cooper. He hung up.

Over the last few weeks, I thought I'd pretty much hit the bottom of the disappointment pit, but now I realized that I hadn't. I hadn't even gotten close. I'd been dangling midway, where there was still some warmth and light. Now I was flat on the cold, dark ground. I guess I'd been looking forward to the party even more than I'd thought.

I stood there for a few minutes, breathing hard as if I'd been punched in the stomach, trying not to cry. And then I called Savanna.

"Poor Gracie . . . What a creep, dumping you like that," Savanna sympathized. "Especially when you were only going as a favor to him. I mean, some people! He doesn't deserve you as a friend."

"We don't know why he changed his mind," I reasoned. "I know Cooper. He wouldn't cancel like that for no reason. Something must be really wrong."

"Oh, please . . . Don't start worrying about *him*. He isn't exactly losing sleep over you," said Savanna. "Anyway, look on the bright side. Now you can go to the dance without feeling guilty."

Well, that was true. Now I could go to the dance feeling like something on the bottom of my hiking boots instead.

"You have to come, Gracie," Savanna insisted. "I won't have any fun thinking of you at home by yourself feeling rejected by someone like that."

I didn't want to go to the dance. I'd never wanted to

go to the dance, but now I *really* didn't want to. I'd rather stick needles in my eyes.

We'll pick you up at seven," said Savanna. "I can't wait to see you in that dress."

The gym was strung with hundreds of clear lights and silver snowflakes. There were tables topped with white paper cloths and snowmen candles all along the walls. Somewhere out on the crowded floor, Savanna—looking like a snow queen in a floaty white dress with silver glitter in her hair—was dancing with Archie. Marilouise and I sat at our table—alone—smiling pretty grimly. Which was what we'd been doing since we arrived. Pete and Leroy had deserted us to stand against one wall with the other dateless boys.

"I knew that I'd wind up sitting on the sidelines. I knew Savanna wasn't going to hang out with me." Marilouise sighed. "You'd think I would've wised up by now. I don't know why I let her talk me into coming. . . ."

I said that Savanna could be pretty persuasive.

"Not persuasive enough." Marilouise lifted her arms in the air. "I mean, look at this dumb dress." She was wearing a red dress with bell sleeves and a bow. She would have looked better in green—because of her eyes. Even with the sleeves and the bow. "Savanna said that I shouldn't get it. She says I dress like I'm trying to bring back the 1950s single-handed, and that it was the wrong color and really frowsy, but would I listen?" She tugged at the bow. "No. And now I'm stuck here looking like Santa's helper."

"What about me?" I demanded. "*Black*—at a Christmas dance! I look like one of the Grinch's henchmen." The short one in the ballet shoes she bought for her grandfather's funeral.

Marilouise laughed. "No, you don't. Gracie, you look great in that dress. I mean, *really*. Like Trinity in *The Matrix*."

"You think so?"

"Everybody thinks so. It looks like it was made for you."

It didn't feel like it was made for me. I felt about as natural in that dress as a chimp in a prom gown. I kept tugging at the hem under the table, hoping I could make it stretch. Even though I was never going to have a good time at the dance, I would at least have felt comfortable if I'd been wearing my own clothes.

"I suppose we can be grateful that we don't have to sit on the sidelines alone." I took a sip of my soda. "At least we have each other."

"Amen," said Marilouise. "I don't know why you decided not to go to the Neighbors' party with Cooper, but I am so glad you did. I would've been like the last doll on the toy-store shelf if you weren't here."

"How did you know about the Neighbors' party?" I

hadn't realized that was public knowledge. "Did Savanna tell you?"

"No." She shook her head. "Cooper told me."

"Cooper?"

"Yeah, last week. We walked home together one afternoon." Marilouise stirred her soda with her straw. "You know Cooper, all he usually talks about is what's wrong with the world, but that afternoon all he talked about was you. And he said you were going to the party together. Which I thought was great. You know, because you're such a cool couple."

Me? Cooper talked about me?

"Yeah, of course." She made it sound like boys were always talking about me. In a positive way. "So when Savanna told me last night that you were coming to the dance, I was kind of surprised."

I was still thinking about Cooper talking about me, and what a cool couple we were. What did he say about me? What made us look like a couple? It took a few seconds for the *Savanna told me last night* part to make its way to my brain.

"Last night?" How could Savanna have known that when I hadn't known myself? "She told you I was coming to the dance *last night*?"

"Uh-huh." Marilouise blushed. "Oh, I'm sorry, Gracie. I guess I shouldn't have mentioned it. It's none of my business. If you didn't want to go to the party with

Cooper, then you didn't want to go." If she blushed any more, she'd look as if she was wearing her dress over her face. "Forget I said anything."

"Marilouise?" I felt calm. Cold, but calm. "Marilouise, what makes you think I was the one who bailed?"

"Well, I—" Her whole face seemed to be blinking. "Well, I guess, you know, I just thought that because he seemed pretty excited about the party. . . . And, you know, Archie's made a couple of jokes about Cooper having a thing about you. . . . And Savanna kind of mentioned that you were only going to the party with him to be nice, but you know . . . I didn't believe her. I thought she just . . . well, you know Savanna. . . . And you don't like parties, so I guess I thought that if you said you'd go . . . Well, you know . . . You and Cooper seemed so good together. Remember at my birthday? And when I saw you together in Java last Saturday, I said to Savanna that I figured you two were going to be a serious item."

"You did?"

But I didn't hear what she answered. There were too many other words in my head. *You can't possibly think Cooper's interested in you, can you . . . ? Archie says he's never said anything about you . . . not as a girl. . . . I'm simply not in the mood anymore. . . . I'd rather stick needles in my eyes. . . . He seemed pretty excited. . . . Savanna told me last night that you were coming to the dance. . . . I said to Savanna that I figured you two were going to be a serious item. . . . I know Savanna has her own way of doing things. . . . Savanna told me last night . . . Savanna told me last night . . . Savanna told me last night . . .*

"Gracie?" Marilouise leaned over and put a hand on my arm. "Gracie, are you OK?"

"I don't know." I didn't. I was trying to make sense of everything, but I was kind of stuck on the part where Savanna knew that I wasn't going to the Neighbors' party before I did.

Marilouise's face looked like a rainy day. "Oh, Gracie, I hope I didn't—"

"You didn't do anything. But I think I have to get out of here." I got to my feet and picked up my coat. "Now. Tell Savanna I'll call her tomorrow."

"Ummm . . ." Marilouise was staring past me. "I think you're going to be able to tell her yourself."

I turned around.

Savanna was charging toward us like a rhino. Her face was flushed, but you could tell from the set of her mouth and the way her eyes were narrowed that this wasn't because she'd been dancing. This was a pretty unhappy rhino.

"I have had it with Archie Snell. I have, like, totally had it!" Savanna was fuming. "I don't care if he crawls over glass with an orchid clasped in his teeth to apologize. There's not going to be any making up after this fight. We are absolutely *finito*." She threw herself into the chair I'd just vacated. "Some season for goodwill to all men this is." Her eyes were suddenly glassy with tears. "There's no goodwill toward me, that's for sure." Her lower lip trembled.

Marilouise and I exchanged a look, but it was Marilouise who said, "What happened?"

"What happened?" The tears starting spilling down Savanna's cheeks. "I'll tell you what happened. Archie got all bent out of shape because he went off to take a leak and when he came back I was dancing with someone else, that's what happened. You should've heard him. He said that if flirting was lethal, I'd be a serial killer! Can you believe that? I was *dancing,* for pity's sake! That's what you do at a dance. You dance!"

Marilouise said, "Gee—"

"I've got to go to the girls' room." Savanna slipped her bag off the back of my chair where she'd left it for safe-keeping. You know, because not everyone goes to a dance to dance. "I must look hideous." She took a tissue from her bag and dabbed at her eyes. "Come on, Gracie." She pushed back her chair. "Marilouise will hold the fort."

I hugged my coat against me. "I can't," I said. "I was just about to leave."

"Leave?" For the first time since she'd landed, Savanna looked at me. "You can't go now, Gracie. I need you."

No, *Why are you leaving?* No, *What's wrong, Gracie?*

No, *But where are you going?* Just, *You can't go now. . . . I need you.*

All of a sudden, I was angry. *Really* angry. I was practically vibrating with rage.

"What did you tell Cooper, Savanna?" My hands were shaking, but my voice was as still as stone.

"Cooper?" Savanna blinked the last few tears away. "I didn't say anything to Cooper." She laughed. "I didn't even know he was here."

"Yesterday, Savanna. What did you say to him yesterday to make him break our date?"

"Nothing." She slid her bag over her shoulder. "I don't know what you're talking about."

"Yes, you do. You told Marilouise last night that I wasn't going to the Neighbors' party."

"I never said that." She didn't so much as glance at Marilouise. "All I said was that I *wished* you weren't going. That's all I said."

It was Candy Russo's twelfth birthday. Candy told me she wasn't having a party that year. I was already in middle school, but I'd stopped by to give her the present I'd bought her. There were balloons tied to the front door. Through the living-room window, I could see more balloons and streamers and kids running around and laughing. I stood there, pretty much cemented to the front path, until someone noticed me, and Candy suddenly appeared in the window. She gazed back at me for a second or two, and then she turned away. My eyes were on Savanna, but what I saw was Candy Russo's face staring back at me, blank with lies — and not caring at all how much she'd hurt me. That's why Candy Russo had been the worst best friend I'd ever had. Until now.

"And, anyway," Savanna went on, "Cooper's your friend, not mine. He doesn't even like me. I mean, what could I say to him to make him break your date?"

I was talking to the wrong person. "That's what I'm going to find out," I said.

My heart was pretty much stampeding and the tears were kind of dripping down my face, but I tried to get ahold of myself as I hurried through the night, taking deep breaths and wiping my eyes with the sleeve of my coat. I didn't want one of Cooper's parents to open the door and find a hysterical midget in somebody else's dress standing there. I wanted them to see a nice, polite, smiling girl. *Hi*, I'd say. *I'm really sorry to bother you, but I'm a friend of Zeb's. You know, from school? And I really need to talk to him.* I wanted to be invited in; not have the door slammed in my face. Probably, he'd be in his room. Brooding. He wouldn't want to see me, but I'd make him listen. I rehearsed what I'd say. I'd say we needed to talk. I'd say this calmly — and reasonably. *There's been a mistake*, I'd say. *A big misunderstanding. I had no idea. I can explain.*

I'd never been to Cooper's house, but I knew which one it was. Everybody did. It was the one that was painted aquamarine and had handmade whirligigs lined up across the edge of the lawn instead of a fence. His parents were eccentric, too.

It was Cooper who answered the door. He must have been coming from the kitchen because he had a steaming mug in his hand.

He didn't say "hello," and he didn't smile. He said, "What are you doing here, Gracie? You're supposed to be at the dance."

And I didn't say any of the things I'd planned to say in a calm and reasonable way, either. I said, "What did she tell you, Cooper? What did Savanna say?"

"I don't want to have this conversation." He had his eyes focused on the top of my head.

"Just tell me what she told you."

He refocused over my shoulder. "You know what she told me."

He took a step back, as if he really was going to slam the door in my face, but I pushed past him into the hallway before he could. Short, but fleet of foot.

"No, I don't know. Would I ask you if I knew? Would I *be* here?" I could hear my voice rising. "I didn't even know for sure that she had said anything. I was guessing." Now I was officially shouting. "That's why you have to tell me. You can't just shut down on me without saying why."

He glanced behind him. "Damn and tarnation, Gracie," hissed Cooper. "Could you lower your voice? My parents are going to think I'm hurting you or something."

I said that he was hurting me. I was trying not to start crying again.

"All right, all right . . ." He nodded. Grudgingly. "Just don't yell or anything."

Cooper walked Savanna home from Archie's on Friday afternoon. He was telling her about Neighbors' and how much everybody there liked me and stuff like that, and all of a sudden she launched into a speech about how much I hated to let people down, and how I was too nice for my own good, and how I was always trying to please everybody, and how I let people push me around. "I figured she meant besides *her*," said Cooper, "so I asked her who we were talking about." And Savanna said they were talking about him.

"She said that you'd only said you'd go to the party with me because you two had that stupid fight, and that really you wanted to go to the dance, but that you couldn't tell me the truth because you didn't want to hurt my feelings. She said that you liked me, but not like that. Because I'm so weird."

"And you believed her? Why would you believe her?"

"What do you mean, *Why would I believe her*?" He sounded as if I was the most unreasonable person he'd ever met. "Why wouldn't I believe her? You walked out of Neighbors' the other day without thinking twice about me or how I'd feel—just because she called you."

"She *needed* me."

"We had a date."

I did that thing where you laugh even though no one has said anything funny. "Yeah, but it wasn't a real date."

"It was to me," said Cooper.

"It was?" I had that punched-in-the-stomach feeling again. "Well, how was I supposed to know that? Did you say that? You never said—"

"Oh, come on, Gracie . . ." I really wished that he'd smile. Even half a smile—or a quarter of a smile. Just so I knew he could still do it. "It's been pretty obvious how I feel about you. Right from day one. Why did you think I went into Java after you that day? Why did you think I asked you to go to Neighbors' with me?"

I said, because I'd thought he felt sorry for me.

"Felt sorry for you? Why the heck would I feel sorry for *you*?" He could still smile. "You're the coolest girl I've ever known."

"I am?"

"Yeah, of course you are." If he'd been, say, Clark Gable in *It Happened One Night,* he would have pushed his hat back and scratched his head in complete bewilderment. "Only I never got to talk to you alone, did I? You were always with *her*. I thought that if I could get you to come to Neighbors' and we spent some time together . . ."

"You did?"

"Damn and tarnation, Gracie. Why do you think I started coming to school early? Because I couldn't get enough of Savanna's laugh? And did you think I couldn't write the language programs by myself?"

It didn't look as if I'd been doing much thinking at all.

"So why did you believe Savanna?" I was shouting again. "I thought you were so smart. Why would you listen to anything Savanna says? You know what she's like."

"And you don't?" Cooper was shouting, too. "But you listen to her. You do anything she says."

"No, I don't!" I screamed back. "Not anymore."

A door opened and Mrs. Cooper stuck her head into the hall.

"Are you all right, Zeb— Oh!" She looked at me. Surprised. "Oh, you must be Gracie." Apparently, Cooper talked about me to everyone but me. She looked at Cooper. Bemused. "Does this mean you're going to the party after all?"

Cooper looked at me.

"Yes," I said. "If we hurry, we can still get some of the three-bean salad."

Cooper slipped his hand into mine as we walked into the night together. It wasn't foggy, but it was starting to snow.

"Hey, Gracie," said Cooper. "Do you think this could be the beginning of a beautiful friendship?"

The correct answer, of course, was *Casablanca*— Humphrey Bogart, Ingrid Bergman, and Claude Rains.

But all I said was, "Yes."

After

There's some famous poem about the world ending not
with a bang but with a whimper, and that's pretty much
how it was with my friendship with Savanna. There was
no big fight or drama or anything like that. She called me
the next day to say that she was sorry. She said that she
really hadn't thought she'd said anything to Cooper—all
she'd done was tell him what I told her—but after I left
like that, she got to thinking about it and she could see
that maybe she'd gone over the line a little. I said that
she'd gone so far over the line, she was in a different state.
"I was just trying to protect you," said Savanna. "From
yourself." I said that I didn't think I was the one I needed
protection from. But I said that I forgave her. And I did. I
didn't need her approval anymore. I was done.

We were still friendly after that, but we weren't really
friends. I'd gotten into the summer project in Costa Rica,
so besides getting ready for that, I was spending a lot

of time with Cooper, and since Savanna had broken up with Archie, she was eating lunch with other people and hanging out with them. We'd already gotten out of the habit of walking to school together and meeting up before classes started. Which made it easy for us just to drift apart, her going her way and me going mine. We'd see each other at school and we'd chat or whatever, but that was it. No more sleepovers where we sat up talking half the night. No more hours on the phone after supper. No more "more." Sometimes, I still missed her a lot—but I figured I'd get used to it.

A couple of days after I got back from Costa Rica, I went into town to pick up the pictures I'd had developed. I couldn't wait to show them to Zeb and my dad. The two of them came to the airport to pick me up, hauling a big sign that said *"Bienvenida, Gracie"* between them, and tonight they were making me a special welcome-home supper. They were really excited, whispering together like a couple of little kids on Christmas Eve. Not only wouldn't they tell me what it was they were making, they wouldn't even let me into the kitchen to fix myself a cup of tea. So I'd come into town to get out of their way.

I'd stopped just outside the store and was sticking the envelopes of photographs into my backpack when I heard someone shouting my name. Urgently.

I looked up. On the other side of the road, a girl was smiling at me and jumping up and down. "Gracie!

Gracie!" It took me a second to recognize her. She wasn't a blonde the last time I saw her.

"Be careful!" I yelled as Savanna hurled herself into the traffic.

Laughing, she ran across the street, waving her hands at the cars that were honking at her as though they were in *her* way.

"Gracie! Omigod! Marilouise said you were back!" Savanna threw her arms around me, whacking me with her bag. "I was going to call, but I've been, like, sooo busy. I mean, it's been the most hectic summer." She pulled out of the hug. "You can't imagine, Gracie. It's just been gogogogogo the whole time. I learned how to sail—well, you know, how not to get hit by the boom or anything— and I went scuba diving and I even went camping, can you believe it?" She did her happy-goose laugh. "But not in a tent, of course. I don't want you to think I've gone all weird. In a cabin right on this, like, incredible lake." She paused for a smile. "Did you have a great time in Guatemala?"

"*Costa Rica.*" I laughed. "Yeah, it was terrific. But I'm really glad to be home. I—"

"Look at you!" She took a step back and held me at arm's length. "You are sooo tanned!" She lunged forward for another hug. "I am, like, so glad to see you!"

"I'm glad to see you, too." I was. But it was then it hit

me that I hadn't thought of her once while I was away. I'd used up all my missing on Cooper and my dad. "You look great."

"Really? It was one of my impulses—you know what I'm like." She touched her hair. "You don't think it's too much?"

"No." I knew what she was like, all right. "It looks really good."

"You look great, too." She laughed. "You know, in a riding-sea-turtles kind of way. And I am, like, totally desperate to hear all about your trip and the lizards and everything."

"I just got my photos." I patted my bag. "What about an iced tea or something? I have a little time before I—"

"Oh God, Gracie, I'd love to, but I can't." Savanna smooshed her mouth in disappointment. "I have, like, a big date tonight." She laughed. "You know how long it takes me to get ready." She rolled her eyes and laughed again. "I guess I'll never change."

"Well, an—"

"Yeah, before school starts. I'll call you. Tomorrow. Swear on a bear." She threw her arms around me again. "Kisskiss, byebye."

"Kisskiss, byebye."

I watched her launch herself back into the road.

She turned for a second when she reached the curb.

"It was great seeing you!" she called. And then she strode down the sidewalk—turning heads—swinging and swaying and shining in the sun. My worst best friend.

She never will change, I thought.

It was lucky that I had.